WHITE ELEPHANT

Also by V.E. Ulett

Code Black series

Golden Dragon

Blackwell's Adventures series

Captain Blackwell's Prize
Blackwell's Paradise
Blackwell's Homecoming

WHITE ELEPHANT
V.E. ULETT

Copyright © 2019 by Eva Ulett

ISBN: 0-9981131-3-1
ISBN-13: 978-0-9981131-3-5

Cover design by James T. Egan of Bookfly Design

Publisher's Note:
This is a work of fiction. All of the characters,
organizations, and events portrayed in this novel are
either the products of the author's imagination or are
used fictiously.

All rights reserved. No part of this book may be
reproduced or transmitted in any form or by any
means, electronic or mechanical, including
photocopying, recording or by any information storage
and retrieval system, without written permission from
the author, except for the inclusion of brief quotations
in a review.

CHAPTER ONE

The ship *Nonesuch* was engulfed in a squall. Strong winds and driving rain beat against the ship's wooden hull. Even with her limited experience, Miriam knew the airship was descending too fast.

"Mr. Dashwood!" Captain Maximus Thorpe called from his position heaving on the yoke, just forward of where Miriam clung to the rails of the fore hatchway companion ladder. "Let go the hundredweights!"

Miriam dashed up the ladder to relay the order that would slow the ship's sickening downward hurtle. She staggered on the top rungs, slick under hand and foot, then brought the speaking trumpet up and shouted Captain Thorpe's order to the upper deck.

It was doubtful any of the officers or seamen on deck heard the order. With her head and shoulders above the coaming of the hatchway, Miriam gazed out on the high pitch of activity taking place on the deck open to the atmosphere. A group of seamen were sliding about the canting deck, struggling to keep the stunsails at the correct angle for descent. First lieutenant Mr. Dashwood raced between the party at the stunsails and the men at the braziers and bellows, shouting to the crew attending the lines of the rapidly sagging, beaten-down, fifty-foot balloons. Mr. Dodd, the ship's second lieutenant, lumbered up out of the dense gray gloom of heavy cloud and choking rain.

"Mr. Dodd!" Miriam screamed over the roar of wind. "The hundredweights, Mr. Dodd!"

Mr. Dodd was staring right at Miriam, raising his hand to his forehead in acknowledgement of the captain's order, when a great fork of lightning flashed out and connected with *Nonesuch's* foremast. An arc of blinding light shot from the foremast to the nearest of the balloons. The silk fabric sizzled and combusted, raining ash and sparks on the men below. *Nonesuch's* bow or nose angled farther down. The ship accelerated, throwing Miriam back hard against the edge of the hatchway. The air rushed out of her lungs with a painful woof. Mr. Dodd had disappeared, picked up and carried away out of sight with a surprised look on his face, the lifeline tethering him to the ship snapping like dead wood.

Miriam clung to the companion ladder, the speaking trumpet long since torn from her grasp. The upper deck was a tangle of men, downed rigging and spars, chunks of charred and still seething wood from the mast, and curls of blackened cloth from the balloon. Out of the wreckage, pulling himself up the sloping deck, came Mr. Dashwood, axe in hand.

Nonesuch's first lieutenant battled his way to the main chains where the hundredweight bags of ballast hung, and began hacking at the lines securing them to the ship.

"Krunk!" Miriam screamed at a seaman, her particular friend. Krunk followed Mr. Dashwood with a drawn *kris* in his hand. "Port side! Forward weights first!"

Krunk instantly about faced, followed by more seamen regaining their feet, making for the ballast near the main chains on each side of the ship. Moments later *Nonesuch's* bow rose and the ship's acceleration changed with a slight upward swoop.

"Miss Miriam!" Captain Thorpe bellowed. "Miss Miriam, Mr. Dashwood, report!"

Miriam backed down two rungs of the ladder, her soaked and dripping head just below decks. She was opening her mouth to shout at Captain Thorpe, who clung to the yoke, his flaming red hair loose and flowing behind him, when the first impact came. There was a tremendous jarring thud, throwing everyone and everything in the ship forward. This time Miriam was mashed chest first against the ladder.

She was one of the fortunate ones. When the second impact happened, the ship bouncing over the surface of the sea like a skipped rock, Mr. Dashwood fell through the aft hatchway and landed facedown with a sickening thud at the bottom of the ladder. *Nonesuch's* crash halted at last with a rending cracking sound.

Captain Thorpe peeled himself from where he'd landed, inside one of the two huge port hole windows all the way forward in the bows of the ship. He clambered to his feet and ran aft, bent over and shouting, "All hands! All hands on deck!"

Miriam descended the ladder toward him.

"On deck, Miss Miriam, we've struck!" Captain Thorpe called, waving Miriam back up the ladder.

"Mr. Dashwood—" Miriam began.

"Aye! I'll bring the laddie."

Captain Thorpe was last up the ladder, pushing the lower deck crew before him and carrying Mr. Dashwood over one shoulder. Amid a steady patter of rain—the squall was moving off—he set the first lieutenant gently down on deck. Mr. Dashwood moaned, his handsome face distorted with pain and so pale it shone like a beacon in the gloom of the surrounding night.

"Mr. Dodd!" Captain Thorpe called, as he strapped Mr. Dashwood's left arm against his chest with the lieutenant's sword belt.

Miriam angled over until she was kneeling beside Captain Thorpe. "Gone, sir," she said, conscious of *Nonesuch's* surviving crew gathering in a little knot round them. "Carried away during the descent."

Astonishment and grief passed over Captain Thorpe's features. It was hard to credit such a thing could happen to the stalwart, bear-like Mr. Dodd.

"I regret it extremely," Maximus said. He gave Mr. Dashwood a tender pat. "Broken collar bone, Valentine, I'm grieved to say. Try to keep the arm still."

Miriam, Krunk, and the captain's steward Saramago were closest, but when Captain Thorpe stood up, all of the remaining seamen pressed closer round him.

"Shipmates," Captain Thorpe said, "the barky is lightning damaged and hulled. We struck a submerged rock or drifting log. The water is risen already to the lower deck. But we are still in one piece and the coast of Borneo is on our lee. We should have made the approaches to Kuching but for that black squall. I mean to fire the braziers and float her to land. Where we will patch up dear *Nonesuch*, and be on our way!"

The men gave a ragged cheer, and then suddenly shrank back. The Hell-Cat, Thrax, attached to Miriam since she'd first sailed in *Nonesuch*, was suddenly among them, pacing the lee rail. Thrax's burning yellow eyes sought out Miriam among the crowd of frightened faces on deck. Once it caught her gaze, as though beckoning her on, the Hell-Cat hurled its sleek body overboard into the churning sea.

CHAPTER TWO

Miriam was in the hospital tent feeding the last of *Nonesuch's* grain—a bowl of mud yellow-colored burgoo—to Mr. Dashwood, when the elephant charged. *Nonesuch* was remarkably close to land just before she wrecked, and though it took every ounce of Captain Thorpe's strength and will, he'd floated her on her one remaining balloon, bow down and dragging over rocks and sand bars, until landing on a low hill beyond a stretch of beach. Matters had not prospered with them since. Captain Thorpe was pressing forward with repairs, in the intervals between fighting off rotating tribes of sea-going Dyaks. These worthies found them within days of their landing. It was during the usual sunset attack, with the screams of action wafting up from the battleground on the strand, as Miriam dipped another spoonful of gruel for Mr. Dashood, that she felt the earth shake.

The tremors were accompanied by a furious trumpeting roar and the jangling of a metal bell. Miriam chucked the burgoo and grasping Mr. Dashwood round his middle, heaved him to his feet. Mr. Dashwood gave a yelp of pain. The tent collapsed overhead as a hulking gray bellowing monster pummeled its way through.

Clear of the path of the elephant, Miriam managed to keep her feet. She still held Mr. Dashwood upright. Together with the other survivors of shipwreck and native attack, Miriam and Mr. Dashwood struggled out from under the collapsed canvas of the hospital tent.

The elephant flew before them in full charge down to the scene of action on the strand, its massive ears spread wide and flapping. The Dyak tribesmen were fearsome fighters, but a charging elephant was not in their line. With shouts of terror, they gave over fighting and fled for their war canoes.

Captain Thorpe, his bloody cavalry sword still in hand, churned his way up the slope away from the elephant, toward Miriam and the encampment. Muddy and stained like a Scottish warrior of old, red hair streaming, the fury of battle lingered on his face and in his parti-colored eyes. Not far behind him followed Krunk, a warrior of a different kind, black, and once a woman—some thought an Amazon—with only one breast.

Emerging from the jungle behind the *Nonesuch's* encampment was a straggling line of pack elephants. Captain Thorpe was hurrying forward to meet them. The rogue elephant's charge scattered Captain Thorpe's little band of defenders, all up and down the strand and slope. The elephant itself made straight for the water's edge before slowing. Then, venturing into the gentle surf of the lagoon only to its knees, the great beast leaned out toward the fleeing tribesmen and blasted them with another trumpeting battle roar.

A dark man in a long-sleeved tunic rolled up to his elbows, and skirt wrapped round his waist, hastened up to Miriam, Mr. Dashwood, and the group at the encampment. He singled out Captain Thorpe, reaching them just then out of breath, as the one most likely in charge. The bloody cavalry sword Captain Thorpe still clutched might also have persuaded the elephant handler to deal with him first.

He spoke rapidly in a language none knew. Seeing the stunned and stupid looks on their faces, he said, "He no bad elephant," in Malay. It was a language both Miriam and Captain Thorpe could speak, thanks to a most prodigious teacher they'd once shared. "Please, Tuan," the man continued, "he no bad elephant. Once a war elephant. He smell blood, he run toward not away."

Captain Thorpe was still gasping from his own uphill scramble, and the after effects of the bloody hand to hand action. Miriam, to offer relief, said, "He is a magnificent creature."

The man looked at Miriam in astonishment, dark eyebrows raised at her *hijab* and gown, or at her command of his language. But then the mahout put his hands, palms together, before his chest and bowed to her.

"He is Hoola. He wise, strong, brave. One day he be White Elephant. See his anger gone, now no men try slaughter and take heads."

Still knee deep in the waters of the lagoon, the great gray elephant was rocking from side to side, gently swiping its curled trunk over the surface of the water, and seeming to delight in the long sheet of spray sent up.

"I do not mean to be ungrateful," Captain Thorpe said at last, "his charge was most timely, but I should like to know who you are. Allow me to make myself known. I am Captain Maximus Thorpe of His Britannic Majesty's Hired Vessel *Nonesuch*." With an unhappy expression Captain Thorpe gestured at *Nonesuch*, not far away on the plateau, lying on her side, exposing a ragged hole six foot across.

"Ah," the man said, "sailing captain. I know you kind." The mahout bowed to Captain Thorpe in that particular way, and then turned to Miriam. "If you Maryam of Persia, for you we sent."

The mahout waved toward the train of three elephants ambling into the encampment. The area was suddenly full of the barnyard smell of the great animals, their rumbling, squeaking, squealing vocalizations, their great flapping ears and mobile, questing trunks. After orders given by their riders, each elephant gracefully folded its back legs, extended its' front, and dropped to a down position. This allowed the mahout to slide from the elephant's back to its knee, and so to the ground. Miriam, Captain Thorpe, Mr. Dashwood, and the rest, stared in wonderment.

"I am Dena, chief uzi and handler of Hoola."

She might be on the wild coast of Borneo, but that was no reason Miriam would forget a lifetime of doing the civil. She curtsied to Dena. "Most honored, chief Dena. Miriam Albuyeh Kodio Blackwell, at your service. May I know who has sent you, and these magnificent beasts?"

"Rajah Broke, Miss," Dena said.

Miriam and Captain Thorpe's eyes met for a fraction of a second at mention of that name, and then they both looked away.

Captain Thorpe's manner changed to one of business. "I must attend to my wounded and see to the hospital tent, Mr. Dena, if you will pardon me. Call upon me this evening, if you would be so good."

The other uzis, as the mahouts called themselves in this part of the world, were already unloading the elephants' burdens. Afterwards they led their charges to a nearby stream that emptied into the lagoon, running below the rise of ground the encampment was on. It was a fresh water stream the shipwrecked party had found most convenient, up to that time.

The chief uzi Dena cast a pitying look round at the downed tent and its sad makeshift neighbors, the ship with the great gaping hole, and the blood-stained white men. "Since I the visitor, allow me host in my hut." Dena emphasized his kind invitation with another deep bow.

"Miriam, m'dear?" Maximus called from outside Miriam's tent, a short time before they were to meet the chief elephant handler.

"Come in."

A great deal of visiting took place between their two tents. No one remarked upon it, because it was a well-known secret that Miriam was *sigheh* to *Nonesuch's* captain. *Sigheh*, meaning temporary wife in the language of Persia, was a concept not unfamiliar to sailors the world over.

Maximus took a seat on a sofa which used to occupy a place in his sleeping cabin, aboard. He'd moved it to serve as a bed for Miriam, and keep her from the sodden ground. There was little to choose between their two tents for niceties and comforts, both were squalid, damp, mud besmirched, and smelling of vegetable rot.

"Did you see how fast those fellows whipped up their shelters?" Maximus said, in his usual direct and easy manner when he was alone with Miriam. "I shall be interested to have a closer look during our call tonight. Not that we shall be here quite so long." Maximus frowned, a serious, grieved expression passing over his face. "But it would be a prodigious great thing to build shelters like theirs—off the ground."

"Much better for the wounded, I should think," Miriam said.

When she'd not been fully occupied assisting with resurrecting the hospital tent, and with the fresh and stale wounded earlier that evening, Miriam had intently observed the uzis and their elephants. How could she not, after Dena declared they'd been sent expressly by Rajah Broke. James Broke was the reason Miriam was there—stranded on the remote coast of Borneo—trying to reach the Rajah's capital city of Kuching.

"A few things strike me as odd—"

"Only a few?" Maximus asked, an incongruous twinkle in his one striking green, and one washed-out blue eye.

"James Broke knew of my coming to his kingdom, his country, his colony—Lord Q will have made sure of it—but how can he be aware when and how I should arrive? Well enough to send an overland party when I did not appear?"

Maximus shook his head, with the pained expression mention of Lord Q and his game always brought to his face. He wanted the world to believe he was at bottom only an uncomplicated Navy man. Miriam knew differently. Aside from being an aeronaut, there were depths to Maximus Thorpe—his sense of honor and justice, his romantic, intellectual strivings—that Miriam was still uncovering.

"And those elephants," she said, "fascinating creatures. Isn't there something odd there too? Three elephants in the pack are females, I believe, and rather work-a-day compared to that great Hoola. Why send such a specimen to collect one person?"

"It is the grand gesture, to be sure. A war elephant!" Maximus shook his head. "His bell is unique too. Pewter or some other metal. Whereas the cows—if you will—have bells of wood."

A silence fell between them. Maximus was adept at avoiding the subjects of James Broke, the private war Lord Q was waging, and Miriam's involvement in the Borneo mission.

"It occurs to me," Miriam said, "whatever the reason that wonderful great elephant was sent, are elephants not used in harvesting timber?"

A genuine smile broke out on Maximus's careworn face, and he clapped his hands together. "Miriam, m'dear, you are the wonder of the world! So they are, too! If I could but convince Mr. Dena to have Hoola knock over one of those fine red hardwood trees, why, repairing *Nonesuch* would be as easy as kiss my hand." Maximus's face clouded. "O' course, it does no speak to the loss of yon balloon, nor the great rent in t'other. But *Nonesuch* can and shall be made to swim, I hope and trust."

"I am convinced of it," Miriam said, extending her open hand to him.

At that moment Thrax came busting into the tent, causing Miriam and Maximus to jump apart as though guilty. Thrax dragged between its four muscular legs a good-sized monkey, its teeth firmly set in the primate's bloody throat.

Miriam pushed down the little shriek that always would rise up, because this part never ceased to disturb her. Thrax heaved the furry black and tan body near Miriam's feet, and dropped it. Avoiding the sight of the monkey's poor crumpled face, its human-like little hands and feet, Miriam lavished praise and caresses on the Hell-Cat.

After a decent interval of affection and gratitude,

Miriam rose and picked the monkey up by the tail while averting her face. "We should be joining Dena now, Captain."

Meat was meat. They would pass by the mess tent on their way, and deposit the monkey for the seamen's stew pot.

Maximus was wary of the uzi camp he and Miriam approached. They had stopped to freshen up in his tent, with buckets of water Saramago hauled from the stream. In half-boots and a muslin gown, and wearing a matching white and silver *hijab*, Maximus thought Miriam as lovely as Persian verse. From gaping too much, he stumbled over the exposed spreading roots of a strangler fig. A burst of laughter came from inside the larger of the two huts before them.

The uzis built the structures at the edge of the jungle, raised six feet above ground. Sapling posts acted as the central supports, and each had a floor of interwoven branches and broad forest leaves, and a thatched roof of palm fronds and tall elephant grasses found at the stream's edge. Maximus admired the two dwellings, so expertly constructed out of what was on hand. There was even a small hut for smoking fish; rows of bony little fishes speared on sticks were already cooking away.

A lively young brown face, teeth shining in a broad grin, poked out at Miriam and Maximus from the platform of the larger hut.

"He never do it, Tuai Rumah Dena, he much too fats," the young person said.

Maximus realized with a bitter shock the youngster was speaking of him. Then he looked skeptically at the single tree branch ladder that ascended to the platform, and at the frail floor of greenery, and almost agreed.

"Good Lord," Maximus murmured, "I never thought I should become the fat man of the world."

Miriam gave a little snort, gathered her skirts in one hand, and went up the ladder with the lightness and grace of a butterfly. Dena handed her to a seat on the frond floor beside him. He turned to Maximus, vacillating at the bottom of the ladder.

"Not to mind heedless youth, Tuai Torp—he name Inghai, we call Ingy-Pingy—my very best friend Rajah Broke a fat man too. You manage it."

Maximus inhaled and swarmed up the ladder as fast as he could go, then spread himself turtle-like on the floor of the hut to distribute his weight. He pushed to a sitting posture once safely at his seat on Dena's other hand. Maximus felt the floor bow and sag beneath his backside. He hoped he could get through the evening without punching all the way through.

Inghai, who appeared to be the mess steward, passed round rice balls and salted fish on broad green leaf serving dishes.

Dena presented the other uzis, and the elephants they were paired with. "Pin Ho, uzi for Miss Chief. Le No has Miss Temper, and Ingy-Pingy, Miss Fat Bottom."

Bows and nods all round. Maximus watched Dena out of the corner of his eye. When the chief uzi plucked up his first rolled ball of fish and rice, Maximus began to eat too. Miriam was tucking in with obvious appetite, which caused a constricted sensation in Maximus's breast—for not providing for her properly. Of course, he and his men fished in the stream and lagoon but it would be rice she was missing. Monkey stew was not to her taste.

When the feast ended; Maximus noticed Ingy-Pingy put down a remarkable quantity of rice-balls; Dena called for arak.

Inghai produced a number of wooden cups, and two pewter ones for Dena and Maximus. He filled them with rice-brandy, and said, "Tuai Rumah Dena, a great man among our Iban peoples, welcome visitors from Inglang. Now we all get drunks."

Maximus put his nose in his cup, and had no doubt of it. Even before he'd swallowed any of the arak, the potent smell of the spirit told him it was not to be trifled with. He glanced sideways at Miriam. She was raising the cup to her lips in toast, but he knew she wouldn't drink spirits, much less remain in the company of drunken men. But Maximus wanted her sharp and focused mind there, should anything of importance come up with the Iban tribesmen.

He turned to Dena. "Rajah James Broke is your particular English friend?"

Inghai refilled cups and Dena grinned. "Jams my very best friend. Muda Hasim, Rajah of Sabah, commander of Sea Dyaks, take my wives and daughters hostage in last war, with one hundred others Iban and Kenyah peoples. Now they home, thanks my best friend Jams. Get all womens but twelve from Rajah Muda Hasim. Defeat Sea Dyaks pretty soon too."

Maximus felt that couldn't happen soon enough. He began to wonder what was so evil about James Broke's empire, that Lord Q wished to quash it so.

"Did Rajah Broke send the great Hoola to honor us?" Miriam said. "I make sure Hoola is no ordinary traveling elephant."

Dena laughed, from the effects of four cups of rice-brandy, and with pleasure at mention of his favorite's name. Miriam had a clear head on her.

"Jams very value Hoola. Know he may be White Elephant someday, sacred to our peoples. After Hoola fight other bull, Jams say send him easy trip. He recover, and will do honor carry Maryam of Persia."

"How very kind and wise." In an aside to Inghai, who was having trouble making the arak reach the inside of the cups, Miriam said, "Shall I pour?"

After a rapid glance at the chief uzi, who nodded his approval, Inghai said, "Cups must never be empties, Maryam of Persia. If man no can drink more, you hold him nose and pour down throat."

Miriam nodded, and taking the arak vessel she began refilling cups with a practiced air. "Hoola must be the greatest elephant in his logging camp, or even all logging camps by the majestic look of him."

"Work Hoola do," Dena said, extending his empty cup to Miriam, "only strongest, finest, smartest, elephants do."

"I should like to know when you wish to leave for the capital, Mr. Dena?" Miriam said. "What orders have you from Rajah Broke?"

Dena blinked at Miriam's rapid change of subject, gazing down unhappily into his half empty cup. "Elephants need rest. Miss Temper, Miss Fat Bottom specially. My best friend Jams, he understand. Say if find, bring before rivers rise."

"I can well understand you should wish to rest your elephants," Maximus said, "though I shouldn't think Hoola needs it. He seems prime to me. Prime and in high fine fettle!"

Dena's eyes shone approval on Maximus. As he opened his mouth to speak, Pin Ho fell face forward on the woven floor between them. Ingy-Pingy looked grave, and Dena pursed his lips. "Hoola great one, true. Rest of us just mens and regular elephants."

"I cannot be ready to leave in under three days, in any

event," Miriam said, extending the arak vessel.

Le No regarded Miriam with unfocused eyes, then slumped slowly backward to lie with one arm flung over his head.

"Quite enough time for a demonstration of Hoola's prowess, is it not Mr. Dena?" Maximus said. "I could not let you go without seeing for myself the wonders the great White Elephant can perform."

Maximus held his pewter cup out to Miriam for the tenth time with a self-satisfied air. It would be odd if he, having drunk whisky, grog, and spirits, man and boy, could not withstand the effects of liquor better than men half his weight and size. Men who, furthermore, were celebrating the successful end of an anxious and tiring search.

Dena swayed toward Maximus. "You see! Oh, yes, I show Tuai Torp what Hoola can do." Dena's forehead hit Maximus's chest, and there he stayed.

Maximus gazed down on Dena's pate through his thinning black and grey hair. He exchanged a glance with Miriam. Understanding came into her eyes—it would be unseemly for any but the chief to go down last—and she turned to Inghai and filled his glass.

"Shall I hold your nose?" she asked.

Ingy-Pingy smiled at Miriam. "I like be naughties with you," he said.

Maximus reached over and gave Inghai a gentle shove floor-ward, the direction he was leaning anyway. Ingy-Pingy continued to grin even as his cheek bounced off the mat.

After arranging the chief uzi in a dignified posture, propped up so that it appeared he'd merely nodded off, Maximus invited Miriam to descend the wood ladder before him. He glanced round at the uzis, all comfortably snoring, none so paralytic they were a danger to themselves, before crawling to the edge of the platform and pushing off from his belly. He tumbled sideways to the ground, gained his feet, and offered Miriam his arm.

"Will you come back to my tent?" she said.

Maximus knew there were serious matters to discuss, but between the arak and his own natural leanings, he said, "Because you want to be naughties with me?"

Miriam laughed. Maximus realized it was that sound, it was her and her lively good nature, that had given him strength to carry on during these last days of hunger, fighting, and desperate work on his wounded ship.

"I do have something intimate in mind," she said. "I want you to read Lord Q's letter."

Maximus was instantly sobered. The little he knew of Miriam's mission in Borneo she'd told him herself. She'd not offered to share Lord Q's letter containing her orders, before now. Professional etiquette Maximus understood perfectly well. And as a gentleman, he would never pry into her affairs. Particularly as her affairs were clandestine, and connected to the highest reaches of British government.

At the edge of the encampment, Maximus caught movement in the shadows. It was Krunk, standing vigil. Watching the uzis' shelters, and then moving away after he spotted them returning arm in arm. How Maximus was to part from Miriam, he did not know. He would also lose two fighters and hunters for his ragtag band of survivors. Krunk and the Hell-Cat must certainly go with her.

CHAPTER THREE

Amid the mildewy smell of the sailcloth tent, Miriam and Maximus sat side by side on the sofa. She watched Maximus unfold her letter from Lord Q. He grimaced at the salutation, written by the head of a secret branch of the British foreign service.

December, 18XX
Aboard His Majesty's Ship *Queen Charlotte*

My Dear Miss Miriam Albuyeh Kodio Blackwell Thorpe,

I must begin by assuring you, your actions here in the Pacific theatre, as well as your assistance in North Africa this year past, have earned the acknowledgement and esteem of myself, my organization, and the Government we serve. To such a degree that you have been suffered to continue in a Vessel ranked among His Majesty's most valued assets. With her captain and crew practically at your own disposal. You are an exceptionally intelligent woman, and will apprehend that this condition cannot exist without Government's requesting and requiring a return.

Your orders are as follows: You will make the

acquaintance of James Broke, gain his confidence, and persuade him out of his delusions of empire. In short, bring him back to his duty as a subject of His Britannic Majesty, the King.

There was a time when many in Government believed James Broke would be a tremendous asset to the Crown—myself not among them I need hardly add. His letters home to his cherished and deeply interested Mother, who lost no time in making them as public as ever she could, extolled the wealth of "British Borneo". Antimony, timber of varying grades and qualities, tin, iron, even gold and diamonds, were claimed alongside a climate and soil ideal for the production of rice, sago, and all the best and richest spices of the East. Spices currently under monopoly control of our allies the Dutch. What counted even more in some quarters, James Broke promised a fertile ground for Missionaries and the sowing of Christian virtues among what he calls his good Land Dyaks, a people without religion and eager for improvement. This abundant wealth—material and spiritual—Mr. Broke claimed, were to devolve upon the Crown for the mere cost of a fleet to sort the piratical Sea Dyaks. A tribe of men, in James Broke's opinion, that "should not be allowed to exist alongside a gentleman."

So far, so much to the good of the King we all serve, I hear you say, Miss Blackwell? But then you would not be counting upon the hypocritical, manipulative, control seeking nature of Mr. James Broke. Sir James Broke it shall be in future, if his mother's campaign succeeds at home. Or if he cannot be discredited for the tyrant he will surely become once England helps him pacify the country. This conclusion is not founded on speculation, ill-will, or rumor, but on the reports of interested parties relayed from the capital of Kuching.

Those reports inform me that James Broke already styles himself Rajah Broke, the First White Rajah of Sarawak. He dashes about the countryside making promises to Rajah Muda Hasim, and other local warlords, in the name of the Crown. Promises that can neither be countenanced nor carried out. His behavior in public is erratic at the same time he seeks to become a Peer of the Realm. An honour that would place him above the Governor of Singapore, and anyone between there and Calcutta.

In light of British Borneo's alleged riches—should it contain a mere half of the resources James Broke has cried up, I would be astonished but well satisfied—and for its strategic importance with respect to our friends the Dutch, the fate of the country cannot be left in the hands of a crack-headed individual with ambitions to rule a private kingdom. Yet because he has cultivated the name of a modern-day crusader, subtle persuasion must be tried before more forceful means are considered.

And there is none, I am persuaded, more skilled in the subtle art of persuasion than you, my dear Miss Blackwell. I know you will not be motivated by the same sense of duty and honour that I, Maximus as captain of *Nonesuch*, and all in Service to our sovereign and country feel. Which is why I must reveal an indelicate aspect of James Broke's character. The public persona he has created of a servant to king, country, and Christian virtues, is belied by Broke's keeping scores of women in his private Rajahs-only harem. He houses them in a ruined temple outside Kuching, and boasts of the many countries and tribes from which these unfortunate fair ones hail. James Broke does not, however, count a woman of Persia among his harem.

And so through careful seeding of news of your travels in the region, this self-proclaimed Rajah has been made to anticipate your arrival.

A woman of your shining parts will know best how to carry out your orders once you are upon the scene. I will not, therefore, offer advice, but merely beg your indulgence of the council of a long gray head. When you leave *Nonesuch* you would do well to remember a man laments not what he does not see. More important, he who keeps his tongue will keep his friend. It is a truth known to all Scotsmen that, in the end, all the water in the sea won't wash out kinship. After you destroy this letter, you may ask Maximus to enlighten you on that last subject.

You have your orders and your mission, Miss Blackwell, and I will conclude by stating that in these you must not fail or you shall answer the contrary at your peril.

I have the pleasure to be, etc.

Q

From Maximus's initial frown at the knowing way Lord Q joined his name to hers, Miriam watched the expression of his face change from annoyance and dismay and then, as he finished the letter, to a fury where steam issuing from his flushed ears and face seemed not unlikely. She let him alone for a moment. He probably couldn't speak English anyway, and would have blasted her in Gaelic. After all, she'd had weeks to mull over the insult, infernal assumption, all the warning and threat in that masterpiece of deception—Lord Q's letter. She must give him time to adjust. Maximus's sufferings of late had been great, and Miriam feared she'd just piled on more.

At last she said, "He never seems to have contemplated my showing you the letter." She reached out and put her hand over the fist in which Maximus clenched it. "He thinks I should have been too ashamed. I almost was. I suppose I really should burn it now."

He allowed her to take her letter. Maximus ran his hands over his beard stubbled, weary, still half-drunk face. He turned red-rimmed eyes on Miriam. "I almost have no words. He is an abominable bastard, is Lord Q, and I am another."

"How can you say so? None of this has to do with you. I was involved with Lord Q long before we met."

"Aye, so you were too, but now! Now it's personal. The ill-will he bears me has extended to you. Lord Q, damn his eyes, with his Blackwell Thorpe, and his insinuations and threats! He is my foster-father, the right old bastard."

Miriam gasped and clasped her hands together over her breast. She should have gotten a clue from the direction of Lord Q's letter *Aboard Queen Charlotte.* "The same as nearly—"

"Oh, aye! The self-same Lord Q as struck me a blow to the noggin so hard as to make me into a freakish piebald creature."

"Oh, Maximus!" Miriam immediately scooted closer to him on the sofa.

Maximus put both his arms around her. He adjusted their positions so her back was to his chest, and clasped both her hands in his. As he inhaled, Miriam felt his shuddering breath and wondered...was he crying?

"My dearest soul," Maximus said, before Miriam could think what to say to comfort him, "only look where we are! How Lord Q would gloat to see me in agonies over sending you away with primitive elephant men to a man who styles himself king, or keeping you here with me. Where any day we may lose our battle with the Dyaks, and then I would lose me head, and you should be taken a slave."

Miriam wanted to claim matters were not so dire as that, but tears rose up instead and choked off that lie. "Is there no chance you would go with me, and the elephant men?" she asked.

"Och, no, m'dear. Being down to one officer, and he wounded, I cannot leave my men and the ship."

They fell silent and listened to the patter of nightly rain on the canvas tent, breathing in the moisture laden air. Miriam reached for a reserve of strength to offer him.

"Didn't you tell me once that in the Navy, one has to choose the lesser of two evils?"

He rumbled out a chuckle. That in itself was a small victory for Miriam.

"We can contrive between us to figure that out. At this moment I'm thinking, since you must stay with your ship, it would best if I went with the mahouts. When we reach Kuching, I will give your coordinates to the British. The Royal Navy will send a ship to your aid."

Maximus seemed touched, for he went silent for a time, only sniffling and clearing his throat.

"It is my kinship with you that will never wash away." His arms tightened round her. Then his voice took on a hard edge. "I am no saying I disagree that the lesser evil is you should go with the elephant men. But before I will see you leave, I need to reassure meself of a thing or two."

Miriam straightened and looked Maximus in the eye. "So do I. I have no intention of skipping off into the jungle alone with a pack of drunkards. But I think, tonight was not the norm. The poor uzis. They were very diligent and tender in their care of the elephants, earlier."

"No doubt they are all very valuable creatures, even Miss Fat Bottom—"

"And Ingy-Pingy?"

Maximus snorted. "You are more than equal to besting Ingy-Pingy, and James Broke into the bargain, this I know. No, if I'm any judge, the uzis are a good set of men. Nor shall you be alone with them. Krunk and Thrax will be with you."

"But Maximus, that will deprive you of two of your strongest fighters."

"Always thinking of others first, you are. But ye know in this case it will no do." He rose and stretched his back. Just as in the between decks in *Nonesuch*, the low canvas roof of the tent prevented Maximus from straightening to his full height. It was something to which he was deeply used. "I admit Krunk and his sacred *kris* will be a sad loss."

He'd told her before that every time Krunk entered the fight, the sea dyaks retreated with horror before the *kris* Krunk wielded with such deadly skill. Miriam had lifted the intricately patterned weapon from the Golden Dragon—another power-mad empire builder.

"Krunk must be the one to decide if he will go or stay," Miriam said.

"That is certain sure," he said. "And so is the choice he will make."

Thrax came sidewinding into the tent, hissed at Maximus, and jumped up on the back of the sofa. The cat began to groom its deeply sodden fur.

"And as to that creature," Maximus said, "who it loves and cleaves to has always been abundantly clear."

Miriam rose and extended her hand to Maximus. "Shall we steal away to your tent and be naughties?" She would not speak of parting. The painful fact of it lay between them like a river, one she meant to cross as often as possible before the actual event.

CHAPTER FOUR

Surprisingly early next morning, considering the events and debauchery of the night before, Dena came to the British camp seeking out Maximus for the tree-felling. Maximus followed the chief mahout into the forest feeling rested and renewed, stronger of body and lighter of limb than he'd been for many a day. The after effects of the loving relationship he had with Miriam. The fact they'd not been attacked at dawn also contributed to Maximus's sense of well-being.

"I am very much in your debt, Mr. Dena, not alone for the rare chance to see Hoola perform his feats of strength," Maximus said, sweating freely and puffing along in the uzi's wake. "It is because of your elephants we were not attacked this morning, I am convinced."

"And I to you Tuai Torp." The chief uzi halted and turned to Maximus with a small bow. "For understand sometime when drink much arak, Ingy-Pingy and others say things no really mean."

Maximus bowed in return. "Let us not go too far into the forest, I beg," he said, brushing his neck where a moth alighted to drink his sweat. "We must not overtax Hoola. He is after all to both fell and drag the tree to my encampment."

Dena gave Maximus a sharp sideways glare, and then began to look about him with the practiced eye of a forest man. Amid tangles of ferns, creeping vines, sago palms and longan trees, jutted the noble trunks of hardwoods. Dena walked about touching the trees, and studying the forest and clearance round each one. At last he decided on a middling sized rosewood tree, with a trunk straight and true and wood that would not even need curing, exactly as Maximus had hoped.

"Now we bring Hoola," Dena said. "Stay behind me Tuai Torp."

They retraced their steps out of the forest, Dena splitting the occasional stalk of bamboo or cutting the tops of ferns to mark their passage. Back at the uzis' huts, all of the elephant men as well as the Nonesuches were awake and about the business of breakfast.

Deep in the tall grasses shoving trunkfuls of sweet greens in his mouth amid contented mastication Hoola heard his man's approach. *La la la, finish your breakfast great Hoola. There is work to do, we need strong Hoola, brave Hoola, La la la.* Reaching for another mouthful of greens, Hoola instead plucked up a wad of grass and mud and stuffed it in the hollow noise maker tied about his massive neck. He snorted. That would settle the little man. Plunged ahead opening his mouth to fold in the next trunkful.

Hoola was keeping his head down feeding and so did not see Fatbottom until he nearly bunged right up against her. The silly cow gave a gasp and tossed up her head, her noisemaker a clang a clang. And then it was *La la la* until your ears ached. The little men standing on rocks and the higher parts of the banks waving singing *Work to do La la la.*

WHITE ELEPHANT

Easiest to do as the little men wished and one by one Fatbottom and the other cows faced round and ambled toward the camp. Hoola didn't hurry catching up mouthfuls as he paced in trunk swinging teeth grinding gut grumbling contented. He wasn't afraid of the men. The cows mere traveling elephants poor dears with reasonable fears. Brought into the life of men from a wild existence in the cruelest way known to men. And this set of beings knew from cruel. Hoola too, who'd been raised by them among them, also obeyed great though he was. Proud Hoola also obeyed.

Back at the men's camp he knew what they wanted. He always knew could smell it their desires see how passionate they waved arms toward the tall trees. Feel the waves of longing. Hoola swung his trunk from the familiar desires of his man — work well for the love of gods do not strain or become injured do not wander away in the forest and find the wild elephants do not do not *La la la* — straight into the crotch of the stranger next to him. Ah, here were interesting new smells desires not so different but such high certainty of gaining them. Not like his poor *La la la* man.

After a long sniff and fondle Hoola knew what the stranger last ate *a stew of babirusa* when he last coupled *in the dark morning hours* and last defecated *an hour since.* Simple frail small vengeful beings. The stranger patted Hoola and said a fair great beast a bonnie great noble beastie. Hoola felt a relaxing of the bowels and let loose a piling plopping mound. A sigh of relief a contented swing of the head. His man and the stranger backed away fast.

But they still want yes they want because the stranger's ship lies on its side with a great hole in it. Every morning the men from the salt smelling water try to take the wounded ship away. Stranger and his men fight blood and sweat smelling and keep their holed ship one more day. Women fight and wrap the wounds, one begs tamarind balls to give Hoola and the cows. Her touch her talk her eyes search his in a different way. Different way from the men. This one most sentient, knows an elephant leads a blessed existence.

Hoola followed them into the forest stands waiting while the men take turns with axes on a great forest tree. The woman next to him. Together ignoring Hoola's men and the strangers' desire to best one another in strokes of the axe. Hoola sniffs her with his sensitive reaching trunk she stands still. He learns she coupled with beastie of the strangers no wonder their head man. She feels the man's desires like Hoola—for the wood that would heal his ship sail away protect her his men his machine—but at bottom she desires like a cows. Let us be safe let our children be happy with enough grass to eat and water to drink and bathe in. Let no bad men arise and beat us and our bodies carried away down river. *La la la.*

Cows. Hoola's head comes up marches forward his turn to show his strength and do his part. Pushing over the top half of the wounded tree. Happy in his strength work done and seen all his life. Hoola's mother a logging elephant. Aims the tree where his man wants it. The great forest spirit falls ripping vines cracking branches a whump. And the earth sighs. Hoola shakes his great head flapping ears to cool his body and paces round. Men will chain the tree to him.

Back to camp dragging man's desire behind him. Pondering a bath green grasses a lie down in the mud.

In the new hospital shelter built four feet above the forest floor, Miriam held Mr. Dashwood's hot hand.

"You will not forget your promise of instruction in use of the Mechanism?" Miriam said. "I must say good-bye for now, but I hope and trust—" she faltered, looking into Mr. Dashwood's fever clouded unfocused eyes. Miriam glanced over her shoulder at Maximus, standing outside the shelter, bent over gazing in at them with a grim set to his jaw. "I hope and trust you will not disappoint my desire to learn from the best, the finest aeronaut with a Mechanism this age. Be brave, Mr. Dashwood, your captain…We all need you."

Mr. Dashwood's eyes found Miriam's face for a moment. She squeezed his hand one final time, and a light of recognition came into the first lieutenant's eyes. He raised his good arm with an effort and brought his hand to his forehead in salute. "Aye, aye, Miss Miriam," he whispered, "not…disappoint."

Miriam folded Mr. Dashwood's good arm over his waist after it fell limp by his side. She leaned forward and kissed Mr. Dashwood's forehead, holding back the cotton cloth of her *hijab* from falling over his sweat damp face.

Maximus placed her hand on his arm as soon as Miriam emerged from the hospital shelter, after she'd said her farewells to all the patients. He led her toward the assembled elephant caravan. This was the parting Miriam dreaded most. How she and Maximus had clung to one another the night before, arms and legs entwined! Now he spoke in a bracing way of the medical stores he had left, with which he meant to treat Mr. Dashwood, and several others.

"I have hopes for him yet," Maximus said of the first lieutenant, "you are no to fret."

He asked her to repeat *Nonesuch's* coordinates, 3° 9' N, 113° 1' E, and desired she should try to track the course of her journey using the navigation he'd taught her. From the corner of her eye, Miriam caught Krunk slipping out through the canvas door of Maximus's tent. Thrax followed at his heels, and then melted into the jungle. Here one moment, gone the next. Krunk took up a position near Dena at the head of the elephant train.

Maximus finished his last check of the contents of a canvas ditty bag Miriam was to carry. Aside from her change of clothes, a hand mirror and a few toiletries, Maximus was sending with her a sextant and compass, an oiled sack with a small sampling from the ship's medicine chest—Dr. James's fever powder, coca leaves, a small stoppered bottle of laudanum—and of course books. They were both great readers, and with the magnanimity and kindness the captain reserved especially for her, he'd allowed Miriam her choice from his cabin's fine library.

She'd selected A Study of the Birds of the Malay Archipelago, The Art of Travel; or, Shifts and Contrivances in Wild Countries, and a few numbers of the Naval Chronicle containing selections from the Journals of H. Cree, Surgeon RN, as Related in His Private Journals of Travel in South-East Asia.

Stopping short of where Dena, Krunk, and the other uzis waited, Maximus wordlessly opened his arms. Miriam walked into them. It was a brief embrace. Miriam felt his heart beat against her cheek one last time. Maximus whispered, "Stay alive, m'dear Miriam, and come back and find us."

Miriam pulled little by little out of his embrace, where she'd like to have stayed a long time indeed, ending with a clasp of his hand. "I promise I shall," she said. She raised a hand to the surviving shipwrecked men of Nonesuch, fanned out behind their skipper.

The elephant caravan set off, fording the small creek that brought the Nonesuches fresh water, and turned upriver along the banks of the Kemena. One of twenty-five rivers to cross before reaching Kuching.

At first Miriam walked at the head of the elephants, in an honored place next to Dena, with Krunk at her side. She'd learned that though Dena, Hoola, and the rest, were sent to carry her to Kuching, she would in fact be walking most of the way. The elephants bore a burden of supplies and trade goods for the journey, but were not actually ridden by the uzis except at river crossings. Or in cases of exigency and incapacity of their human caretakers.

But Miriam couldn't keep the pace of the experienced forest man. She continually glanced back at Maximus, Saramago, and the Nonesuches, until they were swallowed by a bend of the river. Black and red rosewood trees, and tall betel nut palms, crowded right down to the river's edge. A tangle of vines, parasitic orchids, and ferns growing between them—the Borneo jungle itself—choked off Miriam's view of the little group of aeronauts.

"Never worries, Maryam of Persia," Inghai said. Miriam and Krunk, who'd dropped back to walk beside her, were keeping Inghai company at the rear of the column. "Your man here leave sacred *kris* with Inglang captain. That protect him."

Miriam glanced over at Krunk, wiped sweat from her eyes, and considered her companion. "That was handsome in you, Krunk, I thank you."

The *kris* in its finely wrought sheath was missing from the belt Krunk habitually wore slung over one shoulder and across his chest. From it now hung a *parang*, a short sharp dagger, and Maximus's second best light cavalry sword.

Krunk drew the weapon and considered the sharp single-edged blade, adjusting his grip on the hilt with a strong and practiced motion.

"He my captain too," Krunk said to Miriam. His gaze sought Inghai; the veins in his sword arm bulging. "This good blade. Not kill so many as sacred *kris*, but will do."

Inghai sniffed. "Against Lanoon maybe, but how it protect you from Ukit peoples? Blowpipe go *phut phut*, you deads."

Miriam stumbled on an unseen root beneath the leaf mould, and both Krunk and Inghai reached out a hand to steady her. Miss Fat Bottom too paused in her step, extending her trunk toward Miriam, while emitting a low rumbling sound.

"Miss Fat Bottom, she say Miss Maryam of Persia honored guest. I sorrys if I scare. No mean to." Inghai dropped even farther back to walk behind his elephant.

For a time, Miriam tried to follow the plan of tracking their journey the way she and Maximus discussed. Using landmarks, compass direction, and time elapsed between them, to establish the route. But she'd no sooner fixed upon a towering forest tree with strands of curious red fruit clustered high on its trunk, then she passed an identical forest behemoth one hundred yards farther along wearing a similar ruby necklace.

"I shall have to give it up," Miriam said aloud, puffing up a steep hill.

"What up, *khun*?" Krunk said, giving Miriam a little push from behind.

"Navigation," Miriam said. "No doubt Captain Thorpe could do it in this featureless landscape, but it's beyond me."

Silently, Miriam thought that might not prove to be

all that was beyond her. She wondered whether she was equal to this jungle trek. It was not yet mid-day and already her head swam with fatigue, and the heat was beyond anything Miriam ever experienced. The last years of her life, before she'd gone rogue and run away from home, were lived in the mountain city of Tehran.

A brief halt for a meal allowed Miriam to recover her wind. Dena chose an opening in the jungle where wild elephants recently knocked over and devoured a stand of banana trees, creating a clearing. Here the sun penetrated to the ground, a rare circumstance given the fierce tangled canopy overhead. Inghai passed round balls of rice with bits of smoked fish in the middle. Dena, Pin Ho, and Le No, squatted in a group. Miriam and Krunk were seated a little way apart, on the trunk of a fallen tree. Miss Chief, Miss Temper, Miss Fat Bottom, and Hoola, meanwhile, swayed and browsed on left over banana leaves.

The little ball of nourishment, the rest, and water from flasks carried by the elephants, revived Miriam to the extent that she was able to concentrate on the conversation of the uzis. Since entering the primeval forest, the uzis had stopped speaking Malay and reverted to their native Iban. Except when talking to her and Krunk.

So Miriam felt awkward asking Dena, in Malay, "We have strayed from following the Kemena river I find?"

None of the uzis spoke. They looked consciously down at the ground before them, or on the remains of the sticky rice on their fingers. Miriam felt a prickle of fear. Krunk stroked the hilt of the sword on his belt.

Dena uttered a few phrases in Iban, and Le No cleared his throat. "Maryam of Persia, Tuai Rumah Dena, he the head man of our village. No can speak

Malay peoples tongue here. Where Iban, Kenyah, Kelabits, and Ukit mens live."

It was the language of the oppressors, Malay, of these men and their tribes. "I understand that would not be fitting," she said. "It is kind in you to tell me so. Until I learn Iban, will you be so good as to put my question to Tuai Rumah Dena. Why have we left the river Kemena, is it not the first river to be crossed on the way to Kuching?"

The uzis held a discussion, with many a worried glance at Miriam and at Krunk's sword arm. Dena repeated something in Iban while making an emphatic gesture in Miriam's direction. In his eyes, though, what Miriam saw was kindness and concern. She turned expectantly to Pin Ho, Le No, and Inghai.

Silence again. Except for the rumblings and chewing of the elephants, and the ever present calls of forest birds and gibbons. The humans had gone mum.

Krunk cleared his throat and put his hand on his weapon as much as to say, the *khun* asked you a question and you'd best answer. He was particular about her honor. Miriam hoped she might not have provoked a conflict this early in the journey.

But at last Inghai piped up. "Tuai Rumah say, we go upcountry to longhouse of his kinsmen. Cross the river tomorrows. Want distance between us and Lanoons, before they attack Inglang peoples again."

"No one want say so," Pin Ho said, with a sympathetic glance in Miriam's direction. "No one want give Maryam of Persia pain."

"You are all very kind." Miriam swallowed a hard lump in her throat. "And I thank you. But I had much rather know the truth." A vision of Maximus, sacred *kris* in one hand, cavalry sword in the other, swam unbidden before her mind's eye.

Dena rose and the meal was over. Men and elephants moved out of the clearing, Miriam struggling along in the rear.

The elephant caravan emerged from the jungle into a vast clearing. The uniform green of cultivated rice padis stretched before them for some distance on either side of a sparkling river, with a sky overhead full of drifting pink and red clouds. A massive longhouse filled the greater part of the open green space. It was built right down to the river's edge, and extended over it supported on stilts.

Dena halted the caravan near the village landing place, the strand of shore where dugout canoes were beached. The elephants spoke to one another in their rumbling language, and stretched bristly gray trunks toward the water, clearly longing for a bath. Miriam did too. Her *hijab* was sweat soaked, plastered helmet-like to her skull, and her vision blurred with the constant drip drip of it into her eyes.

"Now we waits." Inghai gazed toward the longhouse with the same eager eyes the elephants and Miriam had for the river, and a bath. "Kenyah girls very beautifuls," he whispered, "very naughties."

Dena's kinsman didn't keep them waiting. A procession was approaching from the longhouse, led by a man in a grand feathered and woven rattan headdress. The chief also wore a long red-brown colored cloth skirt, decorated with a pattern of crocodiles, fish, and monkeys. Behind him came his daughters, in tunics made of stacked loops of rattan, some reaching as high as the breasts and some not, with cloth sarongs around their waists. Disks of bone and sparkling shell were tied to the rattan loops, and the young ladies jingled and clinked as they walked. The chiefs' sons and wives and other kin came next, followed by all the families of the longhouse. Everyone not off hunting in the forest, fishing, or working the padi fields was there.

The two headmen, Dena and his kinsman, entered into an elaborate greeting. There was much to and fro of speech and gesture. At one moment they both turned and stared at the white and black strangers: Miriam and Krunk. Miriam tried not to look conscious, but she didn't care to be scrutinized. Beside the young ladies of the jangling dresses she felt like a rag someone used to wipe their brow, and then flung down and trod on in the mud.

Krunk shifted, uneasy, and asked Inghai, "You speak Kenyah, what they saying? Ho, don't give me that stink eye!"

"Please be quiets," Inghai said. "These not our peoples."

There was a score or so children pressing round them now, the mothers clustered behind them. The women wore heavy tortoise shell and colored stone ornaments in gigantic holes in their earlobes, causing them to dangle loose to their shoulders. Miriam felt easier for their presence, and gave the group a bleary half-smile.

The chiefs confabulation broke up with shouts of, "*Makai, makai!*"

A great chatter broke out following the strangers acceptance into the longhouse. Emboldened, the children standing nearest reached out tentative hands to touch Miriam's dress or trouser leg. Many seemed to be repeating the same phrase or question to her. Wits astray, Miriam was unable to understand, her mind reeling with fatigue and heat. Her eyes, meanwhile, met the intelligent brown-lashed ones of Hoola across the way. The yearning for a bath was palpable between them.

Dena was in such good humor, he condescended to speak Malay to Miriam. "They want know if you white everywhere." He nodded at the horde of children.

Miriam was too flushed in the face to make one more blush signify. "Tell them if they show me to the women's bathing place, they may find out for themselves."

With a snort, Dena translated. Instantly every girl, small boy, and woman not otherwise occupied was pulling Miriam away down shore. She resisted long enough to retrieve the canvas bag with her dry clothes. Miriam glanced back as she was dragged down the path. The good uzis—Pin Ho, Le No, Inghai, and Tuai Rumah Dena—after taking off the elephants' burdens, were leading the trumpeting, happy creatures into the stream.

The women's rather inferior bathing spot was downstream of the wallowing elephants. Even so, when they reached the pool formed by a huge tree trunk fallen part way across the river, Miriam went face first into it.

She rolled over, kicking bare feet—she'd taken off her half-boots of course. Her feet were nowhere near tough enough to make the journey barefoot like the uzis. She needed footwear, and meant to husband her one good pair. Diving underwater she ran her fingers through her hair, trying to dislodge the sweat-salt from stuck together strands.

Miriam stood up in waist-deep water, her heart beat uneasy. Not because a number of children and women paddled round her, waiting to have their curiosity satisfied. Suddenly she felt she'd no business there, enjoying cool river water washing her overheated skin. Not while Maximus was left behind. Facing sea dyaks, sickness, wounds, and the hard labor of repairing the ship they both loved, alone.

Many of the children lost interest in Miriam, standing like a statue in the middle of a fountain pool, and went to climb the fallen tree. Once up on its highest point they launched themselves hooting and shrieking into the water. Miriam turned in a slow circle, whirling the water round her. Her brain felt baked, melted by that day's march in the tropical heat.

She tried to keep the important details straight in her mind. Like...where was Thrax? She thought she'd sensed the Hell-Cat, keeping pace somewhere in the jungle, though it was more likely outstripping them by miles. Krunk was with the men and elephants. And Maximus? So much was uncertain. How long was the journey to Kuching? How much longer after that before aid could reach him, the men, and the ship?

Miriam shook her head and plunged underwater. Holding her breath, she scrubbed at her skin and clothes and hair with her hands. *Think! Concentrate! Stop worrying and do someone some good, you ninny!*

She surfaced, gasping, and the scene round her snapped into focus. Miriam shook water from her ears and opened them, the way a brilliant language instructor—another of Lord Q's people—once taught her to do. Little naked brown bodies were somersaulting into the water. The children's piping cries rang out.

"Me first!"

"No, me!"

"I can jump higher!"

The women shuffled in loose circles round her, keeping at a little distance, some feigning at washing clothes. Most wouldn't stoop so low, saying everyone knew that was done at *Mansan jimbio*—the time for drying clothes in the sun. Everywhere there was an amiable chatter and plash of water.

Miriam struggled out of her sodden overdress, and washed it and her duck trousers. She was down to camisole and petticoat drawers. These she'd no intention of removing, since the Kenyah women wore their long skirts in the pool.

A troupe of children a dozen strong swam up to Miriam. "Show us, show us! You white everywhere, lady? Even down there?"

"Hush! Can't you see—"

"White everywhere, I'm guessing, except...you know where."

"She looks at us like she from first family in longhouse."

"And can understand every word you say," Miriam finished for them.

The Kenyah stared in astonishment, then roared with laughter. Women and children laughed so hard—pointing at her and one another, and repeating her words—they began to choke, and were obliged to crawl out of the water and lie prostrate on shore.

Miriam stole past them into the forest to change into fresh clothes. Immediately her dry camisole stuck to her chest and back with humidity. And that was before Miriam pulled a gown over her head. She considered dispensing with the trousers, until catching sight of a parcel of leeches rearing up and sniffing at her from the forest floor. Miriam whipped on trousers and boots, wrapped a light cotton *hijab* over wet hair, and scurried up the path to find Krunk and the elephant men.

Behind her the leeches swayed in disappointment, dreams of bloating on her white skin dashed. Her duty seemed clear. Miriam must urge the uzis along. No stopping for drinking contests, or to be naughties with the local Kenyah beauties. There was not a moment to lose.

CHAPTER FIVE

Maximus ran down the slope from the encampment, cavalry sword in one hand, sacred *kris* in the other, screaming *Nonesuch! Nonesuch!* The only battle cry he knew. His little band of defenders did likewise, charging to meet the sea dyaks. It was the Navy way. The invaders were just pulling their canoes ashore. Long before daybreak, Maximus had been up making his rounds of the sick and hurt, assigning carpentry tasks for the day, and arming and encouraging his fighting men.

They'd no dry powder. Muskets, rifles, pistols, and great guns, were equally useless. Nevertheless, he'd had one of the swivel guns hoisted out and set up on wooden planks at the lip of the camp, overlooking shore. A threat, a show, until the time came when they could dry out their powder and truly rid themselves of the sea dyak's attentions.

The two forces clashed where the strand ended and the slope to the encampment began. At first his Nonesuches had the advantage, descending from higher ground, with the strength of their roared "*Nonesuch! Nonesuch!*" carrying them along.

Soon each of Maximus's defenders was engulfed by dark brown bodies, with black-toothed grimacing faces.

Shouts in Iban and Malay surrounded him. Maximus turned a slow circle, weapons at the ready, surrounded by five men. He struck at the man directly opposite. Yanked his blade back from flesh that yielded with a pop. Whirled to parry a thrust from a *kris*.

A heavy blow landed on his shoulder. Maximus side stepped in time to evade a *parang* aimed at his gut. He spun, and received a slash across his bicep. The heavy cloth of his naval jacket stopped his arm from being sliced like meat. The crowd of screaming, kicking, slashing, bawling, humans shifted. Maximus caught a glimpse of Saramago on his knees.

Several of the Dyaks hurled themselves at Maximus at once, trying to take down the big man, the leader. Maximus kept his feet, bellowing, cursing in Gaelic, hacking and stabbing with sword and *kris*, kicking and slamming around his superior weight.

He lurched his way to Saramago. A Dyak flung himself on Maximus's retreating back, locking hands together round his girth. This left no free arm for his attacker to wield a weapon, and Maximus staggered on. He hauled Saramago to his feet, and bent back. With a violent forward lunge and heave, Maximus flung the man clinging to him over his head. The man's flying body bowled down Saramago's attackers, and cleaved a path in the melee. In the lull, Maximus saw his men clearly outnumbered.

One Jugma Bora, Siamese pirate and polyglot, taught Maximus his Malay. He heard and understood the tribesmen's shouts. "Ransom! Gold, sequins, silver! Don't kill the big *khun*. Don't kill the fat one."

More blows were landing. He was hit on shoulders, arms, and back. Pain at the edge of his mind told him some blows were going home. And he was tiring. A fat man, indeed. Maximus fought back to back with Saramago. The scrappy little Peruvian was a match for any of the tribesmen, an inelegant but vicious fighter, but not for ten of them. Maximus slipped in the churned yellow mud on the strand's edge. He went down into a muck of earth, blood, and spit, his brain in a wild whirl.

Was this how his journey would end? Shipwrecked in the Malay Archipelago, his men slaughtered, his ship taken a prize. His head whacked off by the Iban, after the Malays tried to ransom him. Or dead of his wounds from this day's skirmish, carried off in putrefaction. That best of all women gone but a day. *May you have gone fast, dearest Miriam, may you have gone far!*

Maximus hit the ground sprawling. Several sharp blades were poised above him, only dimly perceived. A shrill panicked screaming started up. The daggers aimed at him faltered, everyone's attention ripped away by the high-pitched wailing.

There was a low woofing bark, followed by an animal roar that cut right through the human screams. At first the Malay and Iban bodies stiffened and stilled. Someone among them yelled, "Ghost-cat!", and they were instantly galvanized into action.

Abandoning weapons, they ran over the bodies of the fallen in a mad sprint for the line of canoes. A snarling, furious, tiger-sized cat, with ticked fur the color of the Thracian steppes, was after them, swiping with enormous paws, lashing a bull whip thick tail.

In the confusion of battle, it was never clear to Maximus if the Malays led the Iban, or the other way around. They were equally eager to quit the scene of action, screaming imprecations against evil forest spirits—elephants yesterday, a tiger today! —and hauled themselves with utmost speed to their canoes. Good, let them think we are allied with the spirit world, Maximus thought, and long may it last!

Thrax came pacing toward Maximus and Saramago, past the dead tribesmen and seamen. The cat didn't turn its huge head, taking no heed of the men's bodies, glaring yellow eyes fixed straight ahead.

Maximus winced with pain and loss. Many of the men the Hell-Cat ignored were old shipmates. He felt their loss extremely. A more immediate frisson of fear crept up his back. Thrax was coming at them with hard glittering eyes, as though it was not done killing yet. And what in God's name did it mean, that the Hell-Cat was here?

"What ho, Thrax!" Maximus called, hoping to stop the Hell-Cat's advance. "Where is Miriam? Why've you left her, eh?"

The Hell-Cat halted at the sound of Miriam's name. It gave a confused shake of its massive dog-like head, and rocked back on taunt haunches. Disdaining to sit in the yellow muck, Thrax crouched, tail whipping from side to side. It half turned away from Maximus, with his straggling band behind him.

"Go back to Miriam, now, do you hear me there, Thrax?" Maximus took a step toward the beast, relieved to see the Hell-Cat become the size of a panther. "Find Miriam and the elephants. Do ye ken, Thrax? No difficult for a great unnatural beastie."

Thrax whipped round on Maximus and hissed. Maximus's heart thudded, it was all he could do to hold himself upright and unflinching. He must keep his feet, and not land backside in mud once more. His men stirred, uneasy. Thrax rose and slinking over to the nearest fallen man, gave the seaman a perfunctory sniff, lifting its lips. Straddling the man as though to drag the body away, the Hell-Cat eyed Maximus.

"Nay, nay! Leave 'em." Maximus fought to keep his voice steady. Thrax had just accounted for half the dead men on the beach. Would he die to keep the creature from taking away a kill?

Swallowing down his fear, the eyes of his men upon him, Maximus took a decided step toward Thrax. Abandoning the first victim, the Hell-Cat moved to another of the dead men. Over the corpse of a Dyak, they went through the same motions. Thrax gathered a nose-full of the man, looked toward Maximus, and being told 'it would no do', slunk farther away diminishing in size. On the edge of the jungle, with a particularly venomous hiss in Maximus's direction, Thrax took off into the undergrowth.

The tight sensation in Maximus's chest eased a fraction. Sagging on his feet, so nearly beaten, he turned round to face his men. Mr. Dashwood came struggling downhill to meet the group of defenders. One arm was still bound in its sling, Maximus was happy to note, while in his other hand Mr. Dashwood gripped a naval cutlass. He was using the heavy sword more as a cane or walking stick, to aid his progress.

"Mr. Dashwood, well met!" Maximus cried, stepping up to support the first lieutenant under his one good arm. "But you should no have stirred yourself so cruelly on our behalf. Isn'a that so, shipmates?"

Faint, very faint, noises of agreement rose from the Nonesuches gathered round.

"Mr. Wagner," Maximus said to the bosun, who sported a kerchief tied round his bald and bleeding head. "Count off five men for burial detail. All other able hands back to camp, and to assigned duties after breakfast. Any wounded step forward, let's have a look at ye."

"One moment, if you please, sir," Mr. Dashwood said, in a faint voice.

Maximus was forgetting naval etiquette in the extremity of the situation, and mumbled, "Right you are, Mr. Dashwood." It was the first lieutenant's duty, when present, to dismiss the company.

"Three cheers for Captain Thorpe!" Mr. Dashwood called, in a shadow of his former youthful cry.

"Huzzah, huzzah, huzzah!"

It was neither loud nor long but, after Mr. Dashwood dismissed them, the men trudged off to camp in congratulatory mood, patting one another on the shoulder.

Mr. Dashwood stood by while Maximus performed a quick triage on the wounded men. Those that could walk were sent in company with two sturdy hands who'd survived unscathed, to cleanse their superficial cuts in the shallows of the salt-water sea. There was one serious case, a puncture of the intestine or stomach from a *parang* thrust. This man Maximus sent immediately up to the new hospital borne between Mr. Wagner and his mate.

All the while Mr. Dashwood swayed, expectant, on his feet near him. Maximus worked fast, not wishing the first lieutenant to face plant into the muck. After finishing with the last man, Maximus was about to send Saramago away with the surgical instruments and the tattered remains of his nightshirt they were using for bandaging. Mr. Dashwood's pale, sweating, serious face, arrested him. If his first lieutenant had something to say, Saramago must hear it. Mr. Dashwood would need help back up the hill, and Maximus meant to stay and join the burial detail.

"Well, Mr. Dashwood," he began, "and so I thank you

for coming. Leading the second wave of boarders, as it were. I will not deny we were in a spot of difficult—"

"Was that Thrax I saw, sir?" Mr. Dashwood said. "Grown to the size of a...of a—"

"Hell-Cat?" Maximus suggested in a reasoning tone, as though it were quite normal for an animal to swell to outsized proportions at will.

"Thrax and no mistake, sir," Saramago said. "Slapping down pirates like a good 'un."

"Now then, Mr. Dashwood." Maximus took his first lieutenant gently under the elbow and turned him round toward the encampment, nodding to Saramago to take his other arm. "We shall hope this appearance of Thrax Gargantua may keep the sea dyaks from our door for a pair of days. We can accomplish much in that time. Saramago will see you back to your berth in hospital. Lie down and recover yourself, Mr. Dashwood, that is an order."

"Aye, aye, sir," Mr. Dashwood replied, his voice weak.

The first lieutenant staggered off, leaning on Saramago, dragging his cutlass in the soft earth until Saramago took it from him. The effort of sounding positive, even cheerful, before his first lieutenant and his steward, had cost Maximus. But it was what was expected of him as a Royal Navy captain, he must lead the men—aboard ship and in shipwreck. Inwardly, Maximus experienced a rush of misgivings. For himself, for his men, and for Miriam. In this hostile, mysteriously spiritual country, he couldn't help but wonder. Did Thrax's appearance mean something had befallen Miriam, that made the Hell-Cat abandon her?

"How was it, *khun*?" Krunk asked Miriam, as she joined the uzis for a breakfast of rice and—the greatest of luxuries—eggs, courtesy of the Kenyahs' hens.

The uzis and Krunk spent the night in individual *bashas* spaced out along the border of the longhouse plantations, to discourage the elephants from wandering in and gorging on their host's bananas. Inghai, as the youngest of the traveling elephant party, and Miriam, were taken into the longhouse for the night. Miriam thought back on the night she'd spent surrounded by the chiefs' daughters, on the floor of their chamber, raised—as was the entire longhouse—six feet over the hogs sleeping and grunting and gassing below them. In the dark hours there also arose giggling and slapping sounds, as Ingy Pingy made his way into the chamber. Apparently, there was no shame to the ladies in being naughties with a traveling uzi. In the morning, as Miriam exited the longhouse, after bowing and giving thanks to her hosts, a pet gibbon kept on the shaded verandah grimaced and made her a lewd gesture. At least, it would have been one in Tehran.

"Tolerable, I thank you," Miriam said. In her mind were Maximus, Mr. Dashwood, Saramago, and the rest. She considered giving voice to her worries, and then said, "How soon do you think we may depart?"

Inghai hustled past them. "Speedy quick, Maryam of Persia. You see."

The young uzi threw glances of mingled apprehension and longing back toward the longhouse. Pin Ho handed Miriam and Inghai broad leaves shaped into cones, with their share of rice and egg inside. Miriam settled on a rock near the river to eat her breakfast with her fingers, highly appetizing after cold monkey stew. Inghai downed his ration by tipping the whole into his mouth, and then chewing furiously with distended cheeks. He hurried after Le No, Dena, and Pin

Ho. The uzis strode into the forest, calling to the elephants in tender sing-song voices, each uzi's greeting unique to his elephant.

The elephants were set loose in the evenings, after the day's work or traveling was done. To wander, forage, commune, and sleep in the forest. Miriam listened to the piping birds and full-throated monkey calls, and watched a jewel-toned kingfisher hunting from a tree branch hanging over the river. Already sweat trickled between Miriam's breasts. She went and washed the egg and rice bits from her fingers, causing a riot among the slender, fast moving fishes in the shallows. Did she have time to visit the women's bathing spot, since the uzis were yet to return?

"Krunk!" Miriam called. Krunk turned toward her from his seat on the rocks. "I'm off to—"

At that instant Thrax broke cover of the jungle and pelted straight for Miriam. Krunk rushed down to the river. He took a stance shoulder to shoulder with Miriam, going so far as to link arms with her. Miriam experienced a shiver of fear. The Hell-Cat rushing them was so wild, so jungle-large.

Thrax drew up at the water's edge, glancing back over its brawny hunched shoulder. A noise of crashing vegetation issued from the jungle, along with the clangor of the elephant bells and the uzis' cries, hailing the return of the traveling party. A short distance from Miriam and Krunk, Thrax turned its leopard-sized head to glare at them. Its muzzle was stained red to the eyes with blood.

The appearance of the elephants caused a commotion ashore. The people of the longhouse came running down to watch the loading of the elephants, to give advice, and bid farewells. Thrax's amber eyes softened for the few seconds they rested on Miriam. It cast a last angry glare at the milling mammoths and people, gave a low snarl, and bounded into the river.

Miriam and Krunk sighed in unison, watching the Hell-Cat stroke for the opposite bank. The cat would go under, and then bob back up farther away. They found they were holding hands and quickly unclasped them. Thrax reached the far bank, shook itself in peremptory fashion, and angled off into the jungle.

"Pisamdeared," Krunk said, using their shipmate Saramago's patois.

"Just what I was thinking," Miriam said.

Dena was calling to them, waving Miriam and Krunk over to join in and witness the leave taking. The chief and Dena went through another ritual of civilities, and at length gifts were exchanged. Everyone in the uzi party, from Inghai to Miriam, wished the banana leaf wrapped parcels Dena received might contain something other than rice and very small and bony fishes. Miriam recognized the velvet cloth Dena was presenting to the chief, while the Kenyah elder beamed satisfaction. It was a fine curtain that once protected Maximus's books in his private chamber aboard *Nonesuch*.

It was like Maximus to provide gifts to ease their passage through the jungle. He was a knowing and kind soul, who judged himself too harshly, Miriam felt. The formalities were over, and Miriam was roused from her reflections by the cries of the children.

"Go along then, white lady! Sorry we not see if you white all over!"

The men, women, and children within hearing laughed, especially when a blush rose to Miriam's pale face. Dena stepped over to her.

"Today, you ride elephant." Dena swept an arm between Miriam and the pachyderms in a gracious gesture. Quietly, he told her, "Only to cross river. Then you walks."

The uzis held a conference to consider the river crossing. Miss Chief was the elephant most likely to lead, but it was left to the elephants to determine which would go first. So Miss Chief, and Hoola, ridden by Dena alone, were ruled out as passenger carriers. Dena decided Miriam was to ride Miss Temper with Le No. Ingy-Pingy and Krunk, he put on Miss Fat Bottom.

Inghai scowled over the assignments, but the other uzis had no patience with him. He'd bragged about his night in the longhouse.

Le No gave a command of, "*Hmit*!"

Miss Temper buckled her back legs to the ground and then her front pair. Le No patted the elephant's wrinkly brown knee where Miriam was to place her foot, instructing her to clap onto the elephant's ear and girth-rope, and hoist herself aboard.

"I do beg your pardon," Miriam said, as Miss Temper's loose hide slipped underfoot. She climbed and pulled her way atop the elephant's back.

The little crowd of on-lookers gave a cheer when Miriam was safely astride Miss Temper. The bristly hairs of the elephant's hide penetrated the cloth of Miriam's trousers, tickling and scratching her legs. She patted the great warm back and expressed her thanks to Miss Temper and Le No, who scrambled up in front of Miriam in a twinkling.

The view from the elephant's back reminded Miriam of when *Nonesuch* was on the verge of a landing. The longhouse, with padi fields and banana plantations surrounding it, lay framed by the deeper green of the jungle. On the other side of the Kemena, waiting to receive the travelers, a few straggling padi fields gave way to thick primordial forest.

Miriam gasped as the elephant lurched forward, and clung to the line round Miss Temper's abdomen. At a gentle urging from their uzis the elephants moved down the bank to the river's edge. Here they paused, swaying and rumbling, and reaching out their questing trunks to the river. Meanwhile the people of the longhouse were still calling out advice, the uzis responding with thanks and farewells. Inghai and a certain young woman were making great cow-eyes at one another. They exchanged waves, nods, and what might have been blown kisses. Krunk, seated behind the departing lover, was puzzled, unable to understand the attraction.

With a determined trumpeting Miss Chief plunged into the river, and the lighthearted moment was over. A river crossing was serious business. The elephants lined up—Miss Fat Bottom, Miss Temper, and great Hoola in the rear—behind the matriarch and waded in to the current. Midstream, water came swirling up to Miss Temper's belly. Miriam bent her knees to pull her boots out of the greenish brown water. Clinging tight, she swayed back and forth with each of the elephant's careful strides.

Overhead Miriam heard the beating of wings. Gazing up from the height of the arched back, with the waters of the Kemena churning below, she caught sight of the banded black and white tail of a great Borneo hornbill.

The hornbill cocked its head and heavy beak, and trained a keen eye on the line of elephants pushing resolutely across stream. A most absurdly frail set of beings rode clinging to their backs.

CHAPTER SIX

Five more rivers were forded that day. At the last stream the elephant party crossed, with the sky above tinged rose and gold colored, Miriam was so weary she nearly fell asleep atop Miss Temper. She jerked awake just before her head struck Le No between the shoulder blades.

The elephants halted on the far side of the Sebauh. The uzis slid down their barrel sides, and at once began unburdening their animals. Le No offered Miriam a hand down from Miss Temper. Miriam was learning to get up and down from the gentle patient creature with some degree of ease, though she wasn't so nimble as Krunk. It had been a hard day's slog through wetlands, rivers, and forests, but there were moments of joy. Miriam was unlikely ever to forget the sight of a herd of Rusa deer leaping and jumping through a flooded plain. Some wore grasses and ferns stuck in forked antlers. It was a landscape that couldn't be attempted without the elephants' amazing strength, their long memories of the terrain, and country wisdom.

There were great stretches of the trek when she'd been afoot, and Miriam got down from the elephant sweat-drenched, with mud caked to her boots and halfway up her trouser legs. Every stitch of clothing she wore was wet and clinging to her skin. Dena led the way up the bank, to a camp site above the waterline. She was no more filthy and weary than the rest, so Miriam helped the uzis and Krunk remove the elephants' packs.

Next the men took the elephants back down to the river. Free of their work attire, the elephants skipped into the stream, raising their trunks and emitting happy noises. They sucked in trunk loads of water that were jetted straight into gaping mouths. After swallowing a few dozen buckets full, Hoola and the cows began spraying water over their backs and heads, flapping their ears in contentment.

Standing at the water's edge, Miriam caught a blast of trunk spewed river water in the face. She picked up a corner of the wet *hijab* plastered to her hair, to wipe it away.

"Can I help?" she called to Le No.

The uzi raised his eyebrows in surprise. He exchanged a glance with Dena, and then motioned Miriam over. Le No gave the fistful of grasses he was using to rub down Miss Temper into Miriam's hand. He drew her forward, while making a scrubbing motion. Lying on her side, Miss Temper rocked toward Miriam, stretching out her trunk. Miriam swallowed down her fear of being squished like a bean, and concentrated on the way Le No placed his hands on Miss Temper.

Krunk was in the water too, with Inghai and Miss Fat Bottom. The elephants finished their baths with luxurious rolls in the water, and staggered to their feet. Krunk waded over to Miriam. The uzis and elephants left the river, marched up the bank to their camp, and formed up in a line. Miriam and Krunk came trailing after.

Dena examined each elephant, running his expert hands over them, seeking out soreness, wounds, troublesome parasites and leeches. The last in line was Hoola, on whom Dena spent extra time and attention, clucking to him in a language of their own. Hoola lifted his trunk and fanned his ears, knelt so his back could be examined, all the while rumbling his approval of Dena's skilled touch.

The inspection over, and the head uzi satisfied, he released the elephants into the forest. Away they went to eat copious amounts of grasses and leaves. Led by one of the cows, the four elephants melted into the jungle with surprising suddenness for creatures of their size.

"Such special beings," Miriam said.

"True that, *khun*."

The uzis were never idle. Le No and Inghai cut and stripped stout saplings, then drove four into the soft earth, suitably spaced as upright posts for *basha*s for the night. Pin Ho and Dena took wooden spears with honed tips from the packs carried by the elephants, and plunged into the river. They swam below the surface for what seemed to Miriam, watching on shore, a longish time. Finally, the two emerged and climbed out on the opposite bank. Pin Ho held up a fat silver small headed fish, and with a whoop he shook it at them from across the water.

"I hope I don't grow tiresome, but I do so want a wash," Miriam said.

On the far bank, the Iban were shouting and gesturing at one another. Dena, apparently disliking Pin Ho's smug triumph, took off upstream after some quarry they couldn't see.

"We help those two," Krunk tilted his head at Le No and Inghai, "with shelters, then look for bathing place."

Miriam and Krunk reported to the uzis. They were told to cut straight trunked saplings as cross-pieces, not the twisted ugly ones, mate, to lash to the posts for the framework. Rattan and jungle creepers, the smooth vines not the ones with thorns that would rip you a new one, were needed to tie cross-pieces to uprights. They cut smaller, supple saplings to form the *basha* floor, two foot off the ground, and fetched palm and fern fronds as a mattress.

Once a roof of latticed branches was added, Le No motioned at Inghai. "Ingy-Pingy know just right leaves for—" Le No steepled his hands, interlacing his fingers like thatch.

Krunk nodded. "We done then? I take Miss Maryam down river."

"You, at woman bathing place?"

Before anyone could react to Inghai's taunt, Le No said, "Tuai Rumah no be pleased he return and no *bashas* ready." He gave Inghai a gentle shove in the same direction the elephants had disappeared. Le No then turned to Krunk and Miriam. "No go far. Jungle like new blood."

With that chilling sentiment ringing in their ears, Miriam collected her second pair of damp, mud stained gown and trousers, and Krunk his weapon belt. They set off along shore upriver. A short walk brought them to a fork, where an island grown up in the middle of the river caused the waters to part round it. A gray headed eagle perched on a dead tree trunk, lying lengthwise across the rock and shingle island. The raptor focused one large intense yellow eye on them, reminding Miriam of Thrax.

"This good spot, *khun*," Krunk said. "Current slows here."

They both stripped off sodden clothing. Miriam

started with the *hijab* over her hair, and ending by peeling wet stockings from her feet. In her small clothes, bloomers and a camisole, Miriam walked into the water. Under the gaze of the unblinking eagle, she took a breath and sank under the surface, picturing Thrax running wild in the jungle.

Thrax unsettled the elephants, and perhaps the uzis too. Everyone knew it, including the Hell-Cat. It was keeping its distance. She admired Thrax's perspicacity, at the same time hoping the cat might not have wandered far.

She popped up out of the water, finding thoughts of the elephants soothed her mind. The birds and forest creatures were gently whistling and calling in the burnished, failing light. It was as though the natural world was taking a breath before a shift change, when the creatures of the night would come out to play.

Krunk was pacing back and forth on the near bank of the river. Miriam was heading out of it to collect and wash her soiled clothes, when a great thrashing and bawling broke out on the opposite side of the island. Krunk rushed into the river, drawing the *parang* he was never without, sleeping, waking, or bathing.

Dena came into view round the fallen tree trunk, wrestling an enormous hissing lizard. The black and yellow reptile thrashed wildly side to side, forked tongue flashing in and out. Braced clear of the ground on four stout legs it snapped at the uzi, trying for a mouthful of calf or leg. Gripping it by its pebbly, prehistoric dragon's tail, Dena was stabbing at the monster with his long spear.

"Cut him head!" Dena yelled as Krunk came charging up.

Krunk, fully prepared to meet an Ukit man, landed on

the monitor lizard with both feet and sliced off its head.

Dena held the decapitated body up by the long tail, high off the ground. "We eat big lizard to-night!"

Stomach churning, rooted to her spot on the far bank, Miriam watched the strange scene unfolding. The broad, pleased grin faded from Dena's face as he took in Krunk's body, revealed by the wet tunic and petticoat bloomers. The fact Krunk had one breast, and no male member, was hard to miss. Miriam plunged into the river and swam flat out for the island.

"What kind of mans is you?"

Miriam heard the Tuai Rumah declare as she scrambled out of the water. Her heart pounded. Krunk was facing off with Dena, who gripped a giant lizard in one hand and a sharp spear in the other. She and Krunk would never make it out of this jungle alive, without the uzis' goodwill. Miriam ran up to stand by Krunk's side.

"None your business kind, that what kind." Krunk flexed his fingers round the hilt of his lizard-gut stained dagger.

"He is whatever he says he is," Miriam said in a strong voice. "It's not up to us to naysay him."

Dena's gaze travelled between the two of them. Miriam was excruciatingly aware of her own exposed body, wet underclothes plastered to her skin. Discomfort and a deep dread of violence caused a painful tightening in Miriam's breast. When Inghai emerged from the forest with an armload of thatching, calling out happily and waving to them, Miriam let out a strangled groan.

Her back was to the far bank, yet Miriam felt Inghai's ogling stare prickling along her spine and down to her butt. She straightened her shoulders and concentrated on the headman. Everything depended on Dena. Miriam prayed Maximus's assessment of the man would be true. She wanted, with a childish desire for reassurance, to reach for Krunk's hand.

Dena raised the lizard and his spear above his head. Would he club Krunk with the corpse and stab him with the harpoon?

In a casual tone, Dena said, "We not Christians or Muslims like you, but we Iban decent peoples. You, whatever man," he said to Krunk, "took off lizard head like a good 'un." He shouted across the river in Iban to Inghai, waded in, and began swimming awkwardly, gripping his weapon and towing his prize.

Inghai ran down to meet Dena as the older man struggled out of the water. The dead lizard was admired in loud excited tones, Dena recounting its stalking in a fierce pantomime. Then the headman herded Inghai back toward camp. Gathering up the thatching he'd thrown down Inghai gazed straight at Miriam and Krunk, still huddled together on the island. He followed Dena into the forest with reluctant steps.

When the uzis were gone, Miriam did reach out and take Krunk's hand.

"I never forget what you say. What you did."

"Stand by you, do you mean?" Miriam nodded in the direction the uzis had gone. "There are good people everywhere. And I only said what was true." Miriam squeezed Krunk's hand. And then she embraced him the way men do, briefly, with rapid shoulder pats. Krunk sniffled.

"I'll tell you another true thing." Miriam headed for the water, clasping Krunk again by the hand. "Lizard for supper is really too sick-making."

The gray-headed eagle, having flown away in disgust at the commotion on the island, returned with a shrill cry. Barreling in low over the island the eagle reached out feathered white feet, and closed its yellow talons round the monitor lizard's head on the backstroke. With powerful whooshing flaps of its wings, the eagle carried its prize into the treetops.

The lump of lizard meat Miriam had been obliged to swallow rested heavy in her stomach. She'd discreetly tossed half her portion of gelatinous yellow tail meat into the bushes. It pained her because the meal was provided with such good spirited generosity by the uzis, but she simply couldn't force it down. The taste was bland and the texture repulsive. What astonished Miriam was the amount of that sickening flesh Inghai, Dena, and the others packed away.

She was infinitely relieved and grateful for the easy manners shown by Dena and all the uzis towards her and Krunk. They laughed over supper, as Dena described the lizard hunt and Krunk's leaping *coup de grâce*. Smoke rose from the cooking fire, and from the little hut where Pin Ho's silver fish and select cuts of lizard were curing, winding its way skyward to disappear in the forest canopy. If anything the uzis were friendlier than ever, making Miriam wonder what Dena told them in private about that afternoon's adventure. She and Krunk were treated with deference. There were no more impertinent remarks from Inghai or quizzical looks when it was time to retire, and Miriam and Krunk climbed in together to share an end of the *basha*.

The shriek of the night creatures was tremendous. Always near at hand, according to the uzis, were chirping frogs and squeaking geckos. There was a furious buzz and whine of mosquitos and other flying insects. Smoke from the curing fire barely kept the travelers from being consumed whole. Fireflies and glowing fungi lit up the darkness round them. Shadows passed darting overhead with a snap of leathery wings—insect hunting bats. At intervals, roars and screams rang out from deep inside the forest.

A snuffling and snorting rose from the bushes ringing the campsite. The uzis lay in a row in the *basha*, alongside Krunk and Miriam.

Into the unquiet night, Krunk said, "Wild hogs finding monster lizard you toss out, *khun*."

Laughter erupted from the uzis. Miriam smiled. She was fooling no one, not in this back of beyond remote and wild place. She and Krunk were lying shoulder to shoulder, fully clothed of course. Because the jungle liked new blood, and they meant to keep as much of theirs as they could. Miriam even wound her *hijab* round her head up to the eyes, like when they were at altitude in *Nonesuch*. She was on the edge of sleep when something in the forest let out a high panicked blood-chilling scream, cut short of a sudden.

"Clouded leopard," murmured the uzis.

Miriam listened to their whispered tales about the big forest cats, ferocious and cunning predators. She thought it kind in them not to bring up Thrax.

CHAPTER SEVEN

Miriam was lying warm at his side. Maximus reached out and grasped slender fingers, was raising them to his lips to kiss, when a voice penetrated through to him, far down deep in his slumber.

"Sir, your honor, four bells." Saramago shook his shoulder.

Maximus sat up, fully awake as all ship captains who mean to make old bones learn to be, ready to meet any crisis. He found he still held Mr. Dashwood's hand, having fallen asleep in the hospital hut beside the first lieutenant. Mr. Dashwood's boyish face was pale and sweating. He fixed a fevered gaze on Maximus, his blue eyes shining. Yesterday's fight, the trek to the strand and back, had taken a toll on poor Mr. Valentine Dashwood.

"You don't suppose that cat, Ttthhhrax, has deserted her, d-d-do you, sir?"

This was uttered in such a weak and stuttering voice that Maximus and Saramago, moved by the same surge of pity, were careful to avoid one another's eye.

"Nay, never think so," Maximus said. "A creature like that, why, it can slip through the jungle, covering miles and miles as easy as kiss my hand. Isn'a that so?" Maximus appealed to Saramago. He might be the captain, but Saramago was the eldest among them and had a great deal of mother wit.

By way of answer, Saramago kissed his hand to the first lieutenant.

"Here and back to Miss Miriam in no time at all, at all," Maximus said.

After performing a quick examination of the injured shoulder, Maximus concluded, "You are to rest in the sick berth to-day, Mr. Dashwood, and never stir. Do you hear me there? That is an order."

"Oh no, sir, I should like to do my part." Mr. Dashwood's head lolled to one side, his voice grew fainter. "I really should."

Maximus and Saramago both reached out a hand and patted Mr. Dashwood, as he drifted into an uneasy sleep.

"Passed sentries, sir, on my way here," Saramago whispered. He'd brought a can of water from the stream and Maximus's shaving kit into the hospital shelter. "No whiff of them buggers."

By 'them buggers' Saramago meant the sea dyaks. Maximus's shoulders relaxed a fraction, and he reached for his razor thinking of Thrax. It struck Maximus how alike his and Mr. Dashwood's apprehensions were, where Miriam was concerned. The Hell-Cat was intimately joined to her, always *her* protector nor theirs. Whether by Miriam's good offices or for its own bizarre purposes, Thrax bought them a few days respite from assault. The price had been dear, and Maximus meant to use every moment of that precious time. He was already working out a duty roster in his head.

He set his razor down unused. "I believe I shall let it alone." Maximus turned to Saramago, passing a hand over his stubbly ginger beard. "I'm told I'm even more hideous ugly unshaven, and I make no doubt tis true."

Saramago grinned, revealing much gum and gaps between teeth. "A true Norte-man, sir. *Confusión al enemigo!*"

A roar like thunder from Valhalla woke Miriam seconds before a wall of rain hit her. She jerked into a sitting position, having to bow her head in order to catch a breath amid the downpour. The *basha* she'd been asleep in folded beneath her, the sapling stakes torn out of the sodden ground. As Miriam struggled to disentangle herself, the palm leaf thatched roof collapsed on top of her head.

She crawled out from under the *basha's* roof, hands and knees squishing in the muddy slush, looking round desperately for Krunk and the uzis. The uzis' *basha*, the little smoke house too, were pelted to sticks by the rain. Straining to hear past the roaring sound that first woke her, Miriam caught high human voices, raised in panicked shouting.

The crash and rush of water was coming from the stream. The night before a mere creek, now it was a full-on swollen river. The waters swirled and licked up to the high bank of their encampment. Miriam scrambled and heaved her way out of the muck. Upright at last, she stumbled toward Dena, Inghai, and the rest. The men were waving their arms and calling frantically upriver.

Miriam turned in that direction and there was Krunk, clinging to a tree root. His lower half was dragging under the mud-brown torrent, while he kept his torso and head above water with a desperate grip. Miriam screamed. The bank with Krunk's tree collapsed, slewing sideways into the river.

A muscular brown arm shot above the surface, and then Krunk's head popped up. Miriam and the uzis ran downstream, trying to keep pace with Krunk. The river was filled with whirling debris. Entire forest giants swirled in its waters. A huge driftwood trunk like the one from the lizard island rushed by, narrowly missing Krunk's head.

A thundering and trumpeting different from the earlier wall of water roar came from out of the jungle. Hoola burst from the forest cover, charging straight for the river.

Dena jumped in the elephant's path, arms waving, commanding Hoola to stop.

With incredible dexterity for such a large moving beast, Hoola veered sideways round the uzis and plunged into the river. Miriam shouted to Krunk, waving and pointing toward the elephant.

"He's there! Oh, get him great Hoola!"

The elephant maneuvered into the torrent. Dena arrived, shouting to Hoola, imploring him to turn back. Hoola, unheeding, maneuvered ahead of Krunk and positioned his enormous body, head downstream and tail to the oncoming rush. Krunk's attention was elsewhere. He was fighting to swim sideways to the current, to reach land and get out of the whirling deathtrap.

"Tail!" Dena shouted to Krunk, resigned to the white elephant's heroics. "Grab him tail!"

Krunk heard, angled off toward Hoola, and thrashing about he flung out a hand. The first dangling appendage Krunk got hold of was not the elephant's tail. Hoola stamped one of his firmly planted feet.

"Oh! You ignorant bugger!" Dena screamed.

Krunk managed at last to find Hoola's tail and the elephant, feeling the weight of the man, his fingers entwined in long stiff hairs, turned toward shore. The great elephant shouldered through the rushing river waters, by a miracle avoiding the spears of trunks and tree branches hurtling by, and lumbered ashore.

Hoola dragged Krunk through the mud and grasses at the river's overflowing edge, almost into Miriam's waiting arms. Shouts of joy rose from Dena and the other uzis, crying Hoola's praises to the bursting heavens.

Her voice too choked with emotion and gratitude to utter a word, Miriam looked deep into the elephant's amber-brown eye. Whatever I can do for you, my brother, she pledged in her heart, shall be done. She reached up and managed to entwine her hand and wrist with the mobile trunk, before the elephant moved away to be properly fawned over by the uzis.

Her arms closed around Krunk. They embraced a moment, before Miriam began searching Krunk for wounds. She lifted an edge of her *hijab*, plastered round her neck and shoulders, and wiped mud from Krunk's eyes and nose.

Krunk blinked back at her. "You face, *khun*! By the goddess, what happen you face?"

It was so unexpected a thing for Krunk to say, that Miriam put a hand up to her face to make sure she still had one. Under her fingers her normally smooth skin was a hilly landscape of swollen insect bites, the worst clustered round her eyes. Now Miriam was aware, the itch and pain of the bites surfaced, and her eyesight past the swelling was not what it should be. If a half-drowned man only just pulled from death made comment, she must be a wretched, bedraggled, feasted upon sight, indeed. Miriam laughed, hugging Krunk close to her.

The rain was abating, it was no longer the 'waterfall of heaven' the uzis were discussing a few paces away.

Their feet making little sucking noises, Miriam and Krunk walked over to the group round Hoola. Miriam had mud in unmentionable places, but there would be no returning to that river to wash. It was more important by far to thank and recognize Hoola for his courage and selflessness. Krunk stepped right between Hoola's tusks and leaned his forehead against the base of the heavy trunk, communicating his silent gratitude.

Five days and three rivers later, the traveling elephant party crossed the river Mina. Miriam and all the people were on foot. The Mina was shallow, peaceable, and slow moving. The last two mornings had dawned cool. Her face was healed of welts, and Miriam hoped the change in weather might keep the insect life down. She enjoyed the heavy mists of these mornings in the jungle, with the tree tops disappearing into fog. The local monkey troupes, unseen in the foliage, winding their calls like a dozen bosun's mates.

Dena, unable to resist anyone who valued and esteemed Hoola, was become fast friends with Krunk since the river rescue. He told Krunk they were on the cusp of a cultivated and populated region, one where the rivers were navigable. They must keep a sharp eye out for inland-raiding sea dyaks.

On the bank of the river Kakus near its joining with the Mina, Dena held up his hand for a halt and silence. The elephants were calling with short squeaking noises, and raising their ears erect. All faced the same direction, with an aspect of concentration as though listening to something happening a great way off. The cows began an odd drumming of their trunks against the ground. The uzis reacted at once to this behavior of unease in the elephants.

Dena turned and set a swift pace upriver, putting distance between them and whatever distressed his charges. Hoola obediently followed the cows, but raised his trunk and gave a full-throated roar. It rang out in all directions, nearly knocking the humans off their feet.

"Tuai Rumah, he knows elephants very wells," Inghai told Miriam and Krunk. "Elephants hearing powerful. Maybe they hear wild elephant sounds. Capture and breaking wild elephants sounds."

Those words chilled Miriam's heart. When camp was made that evening there was a noticeable lack of good cheer, of the relief that came at the end of other days marches. Krunk constructed the *basha* they would share about fifty yards away from the uzis. Fifty yards was no great distance, except in the jungle. The vegetation was so dense it was possible to lose your companions a few feet away. But Krunk had his reasons, and kept his own council.

She was grateful enough to crawl into the *basha* to sleep that night. Not so knocked up from the rigors of the day as she'd once been, she was still powerfully tired. Inwardly she groaned when Krunk sprang to a crouch beside her, all tense and on active alert.

"What is it?" Miriam whispered, as though her voice could be heard over the chirping, trilling, and humming of the night creatures.

A pair of tawny colored furry paws appeared on Miriam's side of the *basha*. Thrax's leonine head thrust up, licking its chops and staring her in the eye. She relaxed a fraction, then realized Krunk was strapping on his weapons and about to jump out of the *basha*.

She sat up, reached out, and grasped Krunk by his muscled upper arm. "What's going on?"

"Hell-Cat and me." Krunk nodded in Thrax's

direction. Thrax was no longer there, peering in. Miriam heard munch crunchy noises coming from just outside the platform. "We go see about wild elephants."

"The ones Inghai spoke of? That was just talk. You know how he loves a tale."

"No, *khun.*" Krunk's shoulders slumped a little. "They trap wild elephants. Mostly cows with they calfs. The men beat and humiliate them—Dena, he say elephants have most sensitive feelings—and it break they spirits. Until elephant spirit broke, she not fit to sell off for work."

Miriam's mouth went dry. She scooted forward to the edge of the *basha* near Krunk. "Do you really mean to go out into that fearful jungle at night?"

She glanced over the edge of the *basha's* platform, catching movement on the forest floor. A squirming, shining iridescence, like a shallow stream passing over a bed of parti-colored pebbles. A crunch-crunching sound drew Miriam's attention. Thrax had a mouthful of long shiny green cockroach. Turning its head this way and that to keep hold of the wriggling roach, the Hell-Cat chewed happily away.

"Maybe you no understand, *khun,*" Krunk said in a hushed tone. "I owe their kind gratitude. Even if small chance this true, I must be there."

Miriam let go Krunk's arm with a squeeze and reached for her half boots, hanging upside down from one of the *basha's* posts. "You are like the heroes of old, Krunk, truly. Will you allow me to go?"

A flash of white teeth radiated from one of Krunk's rare smiles. He put his hand out, palm up, and Miriam took it. Both shod after their own fashion they jumped together off the *basha's* edge, and scattered the cockroaches in the immediate vicinity.

Thrax choked down the last wriggling legs, gave them an attentive stare, then whipped round and headed into the jungle. Krunk took up a machete that had rested at their feet, and followed as rear guard behind Miriam and the Hell-Cat.

CHAPTER EIGHT

They hadn't gone one hundred yards away from camp, before Miriam began regretting the whole venture. The vegetation was so thick, and not to give themselves away by using the machete, they were obliged to crawl on hands and knees through the undergrowth. Their sluggish pace caused Thrax to turn and glare at them in disgust. At every step or hand plant, Miriam feared encountering viperous snakes, outsize prodigious biting insects, thorny stinging jungle creepers. There was even a vine, the uzis warned, that oozed a sap causing blindness. Wouldn't it be lovely to blunder into any of those at night? Dead in the wilds of Borneo from stupidity.

But at last Thrax led them out of the tangled jungle into a wide meadow opening to the river. On the floodplain before them grazed a herd of elephants. Miriam stood, besmirched and be-smutted with jungle muck, and gazed on the wondrous sight.

Overhead arched a glory of southern stars, dazzling in this rare open space, and seemingly close enough to touch. There was Venus, brighter than the rest, shining in the western sky, the direction they'd come from the uzis' camp. Almost without conscious thought, Miriam noted which way was South. Navigation by the stars, using the Southern Cross and the Pointers, was something both Maximus and Mr. Dashwood had impressed on her at sea.

"Like sailing in dear *Nonesuch*," Miriam whispered.

"Over gods own creatures." Krunk nodded toward the elephants.

They were luminous, silver gray in the moonlight; shining like justice, and peace.

Thrax gave a low growl to recall them to duty, and made off, skirting round the edge of the clearing. Miriam and Krunk followed, soon deep in boot sucking mud that absorbed much of their attention. After a long slog they were all the way round the floodplain. Miriam hoped they might stay near the river for a spell, the jungle was a fearful place in daylight much less at night, and the going would be easier.

From out of the tall grasses surrounding Miriam and Krunk, a dark looming shape emerged, and stepped directly into their path. The massive creature flapped its ears with a snap slapping noise, strategically cutting Miriam and Krunk off from the Hell-Cat. They found themselves staring up at the short white tusks of a bull elephant.

Miriam's heart leaped and her throat closed with fear. Then she heard the reassuring, low rumbling greeting of the elephant.

"*Hmit.*" Krunk gave the command the uzis use for *down.*

Hoola's back legs folded gracefully and the great elephant eased his front legs out and down. Krunk took hold of an ear and the band slung round Hoola's middle and swung aboard. Miriam's heart misgave her when Krunk extended a hand to help her up. Hoola was not to be ridden. Dena was his uzi. The elephant was near sacred, would be a white elephant one day if Dena had his way.

Krunk grew impatient. "You rather crawl through jungle whole way?"

Self-interest, then, decided her. Miriam put her hand into Krunk's and scrambled up. "Thank you, dear Hoola," she said, as she gripped the elephant's ear.

Having never ridden a bull elephant before, Miriam was unprepared for the towering height. The view was oh so much improved—the cows grazing companionably in the meadow, the river reflecting the multiplicity of stars overheard, the fringe of dark forest echoing like a living orchestra.

But too soon Thrax, sliding along ahead of them, veered away from the river into the forest. The dense jungle closed round, and the sense of freedom and adventure faded with the light. In its place foreboding and unease crept in. It seemed to Miriam that Thrax and Hoola were stepping up the pace, and moving swiftly through the jungle.

Miriam and Krunk bent low over Hoola's back, avoiding the hanging vines and creepers, many of which had wicked sharp thorns.

"Hoola is Dena's elephant," Miriam said to Krunk, their heads coming together as they bowed over the elephant's gray and pink mottled hide. "Can it be right for us to take him?"

"He take us, *khun*, case you no notice. Not other way round."

Hoola passed into a clear space in the forest, formed by fallen trees. Miriam and Krunk straightened and sat upright.

"Hoola work for Tuai Rumah Dena," Krunk said. "No

belong him."

Miriam recognized the justice of that. She nodded and placed her hand briefly on Krunk's shoulder in acknowledgement, but it didn't lessen her sense of wrong-doing. What if the uzis of these elephants they were going to liberate were good men like Dena, Pin Ho, Inghai, and Le No, and they—she and Krunk, the outsiders—were taking their livelihood from them?

Something changed in the gloom of the forest as the clearing was left behind, here grew a great quantity of eerily glowing fungi, and both Thrax and Hoola, for all his great bulk, were gliding along on velvet feet, barely disturbing the leaf mould above a whisper. Finally, even Miriam smelled smoke, and caught a glimmering light penetrating the jungle undergrowth. The fires and torches of men.

Krunk leaned forward and down, a silent signal to Hoola for kneeling. He'd learned a thing or two from Inghai and the other uzis. Miriam slid to the ground after Krunk, and knelt by his side to gaze toward the winking firelight.

"You beast and me go look close, *khun*. You stay with great one." Krunk made a bow to Hoola, hands pressed together before his chest.

A momentary hush and lull in the piercing shriek of night creatures, and the shouts of men, and the distress cries of elephants reached them. Hoola swung his great head, and shifted in place. He eyed Miriam and Krunk with one large intelligent eye, as though demanding what they would do about it.

"Go then," Miriam squeaked. "Hoola will protect me."

Krunk and Thrax stole away toward those dreadful cruel sounds. Left alone in the dank warm forest with a war elephant, Miriam was afraid. She took a deep breath, willing her heart to stop its pounding, and reached out and touched Hoola.

The loose bristly hide under her hand, the way Hoola curled his trunk round to touch her in turn, his massive size and palpable strength, instantly calmed Miriam.

"We'll be alright," Miriam whispered to Hoola, her heartbeat slowing.

Hoola gave one brief low answering rumble. A short, tense wait ensued. Then Krunk returned, moving with silent stealth.

"This way." He led Miriam and Hoola away from the flickering firelight. "Five men, *khun*." Krunk reported on the way. "Three in camp drinking tuak. Two guarding elephants."

They hid under cover of the trees at the edge of another clearing in the jungle and gazed at the well-constructed pen, illuminated in the moonlight, guarded front and rear by men with spears. The elephant pen was set into a pit dug five feet into the forest floor, and fenced round with stout tree trunk posts and heavy branches for the cross-pieces. Miriam and Krunk found Thrax blending with the undergrowth. Crouched down, whipping its tail, the cat lifted its lips with silent menace toward the enclosure.

Now they were four; two humans, the Hell-Cat swollen to fighting size, and one magnificent elephant; staring at the shocking sight, and listening to the cries of captured mothers and babies.

At intervals one of the two men climbed a wooden ladder set against a side of the rectangular enclosure. From there he jabbed with a bamboo stick, shouting obscenities, and finished off by throwing rocks down on the elephants. The animals set up a desperate trumpeting, that made the two men laugh.

"Gonna laugh out other side face," Krunk said, low between clenched teeth. "Quiet as quiet, we take those two out. Get in there, cut those elephants loose. Sure, they tied up."

"Wild elephants," Miriam whispered. "They're going to squish us like beans."

"Could do, yes, *khun*."

Krunk gave Miriam a weak half-smile, exchanged a nod with the Hell-Cat, and they both leapt up and charged away. Together, they broke cover of the trees. In a flash Thrax raced away round back of the pen, and Miriam heard a muted growl and a cry of panic. Then, nothing at all. Krunk's battle took place right in front of Miriam and Hoola, watching from the ring of trees.

He raced into the clearing, sword in one hand and *parang* in the other, straight at the man guarding the gate of the elephant pen. Krunk's dark skin helped conceal him, so that when he smashed into the guard it was a complete surprise attack. The man had his last laugh at the suffering of others.

Miriam and Hoola hurried into the clearing, to the front of the pen. Krunk, after dragging the guard aside, was heaving up the horizontal wooden post used to lock the trap. He and Miriam pulled wide the tall wooden gate of pointed stakes.

Four frightened cows gazed out at them. Two had calves, only one was left alive. Each of the elephants lifted its trunk and wailed, leaning toward them, pulling at one hind leg bound to the heavy upright posts of the pen. They'd been staked in such a way, calves in the middle, that they couldn't reach each other even if they stretched ever so much. The worst was to see the mother desperately pulling, and straining her trunk toward the body of her baby.

Miriam drew the three-inch blade, the *sgian dubh* Maximus gave her long ago. She strode down the earth embarkment into the pit. "Be confident, be brave." Miriam murmured to give herself courage, plunging among the frightened animals.

Krunk followed with his *parang* drawn. "We smell different, we not mens." He reassured her. "Hoola lead them out, once they free."

First, Miriam went to the cow with the dead calf. She knelt down beside the rattan tether, stroked her hand down the wide ankle, and grasped hold of the loop that was cutting into the elephant's flesh. She sawed with careful determination on the heavy twisted rope. The blade was sharp, and she plopped back on her backside when she'd cut all the way through. The released elephant lurched forward, with no will but to reach her little one.

Two of the other cows were freed, thanks to Krunk's skill with a blade. They met up beside the surviving calf and its mother. The sweet little elephant calf gazed at Miriam and Krunk, working to cut the tough fiber bonds, with mingled fear and hope in its innocent eyes.

"Go!" Miriam urged, when mother and baby were loose. "Take your little one, go!"

The cows were calling to one another and filing past to pat and stroke their condolences over the unmoving baby and mother. Then there were rumblings and the beginnings of triumphal cries, and Hoola's big frame filled the opening of the pen. He rumbled back at the cows, shaking his great head as though to hurry them on. Eager to quit the evil place, the two elephants Krunk released first were moving up the earthen embankment out of the pit.

Miriam and Krunk watched from behind their wide

rumps as the elephants lumbered through the open gate at the top of the embankment. The cow with her calf, little trunk twined firmly round her tail, moved up the ramp and out to freedom.

Only the cow with the dead calf was left in the pit with Miriam and Krunk. She was rocking over the body, moaning and feeling it all over with her trunk. Hoola and the other cows called to her. The poor mother kept pushing the body with her head, and trying to raise it up with her trunk.

A great trumpeting blast rang out. The earth shook with the thud and reverberation of heavy fleeing feet, and the receding crash of frightened elephants. The gate of the trap swung shut. Angry shouts and the cries of men reached Miriam and Krunk, down in the pit with the grieving mother.

Krunk yanked Miriam into the center of the pen, farthest away from the enclosing walls, just as a head and shoulders popped up over the side. The face scowling down was striped with ash in vertical bars.

"You lose us elephants!" A strong arm hurled a heavy misshapen missile.

Dung, fragrant and fresh from a terrified elephant, landed near their feet. From behind came another voice, and Krunk instantly whipped round to face it. He grasped Miriam's hand as he did. "Back to back. You, me, and our sidearms. Old style."

Miriam's answer was a half squeak, half sob.

"A woolly head and a white woman!" The second man shrieked.

He was torn from his foothold, and another man took his place on the ladder. This man, faced painted with swirls of ash, stared down at them as though he couldn't credit what he saw.

Swirly ash-face pointed, baring his teeth at Miriam and Krunk. "You leave us one broken elephant? We gonna cut off black man head, stick our *palangs* in white woman!"

He hurled a sharp ended bamboo spear, one used to torment the elephants. Miriam and Krunk darted away. Krunk crossed his sword and machete blades. Miriam held the *sgian dubh* in a trembling underhand grip. Together they moved in a slow circle, trying to face all enemies at once.

There were three men. Each took a turn yelling insults, and bragging about what he would do to Miriam. One climbed to the top of the ladder, and performed a lewd jerky pantomime. The others hurled rocks and excrement over the pen walls.

The men were drunk on rice wine, but intoxication would fade. Then they would bombard them to wound and disable, so they could get close to her and Krunk in the pen. Miriam gazed at the three-inch black blade gripped in her white knuckled hand. She knew how to use it, thanks to Maximus, but use it to kill she'd never done. She glanced with equal awe and envy at the long-bladed sword in Krunk's expert hand.

Krunk, feeling her eyes on him, said, "Promise I not die before you."

And there it was. The ever present, omnipotent threat to women: Rape. He was offering to kill her, rather than allow her to fall victim to the dyaks. Miriam swallowed hard. How easy it'd been to slip out of the *basha* feeling like a hero on a quest. How her legs trembled now. She strained for sounds of the elephants. Being wild, and after what they'd endured, they'd run when freedom opened to them, poor creatures. Thrax she hadn't heard or seen since the rush of the guard. Please, please let the

Hell-Cat still be out there. Her protector and faithful friend had pulled her from more than one fire.

There came a *pfft pfft* sound, followed by a whoosh of air.

"Merciful God!" Miriam cried.

Krunk and Miriam leaped aside. The mother elephant gave a squealing trumpet of protest.

A dart landed a few yards away, poisoned head buried in the dirt.

The three men hooted. Two were tussling over who should be next up to take aim at the victims in the pit.

"Fire into the black!" Swirl-face yelled.

He turned, grinning, to his companion farther down the ladder. Swirls' eyes went wide, he threw back his head and gave a full-throated scream. Then he disappeared; launched, hurled, or tackled off the ladder.

"Ready, Maryam?" Krunk murmured, crouched and crackling with energy. "Be ready!"

Screams came from the opposite side of the enclosure wall. White tusks thrust between the lower branches of the fence. The cow in the pit made them jump with a sharp, trumpeting roar. The tusks shook and heaved, the great bony skull pressed inward, and one entire side of the pen collapsed into the pit.

Krunk grabbed Miriam's arm, gave her a push toward the fallen wall, released her and sprang. A half dozen vaulting, leaping steps carried Krunk upward over the lattice of branches. Miriam tried to spring after, slipped and barked both shins, fell to hands and knees on the uneven and broken wood, and crawled and scrabbled her way to the top.

Rising out of the pit, her eyes came level with two of their captors. They were squished like burst melons. Limbs bent at unnatural angles, they were lying in ruins near the splintered ladder.

"Maryam, the gate!" Krunk shouted. "Run!"

Miriam heaved open the pen gate, stomach muscles clenching, willing the cow to come out with all her being. Krunk and Thrax sprinted after the one remaining elephant hunter, fleeing into the forest. Out of the pit the mother elephant charged, slewed round, and joined the pursuit, tail held high. Miriam lurched toward the ring of forest. At the edge of the clearing appeared Hoola. Light colored against the dark tangled vegetation, the great pink and gray elephant stood luminous, shining almost white. She ran toward his light.

Hoola led Miriam through the clusters of phosphorescent fungi, and on deep into the forest. She stumbled along as fast as she could in the bull elephant's wake, panting with the exertion of leaping over fallen trees and climbing creek banks Hoola stepped up and over with ease. The elephant never paused in his stride, nor turned or bent his knees so that she could climb aboard and ride.

She kept glancing behind her, searching for any sign of Krunk and Thrax in the weird green half-light of glowing mushrooms. Dreading instead to see that last man, his leering striped face rising out of the undergrowth. Miriam stopped looking back. In turning around once, she momentarily lost sight of Hoola in the thick jungle. The movement of his long swishing tail caught her eye, and relief flooded through her. Miriam pushed her way forward to the great elephant, determined to be Hoola's little bean shadow.

Nothing in the jungle was familiar, except for the constant drip-drip of water, the smell of rank vegetation, and the clamminess of her skin. One section of tangled trees covered in enormous flowering orchids, vines, creepers, and ferns sprouting from every crevice, looked very much like any other. Miriam wasn't sure this had been their route in, she wasn't sure of anything. But with unerring purpose Hoola brought her to another forest clearing, where he finally halted.

Under a patch of star filled night sky the four cows, even the wounded mother, encircled the one surviving calf. The elephants were swaying and touching and joining their trunks. Having smelled and heard Hoola and Miriam long before they appeared, the wild elephants rumbling out greetings of welcome.

Miriam's heart lifted at sight of them. Unfettered, together still. Sadly diminished, but with their little elephant group intact. She glanced over at Hoola, swaying beside her under the trees at the edge of the clearing. He returned her gaze. A glimmer was in his wise brown eye and he waggled his head, as though to tell her she might as well go along.

The calf was allowed to break through the family huddle, and came over in a skipping, zig-zagging trot. Miriam laughed, and then began to weep. She took a few steps to meet it, holding out her hands. The soft little finger of the calf's trunk grasped her hand. In another moment Miriam was surrounded by elephants. The cows rumbled and lowered their bony heads, the better to gaze in Miriam's face. They smelled of earth and crushed vegetation. Many sensitive trunks reached out to pet and caress her.

"Oh!" Miriam exclaimed, wondering if her heart could withstand this joy, coming so hard on the heels of violence and fear. "Oh, it is not me you have to thank! Hoola, Krunk, and Thrax are the ones..."

Her voice disturbed the elephants. She never

regretted anything so much in her life. They pulled away from her outstretched hands, gently shifting round to face the ring of forest trees. Between their large humped bodies, Miriam searched for a glimpse of Hoola at the clearing's edge. She turned in a circle, squinting into the forest, hoping for sight of the great elephant, glowing pinky-white.

Hoola, the great one, the next White Elephant, was gone. The cows too and their sweet baby were moving away into the jungle. Miriam hesitated, her heart pounding. She started to follow the elephants, then stopped. What was she doing, about to trail a group of wild elephants into the jungle? They would go in deep, they would travel far. Miriam was confused, worn out by the terrible highs and lows of the night's adventure.

She'd best sit down, try to assess what in all of merciful creation she was to do now. Make an officer-like decision, that was the way. Miriam had seen Maximus and Mr. Dashwood do it time and again in a crisis. Right. A fallen log offered a seat, and Miriam was about to plop down when she spotted the six foot long cobra pressed along its length, blending perfectly with the leaf mould.

Miriam backed away slow, a small sob escaping her. She moved to the side of the clearing where Hoola once stood, marked by a great moist pile of his droppings. The moon and stars lit a fleet of shiny brown beetles, already hard at work on the dung.

For a time Miriam cried, and watched the busy bugs, longing for Krunk and Thrax. She gazed up at the stars in the patch of sky above her head. Was that Venus, declining in the East? Could she navigate by the stars the way Maximus did—if she could see the entire heavens? When dawn came would the forest be so full of mists that it would be impossible to tell from what direction the sun arose? She was keenly aware of the extent of her own ignorance, but she'd no desire to perish walking around the jungle in circles. Miriam rose, and walked to the side of the clearing where Venus would soon disappear below the horizon and set her back to it.

Sitting on the forest floor, her knees hugged to her chest, more than anything Miriam felt her own smallness. A little speck of a being, huddled afraid and lost in the jungle. No hero, no warrior. Probably unable to find her way in the forest, unable to survive alone for long. What value did her life have, she was little good to man or beast.

Other thoughts began to prey on Miriam's exhausted mind. The striped and swirled and naked leering faces of those men, with their taunts of putting their *palangs* in her. What was a *palang*—a dagger, like a *parang*? Miriam shivered in spite of the close humid atmosphere. What was she doing there, in the middle of Borneo?

Her thoughts were confused, her head lolled down onto her knees. Maximus! She must help him. Poor Mr. Dashwood, dear Saramago, and the rest of the Nonsuches. Send a ship to aid them. Ships and elephants, screams and vulgar shouts, whirled in her head.

There was something else she was committed to do, but it escaped her. Miriam cast about, letting her mind wander away from her physical predicament, her vulnerable little corporeal self. Then she had it, grasped it in her hand, and examined it. Lord Q and the mission to bring James Broke—the White Rajah—to a proper respect for British claims on his loyalty and duty. That was the reason she was here, in this remote unknown corner of the globe.

"Damn you too, Lord Q," Miriam said aloud. "Enough! It's my mission now."

She woke with a start, almost sprawling backward into the forest litter. It was morning, for through the thick mists rising between the massive trees, the patch of sky above was most definitely lightening. And it was brightest, if Miriam did not mistake, over her shoulders. She unfurled from the upright fetal position she'd been in, and got to her feet, careful to keep her face to the west. The direction she meant to strike out, and follow the transit of the sun if ever she could, walking west back to the uzis' camp.

Across the clearing and into the forest Miriam strode, with her heart pounding and her throat constricted with fear. She was determined not to let fear rule her, and the rigors of the forest, like sailing at sea, soon required all her focus. She was out of breath from slogging up muddy hills and controlling her slide down slippery slopes between the boles of massive trees and scattered rock. Her gaze was turned frequently and anxiously upward, trying to gauge where the light was strongest behind the umbrella of tree tops.

She labored on, setting a determined pace, her legs and lungs burning and crying out for a halt. But Miriam was aware if she stopped, and really began to consider her situation, desperation might overwhelm her. And then a tinkling intruded on Miriam's darker thoughts, like the sound of hope.

At last she stopped, swaying where she stood, and tried to stretch her ears. Her hearing was keen, and she searched for a man-made noise underneath the whistles and hoots of the day awakening forest.

And then she heard it again, the sound of an

elephant's teak bell. More than that, there came a faint voice, calling, "Maryam, Maryaaaaaam of Persia!"

She felt pure knee-weakening relief, with her heart on the edge of bursting.

"Here!" Miriam croaked. "Ahoy, mates! Ahoy!"

They kept calling to one another, until Inghai, riding Miss Fat Bottom, appeared directly ahead of her, ambling out of a thicket of hibiscus grown together to form an arched passageway. Better still, Krunk was with them. Sliding down from Miss Fat Bottom's back, he strode up to Miriam and embraced her. They leaned their heads together, fellow survivors—brothers, or sisters—like never before.

"Is Thrax..."

"Well it is." Krunk moved his head toward the surrounding forest. "In its natural element."

Miriam sniffled, nodded, and glanced up at Inghai and dear Miss Fat Bottom. "You are the beautiful sight of the world, Inghai. A flower on your heads," she patted Miss Fat Bottom's shoulder, "for coming to fetch me."

Inghai's expression was sour and disapproving. "You think you do anything this forest we no knows about? Tuai Rumah, he say, 'Take man Krunk, go find Miss Maryam of Persia. Got herself lost chasing wild elephants.'"

Krunk boosted, and Inghai hauled, and Miriam landed atop Miss Fat Bottom. They set off, gratitude brimming in Miriam's heart for this new day. She learned Hoola had brought her very near safety. They emerged from the jungle some five hundred yards later, onto the floodplain nearby the uzis' camp.

The sight of the uzis circling the clearing greeted her, calling out their *la la la's*, with the elephants making their way through the tall grasses, swaying like waves in their wake. A more welcome, homely sight Miriam couldn't imagine.

She slid from Miss Fat Bottom's back when let off, and ran over to Dena. The head uzi was preparing Hoola for the day's travel.

"And here is Hoola!" she exclaimed.

She was dirty, dark circles beneath her eyes, her hair disarrayed, and her clothes besmirched and begrimed.

"Of course, Hoola here." Dena gave her a long considering stare. "He much more sense than go meddling where he no belong."

The head man scoffed at her, but in his eyes there was no derision. Quite the opposite. It was a look of respect, Miriam was certain, for both her and Krunk.

"Today, you ride," Dena said. "Krunk and you, Maryam of Persia."

Before leaving, Miriam had to know one thing. She took Krunk aside while the uzis were busy with the elephants' packs.

"Did you see them again, the wild elephants?" she whispered. It seemed desperately unfair that the elephants should have appeared to her alone.

Krunk smiled, and more relief washed over Miriam. "Every one. Little one…"

"So cute!" Miriam said.

"And they mamas." Krunk nodded. "Yes, they found us. Thrax and they keep some distance. But, thank us, like. Elephants most just beings on earth."

"The greatest sense of justice." She caught Hoola staring at them out of his lashed intelligent eye. "They came back for us."

She might be a speck, an insignificant little bean, but amid the dewy smells and bright morning light, with the mists rising heavenward through a cathedral of trees,

Miriam realized she was not without powerful friends and allies.

CHAPTER NINE

Maximus was behind the breech of the swivel gun adjusting the barrel to track a large war canoe, paddling into the lagoon before the Nonesuches' encampment. The canoe was fifty-foot long, curved at prow and stern, with a double row of paddlers, twenty men per side. Forty lean brown muscular fighting sea dyaks were cutting a swath through the water in their direction.

"One well-placed shot, sir," Mr. Dashwood said, low voiced, crouching beside Maximus, "and we shall dish them entirely."

"Quite right, Mr. Dashwood."

He was grateful his first lieutenant was recovered, had not succumbed to the fever brought on by his wound and the bad humours of the climate, but at times Mr. Dashwood was too young and optimistic by half. Maximus was down to a score of able men, who were lined up behind him and the swivel gun. Able hands was a stretch. Many were suffering from skin fungus, ulcerated cuts and rashes, dysentery. They were ranged up, some of them, with the seats of their duck trousers cut away. Muttering, gripping dirks, boarding axes, and belaying pins, ready to go into battle shite stained as they were.

Would the swivel gun fire? Saramago dried their powder as much as was possible given the humidity, using tightly woven reed trays, carefully corning a portion with saltpeter discovered on the banks upstream of their creek. If the gun hung fire, even if by some miracle they lobbed a shot and missed, the tribesmen would be swarming their position within moments.

Maximus glanced over his shoulder. His band of men were arrayed like a boarding party, weapons in hand. Never pretty at the best of times—many of his crew were missing fingers, limbs, parts of noses—they were much the worse for their stay on dry land. Dry it could almost not be called, the waters of the inlet now lapped just below the embankment of Maximus's camp. At least it should not be impossible to set *Nonesuch* afloat, if they lived to see that longed for event. The canoe full of warriors executed a rapid turn, so their prow aimed in a direct line toward shore. For the thousandth time in the last hour alone, Maximus was heartily glad Miriam was not there with them. He hoped she was far away, in Kuching by now.

"Ready, Mr. Dashwood?" Maximus had never left off adjusting the barrel of the swivel gun.

Mr. Dashwood held a burning slow match in his good hand. "Aye, aye, sir."

The lieutenant raised the sulfur smelling match above the touchhole of the gun.

"Fire!"

There was a booming roar that made Maximus's heart leap. The canoe paddlers fell into disarray, stroking out of time, paddles whacking together, the canoe's prow swinging round the compass.

"Well short, Mr. Dashwood!" Maximus shouted through the deafness caused by the shot.

Their enemies were stunned by the resounding report of the gun. But they wouldn't long fail to notice that no cannon ball had arrived to sink them. The ball had flown in a pitiful arc and buried itself in the sand at water's edge.

Maximus was opening his mouth to call out orders to swab the gun and reload her, when Mr. Wagner cried out in his bawling bosun's voice, "A sail, sir! Sail ho!"

"Prepare to fire another round," Maximus said. "Double the charge."

He straightened and glared out at this revelation, a square rigged ship rounding the headland of the inlet where *Nonesuch* was wrecked.

"Steady, men," he called.

Maximus could feel the sudden pulsing eagerness of his own heart, beating in time with those of his little band of survivors. Did this ship mean salvation, or a greater threat than the dyaks? The dyaks who, against all reason, were pointing their prow at and paddling fast to the square rigged ship.

The schooner hove into the inlet, a shallow-drafted ship like *Nonesuch* that allowed her to approach the shore within a few cables distance. A British flag flew at her masthead, along with two others of unknown nations. A cheer broke from the men at Maximus's back. They'd caught sight of the Union Jack, and the frock-coated figures on the little vessel's quarterdeck. His own first lieutenant was leading the huzzah, with something resembling his former youthful joy. Perhaps Mr. Dashwood wasn't so sanguine about their chances after all.

Onboard the schooner they waited for the war canoe to come alongside, when several of those frock coated figures climbed down among the warriors in the canoe.

"Mr. Gunnerson." Maximus motioned *Nonesuch's* gunner over. "Keep her very well thus, on the canoe, not the ship."

Maximus and Mr. Dashwood exchanged a glance, each patting at his ragged clothing. Saramago reappeared just then, carrying their misshapen and moldering tricornered naval hats. Maximus thanked him and jammed the hat atop his wild red tangles. He passed a hand over his exuberant furry outgrowth of beard, shrugged and gripped his sword hilt.

"Well, and so we cannot help being a wee bit cut up," Maximus murmured.

Mr. Dashwood adjusted his arm in the sling Maximus insisted he continue to wear. "Amen to that, sir."

Then Maximus was stepping forward, removing his hat, and greeting a tall, spare man. The man removed his own hat. His yellow hair started half way back on a sunburned red dome, as though running in fright from his face.

"I am Maximus Thorpe, captain of His Majesty's Hired Vessel *Nonesuch*. How do you do, sir?"

"Charles Vintner," the man said, extending a damp hand, with an odd twisting of his neck and a sour purse of his lips. "Nephew and chief military strategist to James Broke. Soon to be Sir James Broke. Present Rajah of Sarawak, whose lands you are trespassing on. Heard of him?"

The man's tone and accent took Maximus aback. He might be flying the British flag, but this man spoke like no Englishman Maximus ever met. He thought of Lord Exmouth and even Lord Q—damn his eyes—and decided to play the thick-headed Scot.

"No, sir, I have not. All I ken is, I ran afoul of those rocks off the headland in a gale of wind. Been trying to repair me ship ever since."

"That would be her yonder," Mr. Vintner said.

"Aye." Maximus, like most navy men, was impatient of stupidity, and avoided meeting the eye of Mr. Dashwood, or of his men. "If you would be so good as to let me have all the tenpenny nails and spikes you can spare, you should have my eternal gratitude. And a receipt upon the British Admiralty, if you so desire."

Maximus bowed. Charles Vintner emitted an ill-timed snicker. Mr. Dashwood, Mr. Wagner, Saramago, and the crew, shifted and stirred, uneasy for the honor of their captain.

"From the looks of your men, Captain, you need a lot more than tenpenny nails. Never fear, you shall have them. I am a good Christian. But it must be after we've dealt with these mutinous savages. That's why we've come ashore. Weren't no mercy mission. No, we mean to take off the heads of some dyaks."

Moving as one body, Maximus, Mr. Dashwood, and the men of *Nonesuch* drew back.

"Allow me to dismiss my men, sir," Maximus said in a cold tone.

Charles Vintner raised his shoulders in a shrug and turned away. He began shouting orders at his men in a harsh, offended sounding Malay.

Maximus took his surviving officers, Mr. Dashwood, Mr. Wagner, and the gunner, a few paces apart. "Dismiss the men, Mr. Dashwood. Let us try to keep ours from mixing with theirs, if you please, while they do outnumber us so. Mr. Gunnerson, you and Saramago will stay on that gun."

"Aye, aye, sir."

Mr. Dashwood dismissed the company. Some of the men backed away with relief, not wishing to expose themselves, craving only a serious lie down. The less afflicted stayed at the scene of action. Life was hard for them. Maximus was a driving task-master, keeping them at work every daylight moment of their existence, and into the night when they rotated on sentry duty. It was not to be wondered at that they cherished a diversion. The chance to watch their unexpected rescuers and their strange ways. Maximus stood at the head of his men, inwardly uncertain, his guts in a roil.

It took some time for the canoe and the ship's boat to bring all the people from the ship meant to attend the execution ashore. Maximus's discomfort at the numbers of men the ship was disgorging was compounded when Charles Vintner came to stand beside him.

"The Malays keep the plunder, do you see, and the dyaks the heads," Mr. Vintner explained, apropos of nothing.

The word plunder caused Maximus's stomach to churn anew. Was this Vintner—nevvy or cousin or whatever of James Broke—nothing more than a foul pirate? Some men don't know when to shut up, and Charles Vintner drew breath.

"Close on three months now we've been clearing Sir James' coasts and rivers of these pirates. The murdering, raping, thieving, sea dyaks. Me, and my Malays, and good dyaks. When we can bring them to battle, we take back their ill-gotten plunder. When we can't, we chase them upriver where the inland tribes deal with any survivors."

"Pirates fleeing upriver?" Maximus said. Miriam instantly rushed to the front of his mind.

Vintner gave Maximus a pointed, knowing, unpleasant stare. "I shouldn't wish to cross paths in that jungle. Desperate men, capable of any barbarity. Native tribes even worse. Half of 'em with black teeth and nails in their dicks. Cannibals too."

Six small dark men, tied together with rattan cord around their necks, hands bound behind their backs, were at last led before Charles Vintner. Their escort, an equal number of Malays with long curved swords, took up positions behind the prisoners. Maximus stood stony-faced but with a racing heart, the scene reminding him of his youthful days in a grim naval service.

Many of his men, the Nonesuches, lame, wounded, and shipwrecked, were from the same hard service tradition. Maximus caught Saramago's eye. In the brief exchange of glances, did he detect reproof in the older man's eyes? He faced round and concentrated on the condemned men. His heart misgiving him, Maximus realized these men reminded him of the uzis—Inghai, Dena, and the rest.

"Captured sea dyaks?" Maximus asked.

"Land dyaks. Sir James fairly dotes on 'em, calls them *his people*." Charles Vintner smirked, unpleasant red skin pulling back toward his fringe of gold hair. "Like I said, the Malays share out the cargo, and Sir James' good dyaks here take the heads. His people, *these men*, took a money share. That wasn't theirs to take!"

Vintner's voice rose to an aggressive self-righteous shriek, while his skin went a deeper purple-red.

Maximus understood when one of the convicted men spoke in a shaking voice. "Oh Tuai Red-Haired Devil, save us from this mad one. We stole nothing. Malays hate us. Want invade our villages, take our land."

He closed his eyes, half cursing that prodigy of languages, Jugma Bora, who'd taught both him and Miriam how to open their ears and listen.

"Weeelll," Maximus said, "I may be in a position to be

helping you to a better solution, if I may be so bold." Maximus motioned at the Malays with the long swords, and before Charles Vintner could draw breath, he continued. "If your uncle the great man Sir James values these tribesmen, and as I find myself short of hands due to the recent mishap, why not turn them over to me? I shall make topmen of them. And you may rely upon the Royal Navy. Once it has them, it shall not soon let them go."

Charles Vintner stood with pouted lips, rocking slightly on his heels, considering. Maximus watched as the brute thought process churned behind the man's sunburned skull, the row of frightened condemned men before him barely a consideration. At last Vintner arrived where Maximus anticipated he would.

"Your plan's got merit, I won't say it don't." Charles Vintner gave Maximus a sidelong glance. "But what about my Malays? They will either have what was taken restored, or they will have blood."

Maximus heard Mr. Dashwood pointedly clearing his throat. He had an eager expectant *tag me* look on his face.

"Mr. Vintner, I have neglected to present my first officer, Mr. Valentine Dashwood."

Bows and how do you do's were exchanged. Mr. Dashwood cleared his throat again, uncomfortable now. "I beg your pardon for the intrusion, but I should very much like to be of service in this small matter. I have a purse of money, Mr. Vintner, from better fortunes in...er, previous cruises." Mr. Dashwood blushed, and glanced away from Maximus, as though not wishing to offend. "Would half a crown be sufficient to satisfy the Malays' outraged honour?"

Charles Vintner rubbed his hands together.

Maximus's physician's eye took in the nails bitten to the quick, the angry rash on the backs of Vintner's hands. Far down in his mind Maximus wished Miriam might never meet Rajah Broke, if the uncle was half so unpleasant a man as this one. The smug smile gradually left Charles Vintner's face.

"And the nails?" he demanded. "Why was I offered a chit from the Admiralty, and yet here you are throwing down sterling for these worthless wretches?"

"My dear sir," Mr. Dashwood said, in his smoothest aristocratic tones, "of course you shall have a shilling a bag for the nails."

CHAPTER TEN

The encounter with the elephant hunters, which Inghai rightly declared hadn't gone unnoticed by the uzis, caused Dena to turn upcountry. It was a singularly challenging terrain, no one allowed to ride the elephants, who picked their way up steep hillsides with trembling limbs. The uzis led two walking in front, and two shepherding from behind, fully aware of their danger should an elephant slip or fall. Miriam and Krunk scrambled after as best they could.

There were bits that felt to Miriam like pulling herself up a vertical slope. She went barefoot, clinging to whatever rocks or roots offered with her toes. Her pampered upbringing in Ceuta and Tehran was like another life, as she went along with her half boots slung round her neck.

The day they emerged from the jungle, passing beyond the heavy curtain of tangled green into a cultivated uniform hue, the change in the world stunned Miriam. Suddenly there was order, and a sense of normalcy. Walking in the van with Dena and Krunk, an honored position only possible because the going was easier, Miriam was unsure how she felt about returning to the known world. She gazed down the terraced hillsides, planted in dense low growing vegetation, undulating in waves down to the valley floor.

"Tea." Dena informed them. "Inglang peoples like tea." He pointed down the terrace ledges to bright green fields at the bottom of the valley. "Even foreign bugger like you," he told Krunk genially, "know padi when you see it."

Rice. Now Miriam knew she'd returned to civilization. The elephants paced the highest of a series of intricate pathways winding through the tea plantation. The trails stepped down the hillside, access routes for the cultivators, obscured in many places by mature and abundant growth. It was blazing hot, especially in the open, and Miriam wiped sweat from her face with a corner of her head scarf. Just as she was wishing for a hat a cluster of cone shaped reed ones appeared, bobbing toward them like buoys, worn by women working the terraces.

The two groups noticed one another at the same instant. The elephants with their tremendous noses were the only ones not surprised. The group of uzis and women drew back into their respective spaces.

After regarding the newcomers with solemn faces, one of the women spoke. "Say there, brotha, keep them elephants out of tea plants. Headman be angry."

"Who head man here?" Dena called back.

"Foreign man," the woman said. "White Rajah."

A wide grin overspread Dena's face. "I know White Rajah. Jams my very best friend."

A low murmur broke out among the women, that built to a crescendo of voices. Then the bold woman who'd first spoken broke ranks and strode uphill to the high pathway. She approached Dena, her friends behind her. Having halted the elephants, all the uzis gathered round for the meeting.

The woman took off her conical reed hat and offered it to Dena. "You need this, jungle man. Sun gone touched your coconut—" she tapped her head.

Fortunately, Dena hadn't too much dignity to laugh at himself. It helped he was light of heart about arriving in the territory of his benefactor. The women laughed so heartily they had to sit down in the dirt. The uzis joined them. Miriam was always glad for a halt and rest, so her vision would clear and her head stop swimming from the heat. She scooted into the slim shade thrown by the tall trunk of one of the honey-bee trees, interspersed amid the tea plants.

"Who that white Mary?" the eldest woman asked.

Dena shook his head, showing a sudden reticence about throwing names around. They must be close to Kuching, if the influence of James Broke reached these people.

"My name is Miriam."

"Of Persia," Inghai said. "Not Jesus book Mary."

The woman gave Inghai a sharp stare. "You take us for simple or what?"

Everyone laughed, Inghai included. It was wonderful how he reddened beneath his deep brown skin tone. Meanwhile, the old woman kept eyeing Miriam in considering fashion. The woman rose and shuffled over. Krunk laid his hand on his sword, whether in a gesture of threat or respect was difficult to say. Paying him no mind, the woman stooped down and brushed her fingers across Miriam's cheek.

She turned to her companions, holding out her hand, fingers splayed. "Told you white no come off, see?"

Her attention back on Miriam, the woman motioned

to a high ridge of forested mountainside not far distant. A stone structure resting on a summit made a striking sight amid the shades of wild green. "Up there where you belong. With goddesses."

"What god—"

"Time to go!" Dena leapt up. "No good for elephants, stand round in sun."

The tea women gave Dena, Inghai, Pin Ho, and Le No leaf wrapped betel nut and slaked lime to chew. Miriam and Krunk politely declined the local intoxicant. In return, Inghai—their mess steward—fetched from Miss Fat Bottom's pack a bundle of smoked sebarau fish as a present for the ladies.

Miriam studied the stone structure on the distant ridge. In a past age she imagined the stones white and gleaming. The building was temple-like, smaller up top than on bottom, as though reaching toward the heavens. A place of gods and goddesses? Miriam recalled James Broke's supposed harem, housed in a temple. A woman from every country, excepting Persia.

She rehearsed her questions, and demands, ahead of time. 'How far to Kuching now, Tuai Rumah Dena? How hard?' Distances in the jungle were spoken of not in terms of miles or leagues, or travel time, but in the difficulty of the going. This much she'd learned.

Dena squinted across to the structure perched on the mountainside. The path they travelled seemed at the same elevation as the stone temple, in a direct line of sight from where they stood. "If that ruin temple I know, you see Kuching other side. Medium hard, but we no go there."

"Because it's a goddess place?" Krunk asked.

"Silly tea womens. It no goddess place."

"What then?" Krunk wanted to know.

The head uzi cut his eyes at Miriam, seemed to pause out of delicacy, then shrugged. "A falling down temple is all. Some Rajah Broke's womens there."

The elephants paused at the summit of the hill, and everyone gazed across at the ruin. It was a bright clear forenoon, the visibility excellent, the sun glaring and insufferably hot. The temple appeared to be a grand sprawling partially tumbled down pile, the stones a patchwork of gray, green, and black. Miriam gazed between the ruin and the path winding down the mountainside and off through the valley before them.

Her mind was made up the moment Broke's women were mentioned. Miriam was raised in a harem—among the Dey of Oran's wives and children—where she'd learned a thing or two about that kind of community. The tremendous knowledge, cunning, and influence women of those communities could wield was legend. And after all, it was only medium hard to get there.

Miriam wiped sweat from her face for the millionth time, swaying slightly on her feet. "I will sleep there tonight," she said in a decided tone. "If you please, Tuai Rumah Dena."

Dena's face puckered into a sour expression. But he could hardly refuse Maryam of Persia, or continue on to Kuching without her. He jerked his head at her. "You go walk with Ingy-Pingy."

Dena might be obliged to accept her commands, but he didn't have to like them. Miriam heard him complaining to Krunk about "Silly womens," as she dropped back in the elephant train to find Inghai and Miss Fat Bottom.

A few hours before sunset they labored up the last mountain switchback, Dena and Krunk in the lead, with

Inghai, Miss Fat Bottom, and Miriam bringing up the rear. There before them loomed the magnificent pile. A sprawling cluster of ancient structures, some standing almost whole and beautiful, with others no more than stacks of broken stone blocks. The complex had no gate but before the steps leading up through a high archway to a gallery or walkway beyond, facing the jungle pathway stood five resolute hard-faced women. The women barred entrance to the temple.

Dena shuffled up to the warrior women with a resigned, hang dog air. Miriam and Krunk pressed close behind Dena, unwilling to miss a moment of this exchange.

Two of the guard women wore cloth skirts in the manner of the local tribes, with tunics of stacked rattan hoops. Another was clad like Miriam in cotton tunic and trousers. She wore no head scarf, and gazed out of hard black eyes at the newcomers, as though not yet willing to admit their humanity. The last two brown skinned women carried shields and spears. They were muscular, with tight thickly curled heads of hair arranged in intricate braids wrapped round their skulls.

Miriam became aware Krunk was like a coiled spring beside her.

"Eh, Tuai Rumah Dena," the most forbidding of the spear women said. "Why you come away up here?"

Miriam breathed out, relieved to find Dena was known to these women.

"Her fault." Dena jerked a thumb at Miriam. "She say, I gone sleep with Queen of Heaven to-night."

"This White Mary?"

"Not exactly," Miriam said. "No, not Mary. I'm Miriam Albuyeh Kodio Blackwell."

"Maryam of Persia," Dena said.

The woman, wearing a quill through the septum of her nose, scrutinized Miriam. The high shriek and cacophony of cicadas in the surrounding trees reached a crescendo, crashed, and rose again.

"Why you want sleep here, Maryam?"

Miriam squinted into the distance, trying to picture Kuching—the view of it from the mountaintop temple. On the steps of the most impressive structure, the one reaching up to heaven, Miriam was astonished to see large orange-red apes moving about quite at home. This was no place to be telling lies.

"Tomorrow, I go with Tuai Rumah Dena to meet James Broke," Miriam said.

The women exchanged glances. Miriam was uncomfortable with all eyes turned on her. She felt the sweat drying on her skin, the prickling irritation of her matrix of insect bites more keenly. She was like an odd piebald creature. A curiosity; white, brown, with red spots; part European and part not.

"Well then," the woman with the great nose quill said, "we must take her to Nisa."

"Nisa! Nisa!" the other women cried.

Miriam and Krunk took a step backwards in tandem.

"You elephant men, camp round by watering pond. Keep elephants out our cane and bananas."

Dena and several of the warrior women began speaking at once. Miriam opened her ears to a mix of Iban and Malay. She thought she heard Arabic, and a language she wasn't sure was a language, a strange one indeed. Beside her Krunk was ashen faced, every nerve and muscle tensed. The head warrior waved her spear with a horizontal cutting motion, silencing them all.

"Sia! Bring Nisa word another pilgrim's come."

The woman in tunic and trousers peeled off from the

group, and took the steps up to the gallery two at a time.

"Take Maryam in." The head warrior said, pointing at her spear companion, and one of the native women. She glared at them, immobile before her. "Well, what you wait for?"

The woman next turned to Dena, the uzis, and the patient elephants, all swinging their trunks in one direction. They could smell the water; the nearby pond was calling to them.

"Fine for you, Neomi," Dena said to the woman with the quill. He turned to Miriam. "You no forget, you promised. Tomorrow, we see my best friend Jams."

"Yes," Miriam said. She tore her gaze away from the fascinating sight of the temple complex, the eclectic group of women, the orange apes, and concentrated on Dena and the other uzis. Her constant companions these days past, along with the dear, dear elephants. "Yes, I will be with you in the morning—"

"Queen of Heaven, or no Queen?" Dena demanded.

She wasn't sure what that meant, but Miriam promised. "I will be with you in the morning. Peace be with you all, may you have a good night."

The guard women parted to let Miriam pass, their escort ready to take up positions either side of her. Krunk made to follow but, as Miriam stepped through, the last two women instantly closed ranks. Locking arms, they barred Krunk from the stairs.

"No mens," Neomi said, banging her spear against her shield with an aggressive thud.

Krunk didn't reply. Instead he lifted his faded blue seaman's tunic up to his chin, revealing on one side of his chest a network of scarred flesh and on the other a normal female breast. Gasps from the warrior women. Something like a shriek escaped one woman. She pushed her way past the others. She and Krunk stared at one another, and simultaneously burst into speech.

It was the unique tongue Miriam detected before, a language of clicks and tock-tock sounds. Krunk's native language, by the joy shining on his face as he spoke it. Joy was an emotion Miriam never thought to see on Krunk's face again, after what life had done to him. The elephants must have healed Krunk, they were great and noble beings.

"No, no, no." Neomi was unconvinced by assurances that Krunk was one of the countrywoman's tribe. "Show me your spear and I'll show you mine."

Neomi pointed her long wooden spear at Krunk's trousers. Krunk's new found friend protested, disapproving of such an indignity. The other warrior women crowded round, eager for a show. The uzis, standing by their elephants, lingered, craning forward with interest.

Krunk threw back his shoulders. Stepping up close to Neomi, he undid the top buttons of the duck trousers he wore, and pulled the waistband open. Neomi peered in, her companions too were deeply curious. The warrior woman nodded until the quill in her septum was all aquiver. She banged spear to shield, and stepped aside so Krunk could take her rightful place beside Miriam.

"Stay out of cane and bananas!" Neomi called after the retreating uzis. "Or I peel your pods!"

Up the stairs and along the stone gallery Miriam and Krunk went, flanked by the warrior women. Miriam listened to Krunk's excited conversation with his compatriot, Uba, the rhythm of their language punctuated by the slap of their naked feet on the great slab walkway. The smooth stones they trod were oddly inviting after the miles of mud, dirt, and forest mould they'd slogged through. Miriam wished she wasn't wearing her meat-shoes, so she could feel the cool stones on her bare feet. A strong urge came over her to sit down and pull off her half-boots. But odd behavior might be taken for disrespect, and wasn't to be thought of at this particular moment.

The walkway passed between two roofed structures like longhouses extending to either side, and then out into an open central courtyard. Two sides of the courtyard, with clear blue sky and drifting clouds above, were enclosed by the tile roofed long house buildings. On a third side was another dormitory like structure, but out of this one grew a gigantic fig tree. Its column-like pale roots twisted and entangled in the window openings, walls, and roof of the building. Miriam thought the gardens of Babylon couldn't have been half so wonderful. The building appeared to be strangled by the twining roots, its brain squeezed, both on the verge of crumbling and held in place by the forest giant.

That part of the longhouse looked dangerous, uninhabitable. From the other sides of the complex though, Miriam felt many curious eyes peering out. The women of the temple must have their existence inside those ancient walls.

Across a courtyard filled with scattered and tumbled carved blocks, patterned with green moss and grey lichens, forming the fourth side of the complex was a massive stone temple. From a distance, the top of the temple appeared to be a cone shaped tower rising to the heavens. Up close, Miriam saw the stone blocks crowning the temple were cunningly carved into an enormous sculpture.

A huge head, shoulders, and the torso of a woman, rose above the temple roof. The face was hewn of stacked stone blocks, and appeared to smile benevolently down at whoever approached. There was hardly any neck, before the thick and broad shoulders gave way to massive pendulous breasts. Under the breasts were ever increasing cylindrical rolls of stone flesh, girdling the woman's torso.

Miriam stumbled behind Uba and Krunk. They'd suddenly picked up the pace, heading straight for the temple on a well-worn path. Halting before the steep and numerous temple stairs, their guards took a knee. Krunk and Miriam were quick to follow, in kneeling before the temple: Out of respect to the statue, the great mother figure. The awe-inspiring, ancient and enduring aspect of the place, sprung up amid an unforgiving jungle, was enough to humble anyone.

They all sprang to their feet, except Miriam, who rose unsteadily with her eyes on those steep stairs. She thought of pulling herself up vertical hillsides, clinging hands and feet to tree roots and branches.

But their escort veered away from the temple, and marched off to the half-ruined, tree-infested section of the surrounding buildings. Miriam experienced an inward pang. In spite of her qualms about scaling more heights, she would've liked to climb up to the temple platform, examine the carved blocks and pillars. The pillars supported the roof and the massive weight of the statue atop the temple. From up there, Miriam guessed, she'd be able to look down on Kuching.

Underneath a covered portico that ran the length of the dormitory, the two warrior women paused to straighten themselves and their weapons. Gray and white tree roots a foot and a half thick ran through the roof over their heads and the floor beneath their feet, where the roots were intertwined with crumbling stone tiles. Miriam hoped the whole might not come down and wipe out her little speck of an existence.

Uba and the other warrior ducked inside. In a low voice Krunk, head bowed in the direction of the stone mother, told Miriam, "These people we go meet, they worship the Goddess."

The interior was like a longhouse, with individual rooms arranged in a straight row, each with its own window and door openings. Inside the light had a greenish quality, from the growth of moss and lichen on what was left of the stone walls, ceiling, and floors. The dwelling was by no means uninhabited, and Miriam couldn't help gaping. The people were as interesting and unique as their strange overgrown tree-house.

One woman sat on the slab and wood floor suckling a brown bear cub, its long yellow claws and dun-colored muzzle snuggled to her nipple as casually as the child in the next woman's arms. Nothing in Miriam's privileged half-European, half-Persian upbringing prepared her for such a sight. Remembering it was impolite to stare in anyone's culture, Miriam tore her gaze away.

Besides the woman suckling the bear cub, there was a collection of natives, clad in cloth sarongs, bare from the waist up except for necklaces, rattan loops, and long hair worn over both shoulders. There were also women of Africa, like Krunk, Uba, and the bold shield and spear woman Neomi. Black and brown women from other places too, Miriam guessed. India, the Philippines, Johor, Vietnam, Siam, Burma, Cambodia. Women from every nation, she recollected the boast, but none from Persia. A few of the women were Middle Eastern too, Miriam felt sure. An astonishing diverse collection of women, to come across smack in the middle of a jungle.

But the women of James Broke? That Miriam very

much began to doubt.

Their escort halted in a section of the tree-grown building where one of the forest giants was in flower outside. Delicate red and pink petals floated in through the window and door openings. Sia, the woman sent to bring word of their arrival, was crouching beside a middle-aged woman. This must be Nisa. Her pose, kneeling on the floor with her breasts and stomach rolls cascading to her waist, was like that of the temple statue. Unlike the Goddess, Nisa didn't look on them with benevolent eyes.

The woman rose though, and came forward to greet Krunk. Nisa was tall, stately, brown and sturdy like a well-built ship. Not a native tribeswoman by her height and size. Something about the curve of her eyes and nose, her full lips, made Miriam wonder if Nisa was from the Ottoman or Persian empires. A countrywoman of sorts.

She welcomed Krunk with a clasping of forearms, and a few phrases in what sounded like Greek. They leaned together, touching foreheads, and gazing into one another's eyes.

It lifted Miriam's heart. Here was Krunk, accepted by the women of the temple. She was confused as well, for all this time she'd thought Krunk was Muslim. They'd prayed together. And yet...inside a living tree with flower petals underfoot and a millennia-old visage smiling down on them, it occurred to Miriam there might be deeper and more ancient ties even than religion and faith.

Krunk took a step back from Nisa. "Nisa, High Priestess of Queen of Heaven, this *Khun* Maryam Albuyeh Kodio Blackwell."

Thorpe, popped into Miriam's head. She dipped a

curtsey to Nisa. It might be absurd in the middle of the jungle, but it was all Miriam knew.

Nisa's gaze became disapproving as her attention turned to Miriam. "Why does Krunk of the Ancient Companions call you *khun*?"

Miriam licked her lips. *What makes you so special?* She recalled a similar question, from another formidable woman. One like a malevolent force of nature, a menace to the human spirit, the Golden Dragon.

"Krunk has no reason to call me chief, I've said so many times. We helped one another once, escape a horrible cruel...Is that Thrax?" Miriam exclaimed.

An exquisite cat came sidling up, and rubbed its head against Nisa's calf.

Almost at once, Miriam saw she was mistaken. This cat had rounded ears and an elongated snout, with a striking red brown pelt covered in dark spots. Somehow this weird coloration must make the cat blend in the jungle, the way Thrax would on the Thracian steppes.

"I beg your pardon," Miriam said. "I mistook your cat for my—"

She clamped her mouth shut on the word Hell-Cat.

"Your what?" Nisa demanded, bending and putting her face close to Miriam's.

Miriam liked a certain boundary of space about her person, she didn't care for it to be invaded. To top it off, the sleek jungle cat turned bright green hostile eyes in her direction. She had a sudden flash of empathy with Maximus, Mr. Dashwood, Saramago, everyone Thrax ever glared down in that threatening way.

"My Hell-Cat, Thrax," Miriam blurted.

"Hell-Cat!" Nisa bellowed.

"Hell-Cat?"

"Hell-Cat!"

"Hell-Cat?"

The voices of the women echoed round the ancient chamber.

"You have a Hell-Cat?" Nisa repeated, the distrust fading from her face. "This my Hell-Cat, Newt. Where yours, eh? You have a Hell-Cat, you must be a'right person."

Miriam wanted to be an alright person, she wanted it very much. But the truth was she couldn't, never had, commanded Thrax. She and Krunk exchanged an apprehensive glance. The last time they'd seen Thrax was the night of the wild elephant caper.

"Since we've come to your country," Miriam said, "Thrax's been enthralled by jungle life. I rarely see it. I should like to produce the Hell-Cat, but I'm afraid Thrax might not come near this many people, cultivated land, the elephants..."

Nisa sniffed, motioning with her hand to tamp down the whispers of *kittens! kittens!* that kept erupting from the women. "If it smell Newt, this Thrax will be here soon enough. Maybe the Hell-Cat prove you're a'right. Until then, what else you got?"

What else indeed? "I speak five languages, and I know a little anatomy and physic."

"Now that, my fair Persia," Nisa said, rising, "is more to the point. Come with me."

Krunk began to stand up from the midst of a score of African and native women, seated against the wall.

"Stay, Krunk, and take your ease," Nisa said. It was more a command, as though from the captain of a ship. "Have no fear for your Maryam. I am no ogre, I will not eat her."

The women laughed. Miriam, not feeling so merry, clasped Krunk's hand before leaving. She followed Nisa out of the crumbling tree-massacred longhouse.

But outside in the dirt courtyard was a sight that lifted Miriam's heart. The open space was full of children. Released from their lessons or chores, and having been passed the word the newcomers were no threat, they were running, leaping, skipping, and cavorting round the temple courtyard.

Nisa marched straight toward the dormitory on the opposite side of the complex, the building that looked the soundest of the group. Children so young they toddled on unsteady legs, right up to ones approaching adulthood, melted out of Nisa's path. It wasn't the priestess they were interested in anyway. No, they stopped their play and games and intrigues and fights to stare at Miriam.

Miriam had been grinning since first seeing them at their frolics. A small naked body, two or three years old, cannoned into her legs. The little girl wobbled, grasping her hand to keep from falling. Steading herself, she rubbed the back of Miriam's hand hard and gazed at her fingers, the way the tea-lady had done. An older child touched her, and then another, all hooting and marveling at their fingers afterward.

"Eh, White Mary! Can I touch your hair?" an adolescent voice called out, as Miriam trailed Nisa up the steps to the intact dormitory.

Nisa whirled round, and from the eminence of her combined height and the top stair, she quelled the children with such a savage look they drew back in a wave. "No, you can't touch her hair! She is a follower of Islam, and so she covers her hair. She is a person, she has a name. This is Maryam Albuyeh Kodio Blackwell of Persia."

Miriam made a rather pathetic little bow.

"Maryam of Persia, are you white everywhere?" someone called out.

"Have some respect!" Nisa thundered. "Don't be such ignorant brutes!"

This caused an unusual reaction. Miriam and the boys and girls were suddenly straining to hold back laughter.

"She is white everywhere," Nisa said. "And the white doesn't come off!"

Having settled their vulgar curiosity, Nisa whipped round and marched into the dormitory. Miriam ran up the stairs, chuckling, almost light-hearted, and completely unprepared for one of the most horrific experiences of her life.

CHAPTER ELEVEN

Miriam knew by the smell of the dormitory it was a sick place, the hospital of the complex, with its underlying odor of urine and blood. As though having soaked it in from the atmosphere, a lurid red-colored lichen crawled up the stone walls and ceiling of the room.

Nisa turned to Miriam, and in a tone pitched low she said, "Just you wait, by the time we finish rounds, the whole complex will be baying for kittens."

She didn't know how to respond to that remark, and in this place. Five women were lying on mats scattered round the room, writhing and moaning. The nearest to the doorway, a woman of Nisa's age—they were all, Miriam noticed, women of a certain age—held out her hand and beckoned them closer.

"Nisa, when we gonna eat? I want my after dinner *bhang.*"

"Quick and quick, don't you worry."

As though the priestess' words pulled unseen threads, a number of younger women came in. Each one carried a brimming bowl of fragrant soup and a leaf plate piled high with condiments.

"Ma Shwe, concentrate now, this is Maryam."

"My Maryam?"

"No, dear, not your Maryam," Nisa said. "This is Maryam of Persia, she knows physic."

Miriam longed to declare she'd no such talents. The woman gathered her headscarf more tightly round her pain furrowed face, and cast such a look of hope and interest at Miriam that it wrung her heart. At first, she couldn't utter a word.

Working up her courage, Miriam said, "Where is your pain, what ails you Ma Shwe?"

Ma Shwe sat up groaning, but with an eager face. Her dinner had arrived. "She tell you," she waved Miriam off toward Nisa, "Nisa know best physic."

If that was true, Miriam wondered, what did Nisa need her for? She rose slowly, making way for the young person bringing Ma Shwe her supper.

She went and stood beside Nisa. Together they watched Ma Shwe as she scooped from her soup bowl stringy green curling vegetables, and a meat that looked suspiciously like the monitor lizard tail Miriam once ate.

"Too many children are at the root of it," Nisa said. "The women in this room together account for fifty to three score of those children we just waded through. Their wombs drop out."

In her effort to suppress a gasp, a strangled sound came out of Miriam.

"Not dropped out, exactly. Might be a mercy if it did," Nisa said. "Collapsed, detached—"

"Prolapsed," Miriam murmured, her lips oddly numb.

Miriam and Nisa considered one another, the older woman dressed in a cloth sarong and Miriam in her worn remnants of European clothing.

Nisa broke the silence. "You're an educated one, I find. Where did you come by your knowledge?"

"In Tehran, and elsewhere." Miriam asked, "Where did you learn physic?"

Ma Shwe punctuated Miriam's impertinent question

with a loud belch.

"Constantinople," Nisa said. "Half these women are Muslim, two are Copts." She gave Miriam a hard stare. "Well, Miss Maryam of Tehran, what recommend you for these women that are told they must beget and beget until their insides fall out—what for their constant pain, bloating, the discharge and leakage of blood and urine?"

"I wish Maximus were here." The words came out before Miriam could stop them.

A hard, hostile stare settled on Nisa's face. "Is that all you have to say, you wish some *man* were here to tell you what's best? Who is this Maximus?"

Inwardly Miriam struggled. She must force her mind to come up to speed, to keep up with Nisa. But the atmosphere within the stone and wood building, the mingled smells of boiled soup and hospital odors, the sight of the prostrated women, and a strange heaviness in Miriam's limbs, was making it powerfully hard to concentrate. Who was Maximus to her?

"Maximus is my friend, my...partner. He studied physic in Edinburgh, it was from him I learned the little I know."

"Edinburgh, is it?" A change came over Nisa. Her face relaxed and she was once again a middle-aged woman in a worn cloth skirt. Not the towering priestess about to smite the unbeliever. "Then tell me what the great Edinburgh man would say of these women's cases."

The supper trays and empty bowls were being carried away by the young sick room attendants, while the mothers of the multitude began reclining at their ease while sipping thick green beverages. Miriam leaned one hand against the stone wall, in a small patch free of red or black or grey lichen, to steady herself while she reached back in memory. Suddenly Maximus's many remarks in his clear Scottish brogue were running through her mind and, much as when Miriam was learning a new language, she reached out and seized upon a few key factors.

"Sometimes there is no remedy but to remove the peccant part," Miriam said, with something of Maximus's accent creeping into her voice.

The odors, including a rising cloud of belches and gas, were making Miriam's head swim. Nisa gave Miriam a brief nod.

"That was my thought too, a surgery," Nisa said, speaking now in ancient Aramaic. "All the traditional approaches, the poultices, the packing of the womb, give no permanent relief. Would you be one to assist me in such a surgery, Maryam?"

Miriam's knees almost buckled. She sagged against the stone wall, not caring about rubbing against the lurid moss.

"Allow me to think it over," she said in a faint voice.

"This way, we're not done. Follow me."

Nisa walked off into the connecting room. Here a group of women ate together, gathered round a pot of rice with plates of small fishes, boiled vegetables, and the monitor lizard mystery meat, spread round them on reed mats. Their chatter and jests halted when Nisa and Miriam appeared.

"Nisa!" one of the women called. "Eat with us, you come just in time. Who's the White Mary?"

"Miriam," Miriam said, in a sort of knee-jerk reaction.

The atmosphere in this dormitory was even more heavily laden with the ammoniac tang of urine. To her shame Miriam dreaded less Nisa sit down among these women to eat, because she would have to do the same.

"No, no." Nisa spoke in Malay, waving her hands. "Better we don't, more for you." She turned to Miriam, and continued in Aramaic, "These women have complications of childbirth, or from cutting of the genitals as youngsters. They can't control their pee, it leaks out, and so they are ostracized by their husbands and families."

Guilt over her own feelings of revulsion rose up to greet her. Miriam said, "How glad I am they have a community here, protected by guards at the gate."

"Those guards aren't because of them," Nisa said. "That's next. Prepare yourself."

This dire warning was counteracted by a cheerful call of, "Good-bye, mother of Hell-Cats," that wafted Miriam out of the dormitory. But nothing could have prepared her for the shock of that final room of the hospital wing, in the temple of a Goddess.

In this room were the fewest number of patients. But more black eyes, broken lips and arms, bruises, contusions, and trauma than Miriam had ever seen, aboard a Navy ship or in her wide travels. Her mind raced, like a small trapped animal in a cage, bouncing against one horror after another as she looked on the evidence, and listened to Nisa's narration, of the physical and sexual violence. Tears were coursing down Miriam's cheeks long before they arrived at the last patient in the room.

She was a sweet looking girl of twelve or thirteen, with angry sores like burst tomatoes on her young arms and legs. She lay on a mat, with a composed expression on her face. The girl reached out a slender suppurating arm to Nisa and Miriam.

"Married at age nine." Nisa continued her physician's narration. "Her immature body unable to withstand the constant vigorous sexual attentions of her husband. Puncture of the wall between womb and rectum. What you see on the outside not nearly as bad as the internal damage."

Miriam wiped tears and sweat from her face with an impatient swipe, and collapsed more than knelt, taking the girl's outstretched hand.

"Why are you crying?" the girl asked. "Who has hurt you?"

The tender concern in the girl's voice, the willingness to give comfort, touched Miriam deeply and brought fresh tears surging up. It took a moment for her to fight them down.

"No one, no one has hurt me," Miriam said. "Do not concern yourself. I cry for my own loss of faith. Tell me how it is with you today, is to-day a good day or a bad one?"

"Oh, I should say it is about middling." The girl cast a weak smile in Nisa's direction, before turning her dark, luminous, fevered gaze back on Miriam. "What I would like of all things is to be with the children. Do you think that could happen? It's scary here."

Unable to speak, Miriam looked up at Nisa. This was the priestesses' hospital. With a creaking of knees, Nisa knelt on the girl's other side.

"I'm sorry you're frightened here, child, I think Maryam of Persia is too." Nisa nodded at Miriam, who smiled through her tears and shook her head in agreement. "Let me arrange nurses to be with you and then we'll move you. They are not a bad bunch, but it wouldn't do to have you overset by that rabble."

The girl, whose name Nisa informed Miriam was Hawwa, beamed at them.

"Do you know what would make today a good day, the best day of all?" Hawwa squeezed Miriam's hand in a hot, insistent grip.

"What would?" Miriam said. "Do tell me, Hawwa."

Nisa stood up to speak with one of the nurses hustling past. The injured women were attended by several nurses each. Besides their physical wounds, these women had a great need for talking, crying, and unburdening their souls.

Hawwa's eyes shone and she cried out in her shrill childish voice, "It would be the best, best day, the day I found out there were to be kittens!"

WHITE ELEPHANT

Her shoulders slumping, her arms and legs heavy as never before, Miriam trudged up the steep stone stairs of the temple in Nisa's wake. When they reached the high platform, she was out of breath and lowered herself shakily to the stone floor. She pulled off her half-boots, rose, and continued after Nisa as fast as her sluggish body and reeling mind allowed. Miriam didn't know when she'd ever recover from the sights, the shock, of the last three-quarters of an hour. Never, most likely, which was probably just as it should be. After what she'd seen, of what one human was capable of inflicting on another, Miriam felt as though all the joy and promise of life had been sucked out of the world.

Miriam's heart was in turmoil, even as she gazed out over the most spectacular vista the combined powers of gods and mortals ever thought to create. Nisa brought Miriam round the exterior of the temple to the top of the steps, facing away from the temple grounds. Here the stone steps descended and gave way to a series of clearwater pools. The nearest reflected the silhouette of the towering goddess statue against a sky of orange, yellow, and flaming crimson. Where the mountainside sloped away down into a broad valley, brilliant green jungle vegetation rose up to meet the shining edge of the last in the series of pools.

In the distance snaked a wide channel or river, alongside which, picked out by the piercing rays of the setting sun, was a tall white colonnaded building. More at home in London than Kuching, was Miriam's disordered thought. What business was it she had in that remote village, in Kuching?

Nisa sat down on the stone steps facing west. Miriam was only too glad to take a seat one step down from Nisa, after placing her boots at a suitable distance downwind. She splayed her toes on the cool stones the way Nisa was doing. Together they gazed at the tropical sunset over the tops of the giant forest trees, watching the play of light and changing colors reflected in the pools, and in the distant silvery channel of water.

"Do you know the story of Jezebel?" Nisa asked.

"Jezebel of the Bible?" Miriam said. "My step-father may have told it me, but I can't remember."

"I'll tell you Jezebel's story, but this no Bible story."

Nisa paused. Up the stone steps in the dying light a figure climbed toward them. The shadows resolved into Krunk, who sat down alongside Miriam. They were like two disciples at Nisa's hardened feet.

"Nisa was about to tell of Jezebel, of ancient times," Miriam said.

She laid her head down on outstretched arms resting atop her knees, prepared to listen, almost certain another horror was coming her way. Miriam remembered that Jezebel was named a temple prostitute.

"Jezebel was a priestess of Ashtoreth, the name given the Queen of Heaven among her people. Jezebel's mother and father, the king and queen of Sidon, worshipped the Goddess, as did all Jezebel's community. As high priestess she managed the temple's lands, its hospital and finances. She participated in the regulation and government of the people, even sat in judgement upon them: Her word was final, irrevocable. Like all followers of the Queen of Heaven, Jezebel practiced the sexual customs of her faith, periodically selecting men to lie with in the sacred ritual of the temple."

Nisa paused after a small gasp escaped Miriam. She was a product of the narrow views of morality of her formative years, but she was having those views widened.

"And the children of these unions," Nisa went on in a strong voice, "would inherit from their mother, from Jezebel, her mantel of priestess as well as control of all the temple's holdings and business. But into Jezebel's just and balanced world came the Kings of the North, who famously slew every man, boy, and woman who'd been with a man, leaving only virgin women and girls. You can read about it in your Bible."

"It's not mine," Miriam murmured, without raising her head.

"They number the asses and cattle and slaves and untouched women and girls. These the Kings of the North gave as war prizes to their officers and soldiers. The women were forced to forget the Queen of Heaven. Forget their religion, their community, their way of life. What choice did they have but to submit to the male god? A god who demanded they be virgins until marriage and thereafter sexually faithful, submissive to, and dependent on the whims of one man.

They called Jezebel a sinner and a whore. Killed her people, killed her beloved daughters—also priestesses of the temple—before Jezebel eyes. But she would not renounce the Queen of Heaven. She would not accept the new god. So the Kings of the North slaughtered Jezebel too. Put down her murder in punishing detail in the Bible. That is the true story of Jezebel."

True dark night was coming on when Nisa finished the story. A few streaks of pink clouds turning gray remained, while a deep azure was creeping close behind to swallow all up in darkness.

"Not everyone forgot." Miriam straightened and sat upright. "For here you are, in the flesh."

In the growing dark Miriam and Krunk heard rather than saw Nisa smile, a sibilant sound. She rocked back and forth slightly, smiling, and nodding.

"I like you, Maryam of Tehran, you are a nut from the top of the cluster. A fit companion for Krunk of the Amazons. Yes, here am I, abundant in flesh. The high priestess of the last temple of the Queen of Heaven. What would the descendants of the Kings of the North, the children of Abraham, the people of the Book, see when they look at me? They'd see a naked obese old savage, who likes to fuck in the temple."

"Is that still done?" Miriam blurted. Where, she wondered, was her legendary discretion, her sense of...was she really thinking decency after all she'd seen and heard?

"In the temple, yes," Nisa said, "where you cannot go, young Maryam, because it is a sacred place. Reserved for the sacred ritual. It is the only time we, the priestesses of the temple of the Queen of Heaven, invite men from Outside in to the complex."

Nisa and this temple might be a lot of things—a hospice, a place of refuge, a house of worship for an ancient faith—but what they decidedly were not was any man's harem.

Yet Miriam had a hunch how the two came to be confused and conflated, and since she'd abandoned all polite pretext, she asked, "Has James Broke ever been invited into the temple?"

An unexpected snort came from Nisa. "Of course! Someone or other of the priestesses is sure to single him out. He is not an ill-looking man, though perhaps a trifle—" Nisa paused and tapped a finger to her temple. "Broke is not too much of a Christian to accept either, whatever he may claim before his countrymen. We have an understanding," Nisa said, "Rajah Broke and the people of this temple. Except on those particular occasions, we agree to a mutual ignorance of existence."

"How glad I am to hear it," Miriam said.

"Because you mean to keep your rendezvous with the White Rajah?" Nisa asked.

"I mean to keep my word to Tuai Rumah Dena and the uzis."

"Fair enough," Nisa said, shaking her head. "Though mostly women come to us, from their stays with James Broke. Is there anything else you would know?"

A succession of disturbing images ran through

Miriam's mind, Ma Shwe's bloated belly, Hawwa's dark and prematurely aged eyes. "Thank you for allowing me to see your hospital and the women under your care. May I know the name of those great orange apes, down by the pools?"

Nisa's head jerked round in surprise. "Those aren't apes, Miss Maryam." The priestess stood up, regal in the deepening night. Miriam was momentarily afraid she'd blundered, and was about to be kicked downstairs. "They are the people of the forest, the orang-utans. A good night to you both. You may sleep wherever you wish, and leave in the morning if you choose. No one is kept against their will *within* the temple of the Queen of Heaven."

"Good night," Miriam and Krunk said.

They heard the slapping of Nisa's retreating feet against stone slab as she went up to the temple platform and down the steps in the direction of the tree-grown dormitory. Miriam leaned her head against Krunk's shoulder, and Krunk inclined hers so it touched the crown of Miriam's head.

After a time of listening to the chorus of chirping tree frogs and night creatures, and watching the orang-utan ease comically in and out of the pools of water, Miriam said, "I feel sick."

"Me too, *Khun*," Krunk declared. "Oh! Me too!"

Miriam tried to steel herself, and then said, "Tell me."

The other warriors—they called themselves Amazons, like the warriors of old, though they hailed from many nations—naturally wanted to know what had happened to Krunk. And so Krunk had relived in the telling the horror of her capture, abuse, and degradation. Then, just as naturally, Krunk's fellow warriors had their say and told their stories.

"Beatings, rapes. Outrages you not believe." Krunk's words drifted into the warm soft night. "Things we done too. Things we done. Like killings."

Their arms were entwined as they leaned on one another. Miriam clasped Krunk's hand, lacing their fingers together. She thought of her mother taking her hand like this, when she was small. Maybe Zahraa Albuyeh was an adventuress and a bolter, but she'd shielded Miriam from a world of violence and cruelty. A world that wanted to claim her body for its own purposes, to cut it so she couldn't experience pleasure, to assign dominion over it to some man, because he's the one that most resembled God. How far her privileged, sheltered girlhood was from what she'd witnessed that day. From what Krunk had endured, that made her into a warrior and a killer.

Krunk's sob at this juncture scared Miriam badly.

"Forgive me, *Khun*," Krunk said. "All this time I let you believe I follow Islam, so you help me."

"No." Miriam squeezed Krunk's fingers. "Never say so. Between us there will never be anything to forgive. Were I you," Miriam whispered, her voice shaking, "I shouldn't believe in anything at all. Except possibly my own survival."

By way of answer Krunk returned the pressure of Miriam's fingers, and holding up their joined hands gave a defiant fist shake toward the universe in general.

"Oh, look!" Miriam cried, pointing to the bottom of the temple stairs, down near the pools. "Thrax and—"

"Newt!" Krunk said.

Visible in the starlight reflected from the pools, the red coat of Newt and the tawny one of Thrax flashed as the two Hell-Cats circled one another in a dance that smacked equally of threat and courtship. They began a high piercing cat wailing that caused the orang-utan to abandon the pools, furiously shaking water from their orange pelts.

"May be kittens after all." Krunk disengaged her arm from Miriam's, and her head sank atop her own bent knees.

"How happy that will make them all." Miriam waved a hand to encompass the temple and her people, but thought mainly of Hawwa.

"Unless it Thrax bear them," Krunk said. "How you think the skipper take to a half-dozen of Hell-Cats?"

Miriam snorted out a little laugh. "He would say another half-dozen or so self-willed, changeable creatures aboard ship would *no do*."

"Dearest Maryam," Krunk said, startling Miriam again. "Kittens is hope, that why they want them so. I feel so sick all I want is this day should end. But I afraid I stand up, I tumble down these stairs and crack my unbeliever's skull."

Miriam swallowed. Rare had been the times in their friendship, saving at its very outset, when she'd been called on to be the brave one.

"It's time for us to leave them alone anyway." Miriam swept the *hijab* from her hair, motioning with it toward the pair of shrieking Hell-Cats and letting is slip from her grasp. "I'm every bit as scared of tumbling downstairs, to tell truth. But together we shall go down arsey-versey, as the seamen say."

Krunk reached out and patted Miriam's shoulder in agreement. They both inched around to face upwards toward the temple, and crept down one stair at a time on hands and knees. At the bottom, they rose shaking to their feet, and moved away from the prancing, howling Hell-Cats. Miriam put her arm around Krunk's shoulders.

"I told Neomi, she guard captain, I stand morning watch," Krunk said, as they staggered toward the tree-grown dormitory.

"We'll see about that," Miriam said. "You've come out in a muck sweat, and if I could see your color in this black night, I'm sure I shouldn't like it one bit."

A place had been prepared by the Amazons for Krunk. Miriam found the soft mats laid down and made ready for her in the midst of Neomi, Sia, and the rest. Krunk stretched out with a grateful sigh. Tugging the long sleeved tunic she wore over her head, Miriam covered Krunk with it. It was the best she could do by way of a blanket. She shivered slightly in her camisole, with arms bare. Miriam wished she'd asked Dena if any of Maximus's bed-curtains were left.

She fetched a half coconut shell of water and raised Krunk's head to drink. Afterwards, Miriam sat down and held Krunk's hot hand.

Krunk made as though to move over, to make room for Miriam beside her, but in reality only twitched and shuddered. "Lay down, *Khun*. Place for you in *basha*."

"Not yet, my sister," Miriam said. "Go to sleep, rest, I will stay with you till you do. Then I should like to take a turn sitting with Hawwa, a sweet much injured girl I met earlier. I shall sleep beside her, if Nisa permits it. She's Hawwa's physician."

Nodding so that little droplets of sweat fell on the mats underneath her, Krunk grinned, eyes closed. "Hold her hand just so. It give great comfort."

CHAPTER TWELVE

By rights it was Mr. Dashwood who should've decided the tribesmen's fate, since it was the lieutenant's silver that rescued them. But once the sails of Vintner's schooner were out of sight, a collective sigh went up from the six surviving dyaks and the group of castaways alike. Mr. Dashwood, meanwhile, turned bashful.

"I beg you will do with these men as you think fit, Sir," Mr. Dashwood said. "As you know, I do not speak the Malay."

Maximus considered the six men, rubbing their wrists and necks after Mr. Dashwood ordered their bonds cut. Most of the men wore stunned expressions, as though unsure what just happened. All saving one of the men gazed back at Maximus with fear and uncertainty, or avoided his gaze entirely. Maximus addressed the one man willing to meet his eye.

"Are you land dyaks, then? Sir James Broke's people?"

"There hundred tribes from here to Kuching, Tuai Red-Haired Devil, and you white men call all land dyaks. We," the man motioned at his own chest and then toward the other five men, "we Dusan peoples."

"Maximus Thorpe. Of England."

"Alijah, of Durian village," the native man said, and

then named his companions one by one. "Our land near Samarahan river. We farmers. Until mad red-faced devil come upriver, say protect our village. Then steal us away from our land, our homes and families."

Maximus was mulling this over, but before he could make any remark, another of the native men piped up, expressing the concern uppermost in all of their minds.

"We slaves of maiden-faced one now?"

It took Maximus a fraction of a second to realize the man meant Mr. Dashwood. He almost laughed, his mind busy with the glorious windfall of ten-penny nails, what they would mean to the ship repairs and the welfare of his men. And might the Dusans have word of Miriam and the uzis?

"In England, we do not own slaves," Maximus said, in a pompous sounding voice for all the native men to hear. More discreetly, he told Alijah, "In exchange for a small service, ye shall all be allowed to return to your village."

Alijah gave a whoop and spoke excitedly to his companions in their native language. Then they all began speaking at once, and making nervous gestures toward Maximus and his men. Alijah's eyes narrowed, and he turned back to Maximus.

"What you want in return for freedom, Tuai Torp? We decent peoples, we not so sure about you."

In the mess tent the six Dusan men were not treated to anything so luxurious as monkey stew. The local macaques had become wise to the murderous ways of the castaways, the spirit of the Hell-Cat still lingered, and they avoided that particular stretch of coastline. Alijah and his companions ate the few periwinkles and small bony smoked fish served to them, sitting in a long row at a plank table set up on casks. The Dusans made a valiant attempt to draw out the meal as politeness dictated, but gave up and gazed round with pity at the emaciated men and their squalor.

One of the men waved his hand toward the hospital *basha*, demanding something of Alijah.

"My friend Mookit," Alijah said to Maximus, sitting across from him, "want know where your *baboolian*?"

"My ba—, what?" Maximus asked.

"*Baboolian*! Man make herbs and charms against evil spirits, against sickness."

Alijah grimaced, wrinkled his nose, making a bad smell face.

Maximus understood perfectly, and with an inward sigh admitted, "That would be me. I am the *baboolian* for the English peoples. Trained in physic in Edinburgh."

After Alijah translated this there were awkward smiles, and more pitying and indulgent looks from the Dusans. Mookit and several of the other men jumped up.

Alijah and Maximus rose too, moving to stand face to face.

"Mookit and others, they say, if you readies we give what you want. Exchange for go free."

Before passing out of the mess tent, and following the Dusan men into the jungle, Maximus paused to speak to Mr. Dashwood and Saramago. Concern was writ large on both their faces.

"Would you like me to go with you, sir?" Mr. Dashwood eyed the Borneo tribesmen askance.

"Nay, Mr. Dashwood, it will no do." In a low tone, Maximus said, "Stay in camp with the men, if you please. These Dusan fellows have promised to show me what the jungle has to offer in the way of vittles and medicines. I told them I was a *baboolian*, a witch doctor of sorts."

"*Asi es*, sir!" Saramago piped up. "I light along a bucket, be with you this directly minute, sir."

"The Jungle men can have no objection to your steward attending you, sir." Mr. Dashwood sniffed.

Maximus waited for Saramago to return with a canvas bucket, and then plunged into the jungle behind the Dusans. A bare cables length away from camp, under a thick canopy, Alijah began whacking at a fair sized palm tree.

"This tree of thousand use," Alijah said. "Eat inside, we show you how."

Another man waved a handful of severed palm fronds at Maximus. "Good for *basha* roof and floor. Men with shitting sickness foul up. Need change for new." The man shook his head, as though instructing a child.

"Tongkat Ali!" Mookit and another man pulled up by the roots a shrub with fern-like spiraling green leaves. "Walking stick plant, boil root, make you hard. You please womens very much." Mookit stopped, looking diffident, perhaps doubtful Maximus could ever induce a woman to be pleased. He added, "Also good for..." and he rubbed his stomach and groaned.

The Dusans led Maximus and Saramago to a stand of wild bananas, cautioning them against the venomous spiders and snakes that liked to snuggle in the clusters. Next came an investigation of edible tubers and fungi, brown and orange fungi as big as dinner plates, and the honey-bee tree. It was Alijah's opinion the Inglang peoples shouldn't make an attempt on the honey, high up in the boles of the towering, white barked tree. He had his doubts they could even be taught to prepare sago. Alijah tried to distract them by pointing out an orange-barked tree good for constructing *bohongans*, the large carrying baskets used by jungle people, and another—the *langsat* tree—the bark of which, when boiled and drunk brought down fevers.

Like Peruvian bark, Maximus catalogued the tree's appearance and location away in his brain. An idea was simmering in the back of his mind. They'd marked their route with broken foliage on their way in, and when the party headed back to camp it was easy going. Saramago hauled a laden bucket, and the natives had knocked up several palm leaf baskets that brimmed with various edibles and herbal cures.

"Is there such a thing as gum trees hereabout?" Maximus asked Alijah. "Gum dammar?"

Alijah caste a side-eye glance at Maximus. "What you want make torches for, Tuai Torp? Sago and rice better, fill belly."

"Caulking," Maximus said, "to repair the great hole in me ship." It was the great rent in *Nonesuch's* balloon Maximus really had in mind. "May I ask you to bring back both? Rice and gum dammar."

Part of the liberation agreement was this botanical excursion. The other was that the native men, after returning to their villages, would bring rice and other essentials back to the castaways. Maximus knew this second part was extremely unlikely to happen. Once the men returned to the bosoms of their families, their own people, their home village, why should they care about a few stranded white men? Both sides understood he had no means of enforcing the bargain, but for all their sakes Maximus had to aim high and dream big.

Another matter never far from his mind arose, along with a vision of Miriam's lovely face, and he asked, "Did a party of traveling elephants pass through Durian village recently?"

"How I know?" Alijah said. "We gone long time. Taken by red-faced devil man ship, remember?" Something in Maximus's downcast expression must have softened him, for Alijah added, "Hard miss elephants. I bring Tuai Torp and maiden-faced one word, what my peoples say."

When Miriam found Hawwa and Nisa in the children's dormitory, she discovered she wasn't needed. Hawwa and a nurse that looked little older than her were asleep in a quiet corner of the room, comfortably ensconced atop a stack of large mats. Nisa motioned at the unoccupied space on Hawwa's left side.

"No reason you can't sleep there, if you want. What the child has isn't catching."

"Would you..." Miriam stammered, she was worn out to the point of collapse, "would you be so kind as to look in on Krunk? I fear she's taken a fever."

The priestess waved a hand at her and stomped stolidly off, heedless of the children she roused as she cut a path through them. Miriam remembered little after she laid down next to Hawwa. Right before sleeping, during the long jungle trek, she was used to feeling lonely. Not tonight, this night she was perfectly comfortable surrounded by sleeping children. Her hand was taken, there was a whisper of "kittens", and then Miriam plunged into oblivion.

Confused dreams filled her sleep. There was something she must do, but she couldn't remember what, and if only she knew she could decide how best to go about it. Her heart was full of resentment at the unfairness of it all when, what seemed to Miriam moments after her eyes closed, Nisa was shaking her hard by the shoulder.

Miriam sat up and wiped perspiration from her face. There was a pale half-light in the dormitory, creeping in to pick out the sleepers on their mats and the colors of the moss and lichens climbing the walls.

"You better come," Nisa said. "Krunk wants you."

Nisa straightened and about faced, marching from the room in her characteristic manner. Miriam eased away from Hawwa's side, caught up her boots and followed Nisa, her head barely clear of sleep and those awful dreams. Outside the children's dormitory, Nisa turned on her.

"I'm surprised at you, sleeping away from Krunk—your particular friend—and she so sick! What were you thinking?"

Mainly, Miriam heard the words sick and Krunk. "What is it? What's wrong with Krunk?"

"A jungle illness. Fever and debility. Sometimes it passes off and sometimes not. I wouldn't be shocked if you had it too, Missy."

That gave Miriam only a moment's pause as she rushed beneath the archway of roots into the tree-grown dormitory.

"I'm so sorry," Miriam said, on reaching Krunk and kneeling by her side. "Forgive me for leaving you last night."

"Nothing to forgive between us, 'member?" Krunk tried to smile, but produced only a rictus of suffering.

"What can I do for you?" Miriam asked.

"Tell me quick before my senses fly, you go with Dena to-day?"

Miriam took Krunk's fevered hand. The whites of her eyes were tinged yellow, as Krunk gazed intently back at her.

"Yes," Miriam said. "I suppose I must."

A loud cluck of disapproval came from Nisa. The priestess stood nearby, arms folded over pendulous breasts.

"Take black blade and Captain sword." Krunk's hand moved to the weapon belt that lay beside her. Without looking at it she withdrew the *parang* to keep for herself, and handed the belt and sheathed sword to Miriam. "Go and show them, Maryam of Persia only real *Khun* here."

"I will stay if you need me," Miriam said, her tone hopeful, almost pleading. Fear was rising in her. How would she fare without Krunk and the Hell-Cat beside her? Thrax surely wouldn't come with her. It had family—or at least species—matters to attend to. This was its rare, rare chance to breed.

"Captain and mates need you." Krunk wrapped her fingers round Miriam's arm with a sudden, hot, insistent grip. "No white Rajah, no Nisa, no one gone stop you, *khun.* Tomorrow, before sun rise, I be with you—" Miriam began to make noises of protest, and Krunk said,

"—or I send one warriors. Outside rajah's palace, be there so we know you safe."

Krunk raised her voice at the end of this unaccustomed long speech. Her head came off the mats and her jaundiced eyes focused on Nisa, and then Miriam. "Tell me quick, before I go!"

"I will be there," Miriam said in a rush, apprehensive and afraid. What did Krunk mean by *before I go*? "I will meet you, or one of the Amazons. Outside the rajah's palace tomorrow, before the hour of dawn.

"Nisa!" Krunk demanded.

"I promise one of the warriors will be sent to see to your precious Maryam."

Krunk relaxed back onto the mats, her fingers sliding from Miriam's arm. Her eyelids sagged, her breathing became less of a pant, and she folded her hands over her chest and drifted away into fevered sleep. Miriam leaned over and kissed Krunk's forehead.

"Miss Maryam," Inghai said, when she met the uzis beyond the guards at the temple stairs, "your hair most beautifuls."

Dena shook his head at him. "Hush, Ingy-Pingy, you no manners. Where Krunk, Miss?"

Tears rose up and stung Miriam's throat. "Krunk is ill, with a jungle fever according to Nisa, the priestess of—"

"We know who she is," Dena said, amid murmurs of concern from Inghai, Pin Ho, and Le No. "We must go is all," the chief uzi said. "Can't make my very best friend Jams wait longer. We come back way home, see about Krunk."

"Thank you, Tuai Rumah Dena," Miriam said.

She raised a hand in farewell to the guards of the temple of the Queen of Heaven. They'd sent Miriam off in a far kinder manner than Nisa's gruff behavior might have suggested. She left with many assurances of care for Krunk, which was the most important thing. And they'd taken Miriam to bathe and wash her clothes, so she might go before Rajah Broke in some semblance of order. Sia, who was from Syria, had dressed Miriam's long dark hair atop her head and cast her eyes about for Miriam's headscarf.

"I...I let it go," Miriam said. "Last night, after...after I'd seen what's happened to these women. To some of these girls."

Sia's intense, inscrutable gaze rested on Miriam for a long moment. Then she'd stepped back to consider her coiffure of Miriam's hair.

"That'll do," Sia said. "It's the way they wear it in Paris."

Meeting a woman from Syria in the Borneo jungle who'd been to Paris wasn't the strangest thing to happen to her. She trudged along behind Miss Fat Bottom, putting a hand up to adjust a *hijab* that wasn't there, while reflecting on the singular land of Borneo and this strange journey. Now she must be close to its end her feelings were all ahoo, though her strongest desire was that Krunk would recover, and be the one to meet her at dawn. There were other wishes too. The night frights were over, and Miriam remembered Maximus, Mr. Dashwood, and the Nonesuches, suffering on the shore of this unforgiving, beautiful, incredible land.

Her Paris 'do was a sagging sweat sodden mess atop her head by the time Dena called a halt. Before them was a fast-moving stream with water the yellow brown color of the surrounding earth.

"Last river to cross," Dena told Miriam. "Well, next to last. After cross this river, Kuching easy walking other side." The chief uzi paused and eyed Miriam. "Spring other side too, you want wash. We make ready elephants."

Miriam was assigned to ford the stream atop the steady dependable Miss Fat Bottom, with the not so stable but equally good-natured Inghai. At the clear water spring Dena showed her on the other side of the tributary of the river Samarahan, local people had installed a bamboo trough through which mountain water flowed into a pool.

Taking down her hair, Miriam rinsed it, and her face and neck, in the cool spring water. Myriads of iridescent butterflies surrounded her, performing a continuous dance, trading places sipping at the pool's edge. Despairing of dressing her hair up again, she let it fall wet and loose past her shoulders, and rejoined the uzis on the banks of the river. The uzis stared at her uncovered hair. Miriam did some gawping of her own, at the transformation of the elephants, and most especially of Hoola.

Hoola had been scrubbed shiny by Dena, after the elephant sucked up his fill of water and had a roll in the stream. His burden of *bohongans*, crammed with all the necessities of jungle travel, were now distributed between Miss Temper, Miss Chief, and Miss Fat Bottom. Clean and dry so that his mottled pink gray skin shone through, he wore over his high arched back, layered one upon another, the remaining red velvet curtains from Maximus's boudoir. Somewhere, somehow, Dena had laid hands on cloth of gold and fashioned a headdress that draped over Hoola's head, dangling past his bony forehead in front, with a wide triangular tail that cascaded down the back of his skull.

Dena, Inghai, Pin Ho, and Le No, watched Miriam with excited and expectant faces while she approached Hoola and examined him.

"He's perfectly magnificent," she said.

"He elephant of the world," Dena declared, leading Miriam up close to Hoola with a little skip of his splayed feet. "What you think, Miss Maryam? Maryam of Persia enter Kuching riding Hoola the Magnificent, they make Hoola next White Elephant?"

Miriam paused to consider what was afoot. The uzi of a White Elephant would be set for life, much respected, an important man, nearly as revered as the elephant. No more traveling through the jungle, exposed to elephant hunters and the extremes of nature—like rivers of water that fell from the sky. Clearly it was what Tuai Rumah Dena wanted, and what he'd hauled Miriam all this way for. She felt she could not disappoint.

"I don't see how Sir James or any of the headmen can fail to take notice," Miriam said. "I am deeply honored to be allowed to ride Hoola into Kuching."

The uzis burst into praise and exclamations at Miriam's little speech. Dena, in tearing high spirits, even led a huzzah that brought a flush to Miriam's already pink cheeks. Then the uzis rushed off two by two, returning in short order from the clearwater spring changed into fresh cloth skirts and open-fronted sleeveless tunics for the grand entrance into Kuching. Dena gave the familiar commands, and Hoola collapsed to his knees on the forest floor.

Aided by Hoola's crinkly mottled ear and the strap round his middle, into which Dena had threaded different colored fibrous strands, Miriam heaved and climbed her way atop the bony ridged back. Hoola turned his head and considered Miriam. A humorous, knowing glint was in his amber-brown eye, as though they were playing dress up and it was all great fun. In her heart, and mainly because of Lord Q's hand in the matter, Miriam dreaded lest this excursion into Kuching be anything but a happy caper.

The forest path wound first through small villages with their huts raised six feet above ground, where the children and everyone not off working in the padi fields swarmed round to gaze at the spectacle. A parade of traveling elephants, led by a magnificent bull elephant draped in beautifully colored shining cloth, and ridden by a foreign woman with long black hair. The uzis in red, yellow, and brown, patterned tribal dress marched proudly beside their elephants, grinning and yet maintaining a certain dignity.

For her part Miriam hated making a spectacle of herself. She'd done it on other occasions, in her capacity as one of Lord Q's people. Then, as now, she hoped her reasons for doing so had some sense behind them, and weren't just what they appeared—flagrant calls for attention and admiration. Yet with Maximus and his men, Krunk, and the people of the Temple of the Queen of Heaven, firm and uppermost in her mind, she might bear anything. The elephant party left the last small village behind. Children running after them were called back by their elders, and the elephants swaying progress brought them to the outskirts of Kuching.

They passed more huts on stilts, larger and prosperous looking and crowded closer together. Adults outnumbered the children lining the track into Kuching, boldly calling out to Miriam and the uzis.

"Hey, brotha! What a prize!"

"You sell her to White Rajah?"

Atop the noble elephant's back, with a splendid view of the river separating Kuching from a colonnaded white stone and wooden building sitting on a rise of green bank, Miriam gritted her teeth and almost wished she didn't understand the language. Sensing her dismay, Hoola picked up his pace. The uzis were trotting alongside of the elephants, passing through the ramshackle town. The wood and thatched huts whisked by, along with the few tile roofed stores run by Chinese merchants that lined the town's single street. Near the foot of the bridge spanning the Sarawak river, they were forced to a halt by a crowd of people. The great white house gleamed just the other side of the river.

On this side a swarm of men surrounded the elephant party. Miriam looked down on many turbaned and uncovered heads, dismayed that nearly all carried *kris*, *parang*, or both weapons fastened to belts or sashes. For reassurance she reached down and touched the handle of the *sgian dubh* given her by Maximus, then fingered the sword Krunk insisted she take, tied to a belt slung across her body.

She didn't feel invulnerable riding ten feet off the ground on the back of an elephant, because Miriam couldn't shut her ears to the shouts and calls of the crowd. The general sentiment of these natives of Kuching was that she, like some rare beast of a foreign land, was to be presented to the White Rajah for his menagerie.

Shuddering, Miriam called to the head uzi, "Tuai Rumah Dena! Can we not move on?"

Dena waved acknowledgement, and summoned Le No to move Miss Temper forward. Two abreast Hoola and Miss Temper, followed by Miss Chief and Miss Fat Bottom forced a lane through the crowd. At last the elephants planted their wide, spreading feet on the stone bridge spanning the channel.

Dena looked up at Miriam and grinned as they descended the bridge, leaving the crowd in Kuching halted on the other side. "Bridge built by elephants, Miss Maryam," Dena informed her, jerking his head back at the milling crowd. "Bridge for Jams and his people, not for common no goods."

The elephants made their way across a wide cool green lawn dotted with fragrant yellow and white flowering trees, tall swaying coco and betel-nut palms, and black and red rosewoods with orchids sprouting from every crook and branch. Dena lined the elephants up, Hoola foremost, before the tall colonnaded portico at the front of the great white house.

Swaying and shifting their weight, the elephants spoke to one another in rumbling tones. Miriam studied the many window openings in the triple floored manse.

Those on the first floor above ground level were enclosed with iron fancywork, but on the next and highest level of the house were tall windows and doors giving onto a covered balcony. A grand and unusual house, with wood walls ending half a foot short of the floors for greater air circulation. Miriam gazed up at the fine facade, her brow wrinkling over those barred windows. She wondered what someone standing behind those bars looking out would make of the elephant party.

The front door of the manse swung open and Dena and the uzis straightened, coming to attention. A short, squat man rolled out of the cavernous hall beyond the great door, waving his arms over his head, and shouting in Malay.

"You! You there!" The man ran up to Dena. "Remove those great crapping beasts at once. No Dyaks up here, up front of Rajah's house. Land or sea. Do you hear me there?"

Dena swayed back a moment, and then said, "But this is Maryam of—"

"I give not one monkey fart if she Mary of fucking—"

"See here," Inghai interposed, "no need talk coarse, my friend."

The small man hustled over to stand before Inghai. Inghai was obliged to make soothing noises to Miss Fat Bottom.

"I no your friend." The man leaned close in, right in Inghai's face. "No Dyaks, land or sea, front of house. You take big crapping beasts round back of great house, where they belong."

There was a tense pause. Miriam felt the slow burning heat of anger rising off Dena and Inghai like a jungle mist. To have journeyed so far, with expectations of great things, and be met instead with this level of disrespect. Miriam said a silent prayer—to what god or goddess she didn't know—that it might not all end in violence. At that moment, of his own accord, Hoola started forward, jerking Miriam on her precarious seat.

The great elephant veered off round one corner of the house. Miss Chief, Miss Temper, and Miss Fat Bottom fell in line, plodding down the length of the house. Dena reached out his arm, Hoola curled the end of his trunk into the crook of it, and together they marched to the back of the house and took up stations in a large open yard between the grand white house and its out-buildings.

In this space the elephants fell into disarray, for all Dena worked to arrange them in line like he'd done out front. The reason was that the enclosure of the White Elephant was wrapped around one corner of Rajah Broke's manse. The yard became a great milling mass of elephant legs and bumping tummies as each elephant crowded in to greet Maja, the White Elephant of Borneo.

From her high perch, Miriam could see into the White Elephant's enclosure. The tall hardwood walls of her pen allowed Maja only to throw her long trunk over the top of the wall, seeking to touch and caress those of Miss Chief, Miss Temper, Miss Fat Bottom, and at last Hoola.

The elephants rumbled and called their greetings. Miriam felt the vibrations in her legs, which she was obliged to pull up now and again or be squeezed between the great gray and brown bodies. What Miriam observed in those moments of Maja's enclosure caused her heart to ache, in the way it had the previous evening in the temple hospital. The elephant's dung was piled high, there wasn't a scrap of fodder, and the elephant herself had sad and weeping eyes.

A sense of outrage swelled in Miriam's breast. Where was this elephant's caretaker, her uzi?

"Look at all those great asses!" brayed the voice of the man they'd met out front.

This was immediately followed by a clipped, nasal tone. "Shut it, Jay-ar."

The elephants swung round in a body to face the men. From their touching, rumbling contact with one another, Miriam sensed they knew Maja's condition and bristled to face her tormentors. From inside her enclosure came the clanking of the pewter bell that hung round Maja's neck, signifying she was a man killer.

Standing beside the little round Jay-ar was a white man that caused Miriam, and the uzis, to look twice. The man's skin was of such a red as to suggest the worst sunburn ever, his receding yellow hair started half-way back on his skull and fell in long greasy strands over protuberant ears to his shirt collar.

Tuai Rumah Dena went forward to greet the odd pair of Malay manservant and English hobgoblin. "I am Dena Orang Metang, Jams Broke my very best friend. I here to deliver Jams Maryam of Persia, and present Hoola the Magnificent, next White Elephant of Sarawak and British Borneo."

That last phrase gave Miriam a start. It disturbed her to be spoken of like a package of goods, even when she was complicit in the ruse. What was worse, she remembered those words 'British Borneo' in Lord Q's letter. Miriam stared at the back of Dena's head, the leader of their little band, her leader since leaving Maximus and *Nonesuch*. Surely Lord Q's influence, his intelligence arm, couldn't extend this far, even to Iban tribesmen in Borneo?

Jay-ar and the red-faced white man were holding a discussion in English, after Jay-ar translated Dena's words. The head uzi along with Inghai, Pin Ho, and Le No, were shoulder to shoulder, waiting with hopeful faces.

"Tell him Rajah Broke's from home. Returns this evening, to give a reception dinner for the honorable naval captain whose ship he's visiting now off the coast. Tell him come back during the Rajah's regular hours, when he hears native complaints."

"I no complain," Dena declared to Jay-ar and the white man. "Jams my friend, send me away across twenty-five rivers to fetch Maryam of Persia. Here she is."

The uzi turned and gestured at Miriam, and suddenly all the men's eyes were on her. Hoola raised his trunk to his forehead and issued an impressive trumpeting blast.

The white man and Jay-ar took a satisfying step backward.

"Well," the yellow-haired man allowed, "I'm sure m'uncle wouldn't want a white woman turned away. This Miriam of Persia may stay. But make them understand, no uninvited natives this side of the bridge. We have a White Elephant." He pointed a long red finger at Maja's pen. "If he wants to present another, he must come back when Sir James is receiving native petitions."

Jay-ar translated this to Dena as, "White Mary stay, you and great crapping beasts go native side of bridge."

Dena turned in shock to his companions, and they fell into an animated discussion in their language with much indignant waving of arms. Jay-ar crossed his own arms over his breast and put on the same expression of mingled boredom and vexation as the white man.

"Tuai Rumah Dena," Miriam called. "May I get down if you please?"

The head uzi immediately walked over and gave Hoola the commands to kneel. Dena extended his hand to Miriam, allowing her to slide from the elephant's high back without disarranging the fine cloths overmuch.

Once on the ground Miriam gripped Dena's hand, and cast such a look at Inghai and the other uzis as to make them draw near.

"Listen, the white man say already have White Elephant," she told them in her limited Iban. "You must come back when the great man is receiving the Iban peoples, talk then."

"That no better than 'go other side of bridge, you son

of bitch',” Dena said. “Jams my friend, I hard long journey across forest and jungle his orders. I come back tonight, join feast with captain?”

Miriam glanced at the pursed, self-important face of the yellow-haired white man, and swallowed hard. “I doubt it,” she said. “These men no want you and elephants here when rajah return.”

“You remember me, and Hoola, to Jams?” Dena said. There was an uneasy stirring amongst Inghai, Pin Ho, and Le No. “But stay! Jams my friend, but I no like leave you with two poor excuses for mens.”

“I no like either.” Miriam gave a hesitant half-smile to the men she'd travelled so far with, who'd brought her safely to this place. Without them she wouldn't feel safe again, of that she was convinced. “Not like no way. But what choice we have? I remember Tuai Rumah Dena to Rajah Broke.” She had to switch to a whispered Malay, lacking the words in Iban. “But I will tell you another thing, are you sure you want to put Hoola forward? The elephant in that enclosure has no food, and the dung's piled high. What's become of White Elephant uzi?”

This, more than anything that had happened, galvanized the uzis. Their backs were immediately stiff and their looks hard. “I find him out, Miss Maryam. If no find, we come and feed White Elephant.” Nods all round from the other uzis. “Next day sun rising, you meet Krunk, we there too.”

“That right, Miss,” Inghai said.

“Yes,” and “Yes,” said Pin Ho and Le No.

Miriam blinked down tears. “I shall be there first rising, native side of bridge, meet you,” she said in Iban. “Good-bye my very dear friends.”

She cleared her throat, and lifted her head with a haughty gesture, while the uzis struggled with their own tears. “Well, gentlemen,” Miriam said loud, and in English. “Now I've dismissed the native bearers, shall we go inside?”

The white man stepped forward, snickering, and Miriam clasped her hands in front her. She was determined to hold her ground, and neither touch nor be touched by anyone uninvited.

"Excellent suggestion, madam. And what remarkable English you speak. Imagine that, eh, Jay-ar? A white woman popping from the jungle like a daisy. Allow me to present myself, I am Charles Vintner, nephew of —" Miriam stole one glance back at the familiar party of uzis and elephants. The rather thin sense of well-being she'd wrapped herself in, from Maximus's camp to Kuching, was leaving with them. Maja the White Elephant set up a pitiful lowing bellow.

CHAPTER THIRTEEN

The White Elephant's terrible cries of abandonment followed Miriam and the odd pair of men into the mansion. Miriam glanced at Vintner and Jay-ar to see how the heartbreaking sound struck them. Their expressions were insensible. Those cries would rend the heart of a stone, as she'd once heard Maximus say, but these men apparently hadn't a whole heart between them.

"Sir James is a collector of all the curiosities of Borneo." Charles Vintner waved a careless hand at the tall glass-fronted display cabinets lining both sides of the wide central hallway. "He is mad for this country."

At any other time, Miriam would've liked to study the butterflies, beetles, stuffed birds and small mammals that filled the handsome cases, but she was busy counting the doors they passed and watching for potential exit routes to the outside. The animals in the cases became more complex, which was to say they contained monkeys and jungle cats—one resembled the Hell-Cat Newt to such a degree, Miriam jumped—as they neared the vaulted ceiling of the reception room and entrance hall at the front of the house.

In a glass case elevated on a granite pedestal in the middle of the stone tiled foyer, was the most honored artifact. At least Miriam guessed it was by the way the two men led her directly to it, exchanging barely concealed smirks and smiles.

"Do you know what that is, Miss Maryam Kodio Blackwell?" The small man Jay-ar bounced on his toes like a child.

The White Elephant's sobbing cries no longer reached them, the tall rear doors of the manse having swung shut. Miriam eyed the object in the case. It looked like a long section of an elephant's prehensile trunk, but with a cross-piece of flesh set at right angles to the main member. Without that protrusion, forming a *t* four inches from the tip, Miriam would have said it looked very much like a—

"*Palang!*" Jay-ar exploded, unable to contain his glee. "Virile member of Borneo rhinoceros!"

"This one has a hardwood rod shoved into it." Vintner pointed out, rubbing his rash-covered hands together, his pale eyes riveted on Miriam. "To keep it *stiff*. Native men hereabouts in the benighted upland country drive a tube or rod of bamboo, bone, or wood—whatever is to hand—through their members in imitation."

"What do think of that, Miss Persia?" Jay-ar crowed.

Miriam had already taken a step backward, away from the rhino penis. She took another, her head ringing with the taunts of the elephant hunters and their *palangs*. "I should say, I'm heartily sorry for the rhinoceros."

A peal of strong laughter rang out, and all heads turned to gaze at a stunning young person descending the wide winding staircase. She had long wavy black hair, sparkling blue eyes, and was the tallest woman

Miriam had come across in Borneo. The woman glided between Miriam and the men, between Miriam and the monstrous member under glass.

"No one cares for your stupid jokes, Jay-ar," she said in clipped Malay.

"Oh, now, Poonah—" Vintner began in a wheedling voice, as though talking to a child.

Poonah lashed out in broken English, her snapping blue eyes making up for her limited speech. "Why you no see this one here noblewoman? Shame! What Rajah Jams say?"

Vintner blushed, a deeper red suffusing his sunburnt skin. He and Jay-ar fell into temporary confusion, trying to work out what they'd done wrong and whether it would be of any consequence to Sir James. Apparently accustomed to crass buffoonery Poonah came and gently but firmly grasped Miriam by the arm, guiding her up the stairs.

"I settle *ranee* best sleep place. You boys behave, maybe I no tell Jams."

Together they reached the first-floor landing, and Miriam strode forward until Poonah again reached out and touched her arm.

"Not here." Poonah shook her head, agitating her curls so they bounced round her face. "Whites on top floor. This sleep place for servants and slaves. My room here."

Miriam stumbled as they started up the stairs to the top of the manse. As she recovered her stride Miriam gave Poonah a long sideways glance, noting the quality of her gown and head scarf, and the health and strength in her overall bearing and person.

In a soft voice Miriam asked, "Are you in servitude in this house?"

Poonah rumbled out a chuckle. The timbre of her voice had an exceptional range, from the high feminine laughter of earlier, to the low, near masculine tone she used now.

"No, I no slave. One hundred captives taken by Muda Hasim in fight against inland tribes. All but ten released, thanks to Rajah Jams. Me, and my sistahs."

Another wide hallway greeted them at the top of the stairs, mirroring the one that ran the length of the ground floor. Here there was an abundance of light and air, tall French doors and windows let in breezes from the manse's location on rising ground. Poonah led Miriam down the hall, where most of the doors leading off it were left open for better circulation, and Miriam gazed into spacious apartments furnished with an elegant European flair. Miriam shook her head in disbelief. Poonah went ahead of Miriam down the hall, where most of the doors leading off it were left open for better circulation. Miriam gazed into spacious apartments furnished with an elegant European flair, shaking her head in disbelief.

There was more in store when Poonah opened a door into what Miriam could well believe was the best sleeping space in the house. After lying in *bashas* and on stone and forest floors, Miriam was unsure how she would fair in the four-poster bed tucked into one corner of the massive room. This single apartment occupied a whole corner of the upper level of the house, with a grand view of the Sarawak river from a private stretch of covered verandah that continued and wrapped round the entire upper floor. Besides the four-poster bedstead, there were numerous chairs, chaise lounges, and small sofas arranged in little groupings round glass and lacquered wood tables. A screened area near the bed hid a wash handstand, chamber pots, and a hip-bath.

The contrast between Miriam's own ragged and stained clothing, her frankly ragged and stained self, and Poonah's clean, shining person struck her. And yet, because her skin was several shades lighter, because she'd had the good fortune of an education, and most especially because she acquired the English language at an early age, Miriam was a top-floor inhabitant and Poonah a lower one.

"You are a captive, a hostage?" Miriam whispered. Her survival, and her ability to do Maximus or anyone else any good, might depend on how well she understood everything and everyone in this manse. In a remote corner of her mind, Miriam cursed Lord Q.

"That right," Poonah answered in a mild tone, pushing closed the door of the apartment. "Me, my nine sistahs. Not from same family, understand? My mother Kenyah, father Dutch. No more like me."

An ugly suspicion rose in Miriam's mind. Because of her beauty, her dark flowing hair and blue eyes, was Poonah kept here as a curiosity—to be on display like the esoterica downstairs?

"Why were you and your sisters not let go, with the other hundred wives?"

"Ah, wives, we not all. Not ones left. Muda Hasim wants us wives for his sons, something to show for war. Jams, he say no."

"How glad I am—"

"No! Don't set bad spirits upon us." Poonah rolled those enormous orbs round in her head, warning of attack from all sides. "No thing settled, no done."

Miriam hung her head. "How rude I've been. Please to sit."

In the midst of the splendor of stuffed chairs and

cushions, both Miriam and Poonah folded their legs like the elephants and sat down where they were.

"Where Persia find that blade?" Poonah asked in the mix of Malay and her native Kenyah they'd been speaking.

"My name is Miriam. The Persia is because I'm from Iran, an invention of these men here. Not the country, the Miriam of Persia part."

"Iran your tribe? And they say Persia like they do Land Dyaks and Sea Dyaks for one hundred one peoples?"

Geopolitics was becoming too thick, and as she nodded agreement Miriam sensed the topic might sink them. She and Poonah stared at one another. At least Miriam had avoided explaining the sword, and adding Maximus to the confusion. Like any considerate host, Poonah turned the subject.

"I think you must want out those stink clothes."

Stink clothes wasn't far from the truth. Leaving the apartment, Poonah picked up Miriam's leather boots with a disgusted expression and offered to toss them on the rubbish heap. Miriam declined, unable to explain she would need them later when walking out to meet Krunk. And possibly to retreat altogether, back into the Borneo jungle.

"Then I put outside," Poonah said. "Bring up bamboo charcoal later, take away worst stink."

"How kind," Miriam said.

After bathing in the hip-bath with buckets of water Miriam helped haul up using an ingenious pulley and rope driven arrangement capable of raising and lowering anything that fit in a bucket, Miriam set to washing her clothes with the soap and remaining bathwater. After draping her small clothes indoors in the screened off dressing area, Miriam wanted to hang the rest outside to dry. She gazed down at her bare feet and calves, thoroughly covered in scratches, bruises, and insect bites from the long trek, shining red and irritated from the scrubbing. Miriam darted out like Eve, and grabbing a white eyelet cover from the bed, she wrapped it around her body in the manner some native women wore their sarongs.

While she draped her tunic and trousers over cane and wood chairs on her private verandah, Miriam breathed in the moist air, the dank vegetable smell of the river, and stretched her ears for sounds from the White Elephant. She could just see a corner of the elephant's enclosure, but no cries came from it that reached her away up here in her luxurious perch. Or was it her own gilded enclosure, soon to be filled high with excrement no one would take away? With a shudder, inwardly unhappy for allowing her imagination to run in that direction, Miriam turned back into the grand apartment. She would regain her self-command, and just lie down on that bed for a moment.

She made it no farther than one of the gold satin-covered chaise lounge, and awoke drooling on the fine upholstery. Poonah was shaking her by the shoulder. Miriam swung her legs over and sat up, clutching at the coverlet so that it continued to shield her, a woozy sensation in her head. The twilight outside, the dying down of the bird calls and the winding up of the buzz and hum of night creatures, startled Miriam. She'd been asleep for many hours, and felt disoriented and estranged from her immediate surroundings.

"Don't look so wild," Poonah said. "Like one them little forest mini deer."

"Right." Miriam shook her head. She must get back into character; she sat up straighter and stiffened her spine and shoulders.

Poonah smiled her approval. She wore the same neat gown and head scarf as earlier, and carried a flowing shimmery garment of virginal white over one arm. Seeing Miriam eyeing the gown, hands holding up the pitiful bedspread she wore, Poonah outright grinned at her.

"Torsiri 'bout you shape. Spent last long time talking her, hand over gown or White Mary go naked eat dinner."

"You must give Torsiri my thanks, my sincerest gratitude."

Miriam rose, gripping the back of the chaise lounge against a slight dizziness. She bowed to Poonah in the way of the Iban and Kenyah peoples, took the filmy garment, and retreated behind the screen. Her fine cotton small clothes had dried and Miriam put them on at once, sliding the gown over her head afterward. It had a light musty fusty smell, and turning to see her image in the wavy looking-glass, Miriam wished she might instead go down to dine wearing her usual jungle traveling gear. She'd feel better with the weapon belt and sword draped across her shoulder.

She sat down before the small dressing table with its attached looking-glass. If she had any sense, she'd do just that, her face in the glass told her. But no, she was here to play a part; a part within a part. For there was Lord Q's desire that James Broke, his rajah-hood, be brought back, be kept in the fold. It must be British Borneo, no room for other nations, no heed paid to native peoples. Fortunately, part of Miriam's being had not sheered off course with her thoughts, and she successfully looted the small vanity for pins and brushes.

"Who is to be at the reception to-night, Poonah?" Miriam called as she dressed her hair atop her head, trying for an imitation of Sia's coiffure that she'd sweated out earlier.

"Few Chinese merchants of Kuching," Poonah said, ambling round the partition to stare at Miriam in the glass. "One or two Jams' white servants, foreign ship head-man of honor, Red-Face Devil we don't name."

Miriam would have dearly liked to know more of the foreign ship captain, instead she said, "No headmen from the native tribes? Other rajahs, Muda Hasim perhaps?"

"You some kind stupid, Persia? Maybe I give gown back Torsiri, you go naked down eat dinner. Even Chinese go way, no eat with Jams. Just you, four five them white mens."

Jamming the last pins into her dark mass of hair, Miriam rose and faced Poonah. She looked up at her, straight into her big blue eyes and handsome face, and said nothing at all. Poonah just schooled her in how things stood between the white inhabitants of this house, and the natives and local Muslim chiefs. Miriam didn't mind being called stupid to her face, that at least was honest. Poonah, though, perhaps thought she might.

"You like head scarf?" Poonah offered in a hesitant, penitential tone.

I'd like it of all things, Miriam thought, as a shield from the gazes of those four or five men. But she'd made a choice, one she wasn't prepared to take back.

Miriam shook her head with a sad smile, and pointed down at her scratched and bruised bare feet. "Shall I wear the boots, do you think?"

Poonah smacked hand to forehead. "Boots no un-stink by half enough. Here." Poonah kicked off her slippers in Miriam's direction.

Miriam put them on and did a slow flapping promenade about the room, holding the hem of the mercifully long gown—it would cover her scabbed and bitten legs—as her feet swam in Poonah's slippers. Poonah barked out a decidedly masculine laugh.

"Come 'long, Persia. We stop get Siri's on way down."

Stop they did one floor below, with the voices of the men gathering for the reception rising up to meet them. Miriam spent a few awkward moments thanking Torsiri in person, while robbing her of her slippers. In Torsiri's chamber, a hot close room lacking the air circulation of the fine open upper story, Miriam met three more attractive, dark haired, dark eyed women. All residents of this servants' floor of soon-to-be-Sir James Broke's manse. They exchanged pitying looks with Miriam when she rose to join the reception downstairs; the women because Miriam would have no one to support her, and Miriam because these women were virtual prisoners. But of whom exactly?

Miriam said good-night to Poonah, Torsiri, and the other ladies, strode across the hallway outside Siri's door, and gripped the hardwood stair rail. The great thick rail was carved to resemble tree branches, with decorative leaf and vine motifs trailing up and down its length. She took a fortifying breath, straightened and threw back her shoulders, and descended the stairs, endeavoring to sweep in, Poonah-fashion. Without the laughter, naturally, the last thing Miriam wanted was to draw the attention of the gathering.

On that score, Miriam might've known she wouldn't succeed. Conversation and masculine laughter died down when her slippers hit the stone floor of the great reception hall. Looking neither right nor left, Miriam threaded her way between the glass rhino penis case on its tall pedestal and a cluster of Kuching merchants chatting nearby. She refused to meet Charles Vintner's eye, or any of the Europeans with him clustered around a table with a capacious punchbowl full of a ruby-red concoction. The men sipped this drink from small glasses. Miriam felt many eyes on her, in her flowing white gown and gold slippers, as she walked directly to the display cases on the opposite side of the room.

She stood gazing at the stuffed Hell-Cat that had given her such a start, the one that looked like Newt. A young Newt, a little Newt, hardly more than a kitten. Talk resumed in the hall, though Miriam felt the continued prickle of their gazes on her back. She succeeded in ignoring them, while her thoughts revolved on the progeny of Thrax and Newt. What would they look like—the creatures? She was thinking how much she should never wish to see any of them stuffed and on display.

"Are you an admirer of natural artifacts and ethnography, Madame?"

Miriam was taken aback by the suave French voice, coming out of nowhere, and in this setting. She hadn't felt the man come so close to her, and she gave a ridiculous little skipping jump.

"Forgive me, Madame." The man bowed, showing Miriam the top of his curly blonde head. "And allow me to make myself known to you. I am Jules Sébastien César Dumont D'Villiers, *Capitaine* of His Majesty's Hired Vessel *l'Astrolabe*, at your service, Madame."

Straightening from her answering curtsey, and raising her bowed head, Miriam said, "Miriam Kodio

Blackwell, Sir. And yes, I am interested in the natural world and all its creatures, so brilliantly on display here." She added rather lamely, in case he should mistake, "In Borneo, I mean to say, not..."

She left off; she must not insult their host's prized collections.

D'Villiers gave her an understanding smile. "It must be sad to see specimens under glass, when you have witnessed them in their native surroundings, and in the full flush of life. As you must have done, Madame, in crossing Borneo?"

"If I crossed anything, it was a mere corner of this vast land, Sir. But certainly, there was much in it to delight the natural philosopher." Had she not been so busy slogging up and down mountainous hillsides, trying not to lose her footing and head plant in the muck, covered with sweat, made dizzy by it, she might indeed have appreciated the wonders of the country more.

Captain D'Villiers was regaling her with an account of the collections of fauna and flora, weapons, and a myriad of ethnographic and cultural objects, he had on board *Astrolabe*, when Charles Vintner sidled up to them. Vintner was holding two little glass cups full of the evil looking bright red beverage.

"I say Captain D'Villiers," Charles Vintner said, aggressively pushing the cups at them, "you must not keep our fair guest all to yourself, and talk in French. Some of us ain't so gifted."

There's an understatement, Miriam thought, hoping her feelings didn't show on her face. Captain D'Villiers, meanwhile, was gazing at and swirling the glass of suspicious red liquor.

"Ratafia!" Vintner barked out, misinterpreting D'Villiers's look of dismay. "A lady's drink to be sure, but there is a lady present."

Vintner wiggled his near invisible eyebrows at Miriam, believing somehow his remark was original and charming. D'Villiers' fair face flushed and he shifted uncomfortably. Miriam eyed the room, her gaze sweeping past the groups of chatting men, in search of a convenient surface on which to abandon the alcoholic ratafia. Some things would never change—she didn't drink ardent spirits—no matter how many times her worldview was revised.

The tall front entry doors swung open, producing a general stirring in the room. Two bare-chested warriors entered, holding long, curved *kris* to their bosoms. Behind them followed a slightly built Englishman with a shock of wavy dark hair and a pair of fine white hands that he fluttered at the men he passed with the beneficent air of a king or Pope.

The gathering parted before this rather delicate looking white man—James Broke, the great man, the White Rajah. Broke nodded regally round at the Kuching merchants, waving his hands as though they stood at some distance instead of two feet in front of him.

With two warriors in front and two behind, inclining his head and fluttering his hands as he went, Broke strode up to the refreshment table with its knot of Europeans gathered round it. Broke locked eyes with Charles Vintner, Captain D'Villiers, and finally glanced Miriam's way, making sure all eyes were on him. Then, breaking out in a wide grin, and giving a decided whoop, he dashed his whole head down into the enormous punchbowl of ratafia.

Everyone jerked back and a collective gasp ran through the reception room. Even the Dyak guards wrinkled their painted faces in surprise. Broke lifted his head from the bowl, whirling his sodden hair in a circle so that wet red beads of ratafia flew in all directions, laughing uproariously.

The gathering of sycophants and dependents immediately set up a titter and then a howl, congratulating Sir James on his splendid joke. Pretending to be the great man...and then...oh, hahaha! Miriam and Captain D'Villiers exchanged raised eyebrow looks.

All this way—*all this long weary dangerous sick-making way, Krunk incapacitated, dear Maximus and his ship and crew wrecked on a remote and hostile shore*—to treat with a mad man. Thanks to you, Lord Q!

CHAPTER FOURTEEN

Toward the fag end of the dinner for Captain D'Villiers, which turned out to involve only Miriam, Sir James, Vintner, and the guest of honor, an impassioned discussion was underway. It was between Broke and his odd unlikely nephew, a man Broke appeared decades younger than. The passionate nature of the discussion—upon the subject of what Sir James considered *his* Dyaks—was in great part a consequence of the growing pyramid of wine bottles stacked in a corner of the dining parlour. They drank not execrable wine, for Captain D'Villiers was partaking of it within having to hold his nose. The Frenchman, however, was far superior at holding his wine than the two English roast beefs.

"He's very demanding over that spot on the Tatau," Vintner was saying of a Seventh Day Adventist missionary. "Perfect for rice cultivation, an orchard, and a school, he says. A bend in the river where a dock can be built. From where he'll launch his campaign upriver to gather in souls from the hill tribes." Vintner gave a derisive snort. "I wish him luck with those stupid, feckless, depraved people. They'll probably take his head."

"If what he wants is a red-hot missionary crusade," Sir James said, "to begin by telling the natives that their religion is a lie, and their prophet an impostor, is not the way to get on. For, though it is true, it should not be told. One must remember Muslims are in the majority here. What are your thoughts on Islam, Miss Blackwell?"

Miriam was still trying to wrap her head around that impostor remark.

Sir James didn't wait to hear her opinion and forestalled her, beginning again in a tone of eminent reason. "Now, if he wants a mission of reasonable and educated men, who know when to speak, and when to be silent—who hold civilization and education as a means of religion, who will strive to enlarge the native mind, and to give them the outlines of our religion—then he would be welcome to the place at Bukit Nyala."

"'Tis a prime piece of land, rich in ironwood and red and black rosewood." Vintner cut a sideways glance of mingled cunning and cupidity at his uncle. "You must see it for yourself, before letting it fall into the hands of the *Americans*. You must think of your people."

"Quite right, dear Charles. You always have an eye on my best interests." Sir James turned pointedly to Captain D'Villiers. "Charles is too modest to speak of it, but he is only just returned from leading a successful campaign to put down the piratical Sea Dyaks."

"They murder, rape, and pillage all up and down these coasts," Vintner said with relish. "And when the pickings become too slim on the water, they turn upriver and plunder the inland tribes. Of course, Sir James will not suffer abuse of his good Land Dyaks."

"How did you find the people of the countryside, Miss Blackwell?" Captain D'Villiers said. "Having so recently traversed it?"

"Yes, do tell us." Sir James leaned forward with the regal air of his earlier, pre-head soaking self. "Are not my people in a tolerable state of existence?"

"Those I was privileged to meet may not be Christians or Muslims," Miriam said. "But they are decent people, with a great generosity of spirit, and their own particular skills and wisdom. May I especially bring to your notice, Sir James, how grateful I am to have travelled with, and been under the guidance of Tuai Rumah—"

"Have I invited you to sleep in my chamber yet?" Sir James suddenly trumpeted.

Everyone froze; Captain D'Villiers with his wine glass halfway to his lips, Vintner in mid-sneer. Miriam blinked, and then fixed Sir James with a hard glare. Why had she not strapped the three-inch black blade to her calf under her long flowing gown?

"All the great men do it, all the rajahs hereabout." Sir James gave a high-pitched laugh. "It is the highest honor to be invited to sleep on the floor of the Rajah's chamber. Have I invited you yet, Captain D'Villiers? For I assure you, I honor you, your mission, and your country much."

Captain D'Villiers coughed, and Charles Vintner rose from the table with a mumbled excuse and exited the dining room.

"No, Sir, you have not," Captain D'Villiers said in a severe and decided tone. "And I do not intend to sleep out of my ship."

"Missionary Youngberg has it right," Sir James said. "In his notion of a school, we must instruct the child to benefit the adult. I find it very odd none of the local headmen have seen fit to send me a boy or girl to sleep in my bedchamber, it being such a great honor. But they have strange ways when it comes to children." He turned pointedly to Miriam. "Do you know, not far from here is a temple where no men are allowed? Can you imagine?”

"I can well imagine," Miriam said.

"Only women, and children up to a certain age," Sir James continued, as if Miriam hadn't spoken. "This shall interest you, Captain D'Villiers, for I know you share my fascination with native customs. Because they value children so, once or twice a year this society of women permit men into their inner sanctum. To perform the act of Venus, to beget children upon them, to fu—"

"I take your point, Sir, indeed I do." Captain D'Villiers blushed to the roots of his fair hair.

"Here is Poonah!" Vintner came in, herding Poonah before him.

Sir James jumped to his feet, clapping his fair white hands, and knocking over his gold-leafed dining chair. Miriam and Captain D'Villiers rose more decorously, the evening was taking another bizarre turn. Since Broke's remark on the Prophet Muhammad of her former faith, Miriam had been trying to think of a way to extricate herself from this nightmare dinner party.

Poonah had eyes only for Sir James, gliding round all of them to take his head against her bosom.

"None of them want to sleep with me, Poonah," Sir James's muffled voice complained.

Poonah glanced up at Miriam.

"To be fair," Miriam said, "Captain D'Villiers merely said he could not sleep away from his ship. A naval captain has great responsibilities."

"And you?" Broke raised his head with a hopeful expression.

Miriam felt all their gazes on her, four masculine stares full of expectation. "I'm content where I am. It is quite the loveliest sleeping place I've ever been offered. I thank you."

"You see?" Sir James wailed.

Poonah patted Sir James and murmured soothing words while gazing daggers at everyone else in the room. She and Vintner, in particular, would have murdered one another with the malevolence of their gazes. Instead, and at last, they exchanged a few words in Malay that would've made Captain D'Villiers blush anew if he'd understood them.

Charles Vintner won the point, and Poonah instructed Sir James to say good night to his guests. After taking leave of them, Sir James, fluttering his hands about, left the dining room speaking to Poonah in a wheedling tone. "But you will sleep with me, won't you dear boy? You and the others? Tell me I shall not be left quite, quite alone."

The door closed behind Poonah, Sir James's head resting on her tall shoulder, with Vintner practically booting them out from behind. Miriam and Captain D'Villiers were left alone, holding onto the backs of their chairs.

"That was weird," Miriam said.

"True words, Madame." D'Villiers made a little bow. "I must take my leave at once now our host has left us. I'm sure you will forgive me, as I must be brief—" Miriam's heart beat oddly at those words. If he'd invited her, she believed she would've abandoned all, and joined him aboard his ship *Astrolabe*—"and respectfully ask what you have to say to Code Black?"

Miriam's knuckles gripping the carved chair back turned white, her heart thundered away in her chest. Here—in Kuching, Borneo—on the far side of the world: One of Lord Q's people.

"Kodio Blackwell, sir, at your service," Miriam said, feeling stunned.

Captain D'Villiers nodded, an almost tender look in his eyes as he gazed at her. "The rendezvous is at Bum-Bum-Too-Too."

They both heard the heavy flapping footsteps approaching that could only belong to Charles Vintner.

Miriam repeated, because she understood the ways of the Navy, "Aye, aye, sir. Rendezvous at Bum-Bum-Too-Too. Sir, the ship *Nonesuch* is in distress, Captain Maximus Thorpe commanding. She lies in 3° 9' N, 113° 1' E."

"I very much regret," Captain D'Villiers said in a louder tone, and in English, "that I must bid you good evening and take leave of you, Madame, and return to my ship."

As Charles Vintner's hand fell on the door latch, Captain D'Villiers bolted round to Miriam's side of the table. He took her hand and bowed over it, saying in a whispered rush, "*Nonesuch* lies in 3° 9' N, 113° 1' E. Forgive me for not offering you the hospitality of my ship. I do not care for leaving a woman of your obvious qualities among mad men and fools, Madame, but such is the will of—"

"I wish you Godspeed," Miriam interrupted as Charles Vintner's shining red face poked in the doorway. "It was a pleasure to make your acquaintance, Captain D'Villiers. May you have a safe passage wherever duty next takes you."

Captain D'Villiers made Miriam a deep bow, mingled concern and appreciation on his face. Straightening, he turned to Charles Vintner and spoke in a hard quarterdeck voice, full of authority and command. "Mr. Vintner, you shall see me out."

Miriam followed them through the dining room doorway, the men turning for the staircase, while she went in the opposite direction toward the bedchambers. As soon as Miriam turned the corner of the corridor, out of line of sight of the main hallway, she ran to her luxurious apartment. Flinging wide the door, she rushed in and latched it closed behind her.

Up and down the wide space she paced in a fevered state, her heart and head pounding. Had she given Maximus's location to a good and trustworthy person? Even among Lord Q's people there must be all kinds, those who'd do their fellows evil just as soon as good. Suddenly it felt to Miriam that she must be rid of Torsiri's elegant flowing gown, and she ran out on the open verandah and snatched up her long tunic and trousers.

Miriam put them on, leaving Torsiri's gown draped carefully in the dressing room with the gold slippers alongside. Her head swam and Miriam felt at once weak and compelled to action, as though should she stop moving she must fall down into inertia never to rise again. An image of Krunk rose in her mind—the fiercest warrior of Miriam's personal acquaintance, including all the military men she's ever known—lying helpless on the stone floor of the temple.

She took up Krunk's weapon belt and draped it across her body, with its sword dangling from a leather strap. Barefoot, Miriam went out on to the verandah to fetch her boots, removing the sachets of bamboo charcoal, and strapping them on her feet. Voices rose up to her, and Miriam eased into the shadows so she could peer down unseen at the manse's dock.

Captain D'Villiers was stepping into his boat. The regular order of his men, waiting at the oars, somehow comforted Miriam. Her hopes reached out to the French captain, a man she knew nothing about. D'Villiers might be as power-mad as Lord Q, or straight up mad like Broke. And she'd told him Maximus's exact whereabouts. She wished she could call down God's protection but, having so recently forsaken her faith, Miriam doubted her prayers would be of the least import to any Divine Creator. She said a silent prayer for Maximus and his men anyway. She knew she was a faithless bean, but that dear man and his crew were not.

By the snatches and tone of the conversation that reached Miriam, she guessed Captain D'Villiers and Charles Vintner were exchanging a few unpleasant words before parting.

Then the captain's gig was pushing off from Sir James's dock, and a strong voice issued the command to, "Pull away!"

Jay-ar shot out from the shadows to join Charles Vintner as he headed back toward the front door of the manse. Miriam heard Vintner instruct Jay-ar to, "Lock her down." Jay-ar retreated into the mansion on Vintner's heels, leaving two native guards outside the tall front doors.

Miriam leaned carefully forward until she had a good view of the guards below. Light from the interior of the house shining through the window openings glinted on their curved blades, and picked out parts of their painted faces in a shifting, eerie pattern. By degrees, moving slowly so as not to attract attention from below, Miriam sank into the shadows against the wall and eased around the corner of the extensive verandah outside her room.

From this section of the third-floor verandah, Miriam could see up river and down. In the distance she spotted Captain D'Villiers's gig, by the single white sail they'd raised. She gazed at the fleeing whiteness, like freedom and sanity racing away into dark night, until the sail was no more than a speck between dark water and star filled sky.

She leaned back, drew breath, and closed her eyes. Two things struck Miriam once she was calm enough to consider; there was a faint smell of smoke in the air, and a distinct hollow thumping or drumming sound. Opening her eyes, Miriam turned toward the White Elephant's enclosure, and the direction of the thumping noise. She was by no means wise in elephant ways, but Miriam did remember Hoola and the cows thrumming their trunks on the earth. Whether they were signaling, or communicating with one another, and their moods when they did it, was where her knowledge was lacking.

Straining every nerve in the direction of Maja's pen, trying to decide if it was the source of the repeated whumping sound, Miriam's heart gave a sudden thrum of its own. At the edge of the Sarawak river, her eye caught movement. From the shallows at the river's edge, four creatures rose up and crawled out on the bank. When they reached the cover of the tall grasses farther up the slope, the mud caked beings rose to stand on two legs. Almost as one, their heads swiveled in the direction of the tall looming mansion.

Even from her perch of privilege, Miriam couldn't fail to recognize Inghai, Pin Ho, Le No, and Tuai Rumah Dena, their faces smeared with mud. She would have known them by the way they turned to and began to hack down blades of elephant grass, if by nothing else. Taking a swift appraisal of her surroundings, eyeing what was above and below her balcony, and once she was sure she couldn't be seen from the front of the manse, Miriam came to a decision.

She sat and removed her boots, hanging them by tied laces round her neck—they were certainly less ripe than before the charcoal treatment. Miriam crawled across to the edge of the verandah, and eased over the wooden ledge. She hung by her hands, clinging to the ends of the plank floor, her feet seeking the bowed iron railing over the window below her. Miriam's toes found the iron rails, and she shifted to find firmer footing, like when negotiating her way up and down those sheer jungle slopes. She loosened her grip with one hand and dropped half way down atop the iron railing, catching hold of it with first one hand and then the other.

Miriam paused, crouched like a primate, clinging to the protective iron bars with all fours. The ornate ironwork gave a groan and pulled away from the house on one side. Really, Miriam thought, exasperated, am I so cumbersome and out of place here that even the fancywork must complain?

More importantly, what if Torsiri or one of her sisters heard her making such a great noise and looked out to see Miriam perched there like a gibbon. She took firm hold of the iron bars and, letting go her toe-holds, allowed her legs to hang free. Hand over hand, Miriam worked her way down till she clung to the underside of the grillwork. Her legs were swinging near the tops of the tall ground floor windows, the weapon belt thumping against her breast.

Dangling there with a fifteen-foot drop below her, no more grillwork, verandahs, or even open window shutters or doors to land on, Miriam thought this must be the end of her monkey capers. Even supposing she made it down without breaking her nut, how was she going to get back into the manse? Miriam's breath came out in a huff, and then something whacked her in the head.

It was more like a lash, as from a whip, though gently

delivered, and scared Miriam far more than hurt her. When no more blows fell, Miriam looked up.

Poonah's face was at the window above, the interior shutters open. "Say, Persia," Poonah whispered, "think you first one ever think of that? Give me long blade, you have this rattan vine. Best long strong rattan vine. Blade weigh you down anyway."

With great effort Miriam hauled herself up again, to cling to the bowed frame, her feet curved over the lower half of the iron bars. She removed the weapon belt from over her shoulder with one hand and hesitated, thinking of Krunk. The real power of a weapon, Miriam knew, lay in the hand of the warrior wielding it.

"You have Sir James in there with you?"

"You suspicious one. What you think? White peoples sleep top floor."

"Last I saw, you and Sir James were toddling off to bed."

"Show what you know. Jams, one moment he bad next one good."

That gave Miriam pause, sending a slight shudder through her. She was growing exhausted, clinging there, panting slightly.

"Toss down that line," Miriam said in a low voice, "so I can see it reaches. What's it tied to?"

Poonah gave her a disgusted look, pointed to a bollard like upright support to one side of the window opening, and tossed out the coil of line. The brown green color of the vine lay perfectly concealed against the house facade. Miriam reached the weapon belt through the open window and gave it into Poonah's hand. She wasn't sure she cared for the gleeful avaricious glint that came into Poonah's eyes as she grasped the sword.

"It is only a loan, you understand," Miriam said.

"That weapon doesn't belong to me, or to you either."

"Sure, Persia," Poonah said. "That much clear. You go now, you about fall off."

That much was clear too. Miriam took firm hold of the vine, first one hand, then the other, and, bracing her toes against the house, walked down and jumped at last to firm earth. She looked up but Poonah had wisely retreated back into her room, like a turtle into its shell. Except this turtle was armed with a deadly weapon. Another shudder passed through Miriam as she forced the uses Poonah might put the sword to out of her mind.

She leaned against the house and laced on her boots, her upper arms shaking slightly from all the clinging and climbing. Miriam thought about the double effort it would be to climb back up into her room, but then...perhaps she wouldn't return. Leave the sword, and half-mad or all the way mad Sir James. And do what? Set off with the uzis downriver and find Captain D'Villiers' ship. Why hadn't she just thrown herself on the good captain's mercy after dinner, wouldn't that have been easier?

Miriam pushed away from the house and set off moving diagonally down to the river bank, below which she'd be blocked from view of the house. Once she hit the muddy reed choked bank, Miriam pushed and slogged her way to where the uzis were cutting grasses.

Her appearance at their backs almost caused Inghai to scream.

"By the Supreme Creator, it's Miss Miriam!"

The other uzis stopped their threshing and stared, arms hanging at their sides. Amazement was on all their faces.

At last, Dena said, "What you do here? You give us all away, you with white face!"

Miriam's cheeks flushed as she realized the danger she'd put her friends in, with her impulse moves. She stammered out, "I wanted to help. Help feed the White Elephant."

Dena shook his head, but leaned down and scooped mud with his fingers. He smeared Miriam's face with the mud, not unkindly. Afterwards, having none of his own, wiping his hand on her tunic. He grasped his *parang* again.

"You bring knife?"

Miriam bent down and pulled the *sgian dubh* from the sheath strapped round her calf. Dena smiled.

"Over there," he motioned with his own knife. "You cut. Stay low, face away from house."

Miriam did as she was told, moving to her designated position where she gathered far less grasses and reeds than her four companions. Nevertheless, a sizable heap of fodder was piling up. Just when Miriam thought her hands, scratched, scrapped, and cramped, could cut no more, Dena held up his hand for a halt.

They gathered beside the heaped grasses, just below the lip of the river bank. Miriam's chest heaved with the effort and exertion, and she stood catching her breath. The uzis, meanwhile, were perfectly composed, alternately poking their heads above the bank and discussing the difficulty of crossing the open space to the elephant's pen.

"Maja, the White Elephant," Dena said to Miriam, "her uzi dead."

"I'm very sorry to hear it," Miriam said.

"Don't be. He stupid bastard, his assistant another one. That one so afraid of *Maja the man-killer*, he no want feed or go near her."

Miriam gasped, clasping her hands together over her

breast. Dena nodded his head, grim, and began to give orders for carrying the fodder across to the elephant.

Next moment they were all dashing across the yard in back of the great house, holding bundles of grasses like so many animated bushes. Miriam wondered if an observer in the house would think the jungle was come to life. Fortunately, the windows were dark on the side facing the outhouses and elephant pen. The uzis and Miriam saw no native guard at the back door of the manse.

Breathless, the party arrived at the elephant pen and piled up the fodder. On the other side of the wall of logs, Maja began to rumble and snort with excitement. She flung her trunk over the top of the wall.

While Pin Ho and Le No scrambled back to the river bank to bring more of the cut fodder, covering themselves with a few fistfuls of grasses, Inghai, Dena, and Miriam scrounged around for a ladder. The uzis, though valiant, were not brave enough to let Maja from her pen to feed. Miriam thought of the long vine rope dangling from Poonah's window, but it would not do. How was she to signal Poonah to untie the vine and let it down? And there was candle light shining from rooms on that side of the manse.

The best they could come up with was a log ladder, like one used at a longhouse entrance, that they wedged against the far wall of the elephant's enclosure. The grasses and reeds were heaped up, and the uzis and Miriam were gathered at the bottom of the ladder. Maja was becoming impatient, alternately thumping her trunk in frustration against the dirt floor of her pen and trumpeting in protest.

Dena cleared his throat with an uncomfortable sound. "I, Tuai Rumah, go first up ladder to face White

Elephant. Until you show face, Miss, now—"

"You must go, Miss," Inghai blurted, "you no mans. Maybe Maja not kill you."

Miriam saw at once how she was more expendable than Tuai Rumah Dena, and she shook her head in agreement. She eyed the ladder pole, and sat down to remove her boots. Barefoot, Miriam scrambled up the ladder. Where the pole met the top of the elephant enclosure, Miriam reached out and touched Maja's extended trunk. The elephant immediately snuffled her through the nostril tip, and wrapped her trunk firmly round Miriam's slender arm. She felt the gentlest of tugs from that trunk. Maja could rip her arm straight out of its socket if she chose.

"Please," Miriam said, "the food."

Just below her on the ladder was Dena, handing up the first bundle of grasses. Miriam stretched one arm awkwardly down while Maja held the other. But the elephant smelled the fragrant grasses and abandoned her grip on Miriam. Maja snatched up that first bundle and brought it instantly to her mouth.

The uzis were formed up in a chain below her on the ladder, with Inghai at the bottom handing up the bundles of grasses and reeds. Each one disappeared over the enclosure wall and into Maja's maw. With the great elephant distracted while feeding, Miriam was emboldened to climb as far up the ladder as she could to look down into the pen.

Now there was a stack of feed piled up next to where Maja stood. The elephant rumbled contentedly, picking great quantities of the grasses up and stuffing them in her mouth. Some straggling bits she put on the pile again, patting it with satisfaction, even lifted the grasses up to swish them against her hide in luxuriating fashion.

"Water in pen, Miss?" Dena said from behind her on the ladder.

"Yes, there's a trough and cistern." She looked down at the confused expression on Dena's face. "The White Elephant has water."

"This last one, Miss." Dena handed up another stout bundle. "Best come down slow."

Miriam tossed the bundle down onto the elephant's stash. She said, "You shall see me again, great Maja. This I promise you." Maja paused in her munching, stretched out her trunk, and patted the top of Miriam's head.

She backed carefully down the ladder. At the bottom, with the sounds of rumbling and mastication emanating from the pen, Miriam was about to ask Dena and the others how they were to manage the next of Maja's meals. An elephant requires a great deal of food to fuel its enormous bulk. Then a shout in English rang out, making them all leap like hares.

"You there! What are you doing near my elephant?"

"Run!" Miriam urged Dena and the uzis. "Swim back across river. I see you first rising."

Dena and the others rolled their eyes at Miriam, the frightened whites of them glinting in the night, and shot off toward the river. They ran bent double and reaching the water's edge, plunged in. The uzis barely rippled the surface of the river, swimming away fast underwater.

Miriam leaned down and, shaking, pulled on her boots. She straightened, and walked with purpose in the direction of the English voice.

Sir James stood framed in the open half of one of the tall French doors, backlit by a brace of candles shining out from the room behind him. In one hand he held a pistol, he was pointing it at Miriam's chest as she approached. Clutched in his other hand was one of the delicate ratafia cups.

"Who's there?"

She heard the click of his pistol hammer. "It's me, Miriam Blackwell."

He sagged with relief and turned back into the downstairs library, waving Miriam in after with his pistol. "You gave me such a start."

"I do apologize." Miriam stepped over the threshold into the blaze of candlelight.

"What were you doing out there?" Sir James settled into a large wicker chair, where he looked child-like with his dark tousled hair and petulant expression. He set the pistol on a low wood table before him.

"I was feeding the White Elephant," Miriam said. "Her uzi has died."

"Yes, I know. The ridiculous blighter got himself killed. In a knife fight."

Sir James gave a sudden high shriek of laughter that scared Miriam badly. "Do you know you're covered in smuts? Hahahah! Never mind, I suppose it's ungentlemanly of me to point it out." He flipped a delicate white wrist upward, and continued as though to himself; "On the other hand, what's a gentlewoman like her doing out mucking round with elephants?"

Miriam was seated in a chair near Sir James, with her trembling hands clasped together in her lap. She leaned closer to the table with the pistol atop it, and Sir James flashed out a hand and took the pistol up again.

"What were we speaking of?" He brought the pistol up, and pensively laid the barrel against his forehead. "Of yes! The Malays and Dyaks are passionate creatures. And they love their knives, their *kris* and *parang*. Have you ever seen a man run amok, Miss Miriam?"

"I don't—"

"They go on a killing spree with their sharpest deadliest *kris*," he said. "It usually starts as some sort of revenge or affair of honour, and then they cannot stop. Fall victim to blood lust and kill everyone in sight."

An image of Poonah, and the cruel glint in her eye when she'd gotten hold of the cavalry sword, rose in Miriam's mind. Should she have fled with Dena and the uzis into the black Sarawak river? Miriam swallowed hard.

"You're thirsty!" Sir James declared. "Of course, it's thirsty work hacking down elephant grass, and I am a deplorable host. Do reach yourself a glass. The decanter stands just at your elbow. I could use a refresher myself."

Sir James waved his little cup. Miriam poured a noxious red liquid—the remainder of Sir James's hair tonic?—smelling of alcoholic tincture of laudanum, from the decanter into his glass. She set another empty one on the table before her.

"I don't drink ardent spirits," she said.

Sir James shot a hostile glare at her and waved his pistol in her direction. "Oh, I think you shall. To oblige me, don't you know. And then we will see what we can do to knock all that dirt off you."

CHAPTER FIFTEEN

Miriam woke in a hot clammy atmosphere, one she felt both inside her body and out of it. In her nostrils blew a horrid smell, a mixture of stale alcohol, foul breath, and dung. She opened her eyes to Sir James's tousled head on a pillow inches from her face, his fetid breath aimed right at her.

She let out a shriek and leapt from the bed, heart pounding fiercely. At this point Miriam realized she was naked, and with another cry she reached forward and snatched the coverlet from the bed, wrapping it around her and tying it above her breasts. Somehow all this fuss hadn't wakened Sir James. He snored on with an idiot slack-mouthed expression.

Miriam filled her lungs, ready to yell, "Get out!" She was rearing back to kick the bed as hard as she could, when her eye fell on the decanter. Two or three fingers of lurid red liquid remained.

Moving quickly, Miriam planted one knee firmly on the bed, and seized hold of the decanter. She clamped the snoring nose viciously shut, and emptied the decanter in Sir James' gaping mouth.

Spluttering and gagging, Sir James snapped to a

sitting position. Miriam jumped back. He wore a nightshirt now splattered red and a nightcap resting askew on his disarranged curls, ludicrously held on by strings fastened under his chin.

"What the devil—?"

"Get out! Why are you here, in my chamber?"

Her breath caught on those last words. Miriam wasn't in her airy top floor chamber. No, this was one of the first floor rooms. For servants and captives. With bars upon the window. She thought her heart would pound itself out of her chest.

Recovered from a fit of gulping and coughing, Sir James said, "My dear girl. Don't you remember? You were frightened, you invited me."

"I doubt it," Miriam said.

Yet she felt disoriented, as though her head were swollen, and she couldn't remember any of how she'd come to be in this room. That fact, let alone the more frightening one her mind wouldn't go near, because it might make her physically sick, of who'd removed her clothing and cleaned her of the mud and muck kept Miriam's heart racing. Meanwhile, her body felt near collapse.

"Where are my clothes?" Miriam gazed round the room, looking also for the pistol from the night before. "Where are my weapons?"

"My dear, I do assure you," Sir James said in a reasoning tone, "you were perfectly willing last night."

Miriam snatched up the first suitable object that came to hand, a heavy pewter candlestick holder, and rushed Sir James. She leapt atop the bed, wielding the candlestick like a belaying pin. Part of her wanted to smash Broke's head with it, but she mastered herself. There was no need to subdue him, the alcoholic ratafia was taking effect. Broke lay slumped against his pillows, on his way to paralytic drunk.

She backed off the bed and stood a few paces away, a plan taking shape at the edges of her mind. She'd need co-conspirators, Poonah and others in this house, as well as a great many more besides.

"You think you're on the right side, the side of virtue," Sir James said. "Let me assure you, if you've anything to do with Lord Q, you are not."

Miriam wouldn't be baited. Her head was muzzy, but she wasn't the one who'd just downed a snoot-full of alcohol and opium.

"And what do you subscribe to?" Miriam asked. "Private kingdoms where you can hold women and innocent elephants captive without consequences?"

"Shrill self-righteousness doesn't become you, dear girl. Is it my fault these women, Torsiri and the rest, come from a backward people who believe in forest spirits? Too frightened by these imaginary—" he paused and tried to train wandering eyeballs on Miriam, "—and very real evils we both know lurk there, to venture into the forests alone and find their way home?"

"You could easily give them an escort. The uzis—"

"No I could not!" Broke snapped. "I know what's best for them, that's what you fail to understand. For them, and for this country. Under my protection, the people will flourish. Without me they will languish back to the benighted state I found them in."

Miriam listened to his rant with half an ear, she'd discovered a lady's scarf draped over a chair back. Taking the long length of linen, Miriam moved to the bed and flipped back the bedclothes from Sir James' delicate, white, immobile feet. She hobbled his ankles together with the scarf, the way she'd seen the uzis do to the elephants on rare occasions. Bundle him up like a package, enlist Poonah, the uzis, Krunk, in finding a boat, bring him to *Capitaine* D'Villiers—was it not a Code Black? Clap him under guard, problem solved. Lord Q could have him, in exchange for her remaining aboard dear *Nonesuch* indefinitely.

"And what do you think would happen to those women of the temple I told you of?" Sir James cried. "Were I not here? What would become of them under Lord Q and the British? I am their protector."

When the words of a madman and an addict made sense, Miriam really had to wonder. She shook her head. Her thoughts were disordered was all, there was a mission. A commotion broke out the other side of the chamber door, a confusion of voices was heard, most of them female.

"In here!" Broke shouted. "Poonah, Charles! To me, to me! Help me!"

If he thinks those women bear him any love he's much mistaken, Miriam thought. She moved to open the door. Poonah burst into the chamber, lips pulled back from her teeth in a grimace. In that moment, Miriam felt sure of securing Poonah's help.

Poonah went to the bed, threw back the bedclothes, and hauled Sir James to his feet.

"Oh, thank you, dear boy! You've no idea, she's a witch, an evil spirit. How I've suffered!" Sir James babbled, stumbling in the long nightdress, with his ankles tied. Poonah marched him toward the door.

Miriam followed, gathering her thoughts, preparing to give orders about Sir James' removal. Torsiri and a half dozen other ladies were crowded outside in the hallway, some with frightened faces, many more wearing the same angry expression as Poonah. For the first time Miriam noticed her weapon belt draped over Poonah's shoulder. Poonah was prodding Broke with the sword tip.

"I'll take my sword back now," Miriam said.

"No, you won't, Persia. You done good." Poonah waved the sword at Broke's feet. "But this here don't concern you."

The other ladies nodded, closing in. Miriam reached for the weapon, and Poonah shoved her hard in the chest. Torsiri and a fierce, dark-eyed woman caught hold of Broke, leaving Poonah free to come after Miriam.

"I'll take him back to England—" Miriam began.

"You take others too? Evil red-faced one and—"

"Charles! Charles!" Sir James shouted.

They all heard pounding steps coming up the stairs, the shouts of men.

Poonah pushed Miriam back into the bedchamber, emphasizing every word with a hard backward shove. "This. Not. Your. Fight."

Miriam landed skidding on her backside on the bedchamber floor. She bounced to her feet and hit the door as it was closing. Beyond it Vintner and Jay-Ar made it to the top of the stairs, Poonah was gripping the sword and turning round to face them. The door slammed shut and Miriam heard a bolt slide to, locking her in. She pulled on the door handle and pounded on the frame.

"Poonah, Torsiri, are you there?"

No one heeded her screaming and pounding, they were doing their own on the other side of the door. There was a shout of, "I kill him!", and all went dead quiet. Leaning exhausted on the door, Miriam felt foolish and sick and done. She slumped across the room, and pulled open the window shutters. The smell of dung, with an underlying tang of sulfur, filled Miriam's nostrils. A strange shadowed sunlight fell across her face.

"Oh, no, I missed it!" she wailed.

Outside the barred window, though the light and the very air had a filtered grey quality, the sun was well up in the sky. She'd missed the meeting at first light with Krunk, and Dena, and all her friends. It was well on in the morning, if not noon of the day.

With a sob, Miriam crumpled to her knees on the floor in front of the window. She realized she wasn't sure what day it was, or how many had passed since she'd been with the uzis feeding Maja, the White Elephant. Or had she imagined that too, like she'd imagined away the sequence of events that brought her to be lying in bed with Sir James Broke?

She stretched prone on the plank floor, reaching a hot hand toward the window. The dung smell was strong because her window gave on to Maja's pen. She'd glimpsed the elephant on the far side near the gate, swaying and emitting low moans. Hungry, isolated, captive, and forgotten. For both their sakes she needed to act, to try the strength of those bars outside her window. A vision of a long vine cord tossed to the ground passed before her mind's eye.

Yet all Miriam managed to do was roll about a little, groaning, wishing for a cool hand on her forehead, a comforting voice in her ear, and the pounding in her head to stop. She knew there were things she must do, vital things, but her thoughts were strangely awry. Make a reconnaissance of the room, was that it? For weapons, bedsheets, clothing, and boots that smelled of meat. That didn't seem quite right, but wasn't there something about Bum-Bum-Too-Too?

Feeling as sick as she was, Miriam couldn't imagine

why her mother didn't come in and bring her a sip of water. She would give anything for that, she was so thirsty. And sore of head and body. Miriam wanted to go lie in the bed, but it was too besmirched and far away, too difficult to rise from the floor. There was another reason she couldn't lie there, and she struggled to remember what that was.

Into her mind popped a man's voice, "...knock the dirt off you." She shuddered and retched ever so slightly. Get ahold of yourself, an internal voice commanded, you know what sex feels like. Miriam thought about the not unpleasantly reamed sensation in her body that resulted from her relations with Maximus. No, that feeling was absent, not there deep inside her, she was untouched in her innermost core. While the realization eased her horror, a smoldering rage remained. Someone had taken the clothes from her drugged, insensate body, and dared touch her unbidden. Her fists clenched and hot tears squeezed from the corners of her eyes.

With visions in her fevered head of vengeance—it looked like Poonah and Torsiri—and what she herself wanted to do to that someone when she caught up with him, Miriam fell into a troubled sleep.

She woke to the sounds of actual violence. From all corners of the manse, upstairs and down, came the sounds of smashing furniture and breaking glass, slamming doors, voices shouting abuse, and terrible chilling shrieks and screams. Twice, pistol shots rang out. Those shrieks—male and female ones, Miriam judged dispassionately—she'd heard last in the jungle. When one animal was acting the predator, and another crying out with its last breath on earth. Miriam tried to wet her lips but she was too dry. Mayhem was just outside her door, and the only thing Miriam could do was stare longingly at a jug of water on a wash handstand nearby.

Waves slapped the prow of *Nonesuch's* jolly boat, with Maximus sitting in the sternsheets, beating upriver to Kuching under a low gray sky. Alijah, Mookit, and the Dusan men, had shamed Maximus in his expectation they wouldn't keep their end of the bargain. The rapidity with which the native men returned bearing rice, gum dammar, fruits and roots, exceeded Maximus's fondest hopes. Alijah actually rode in the jolly boat with Maximus and his boat's crew, to act as local guide ashore.

Mr. Dashwood's good deed of buying the Dusans' freedom from the rapacious Charles Vintner had been paid back in full. With the fiber and sustenance brought by Alijah and his companions, Maximus's men recovered. The repairs to *Nonesuch* were completed in a trice, and the barky floated off its resting place when the waters of the lagoon were still high.

It was a joy to be at sea again, in his element and aboard his dear ship, crippled though she might be, for the gum dammar hadn't worked to seal the rent in one balloon. The truth was, he'd made rather a cock of it and succeeded in ruining the greater part of the delicate fabric of the damaged balloon. Though they could not fly, they could certainly sail. The ship encountered still more good fortune when, after leaving their lagoon, and rounding the tip of one of the countless archipelagos off Borneo, *Nonesuch* sighted the French ship *Astrolabe*.

Jules Sébastien César Dumont D'Villiers was *Astrolabe's* captain, and since their two countries were not presently at daggers drawn, Maximus brought *Nonesuch* right alongside and hailed him. Captain

D'Villiers actually reeled in shock at sight of Maximus's phiz, jerking his head back in surprise. Sure, he'd had the beard of Methuselah, and many were shaken by his parti-colored eyes alone.

Captain D'Villiers, a well-bred man to the tips of his golden locks, quickly recovered of his shock. Since he and Maximus were long acquainted from their days together at the *lycée* that covertly trained airship officers, they were soon *mon ami*"ing one another in an old, familiar way.

But Maximus dropped the casual, hail-fellow-well-met attitude when Captain D'Villiers began speaking of matters closest to his heart.

"Yes, I had lately a visit aboard *Astrolabe* from Sir James Broke, he they call the White Rajah. He returned the favor, inviting me to dine at his Astana in Kuching. There I met a most interesting Persian woman."

Maximus bent forward all eager attention, for surely to god there could be only one Persian woman in Borneo.

"I hesitated very much, I may say, leaving such a woman in that house."

"And why would that be?" Maximus asked, his French coming out a perfect growl.

Captain D'Villiers started, and gave another backward jerk of his head. "I trust I may speak candidly—" Maximus and Captain D'Villiers were by this time closeted in *Nonesuch's* cabin, "—as between brother officers in the airship service, when I tell you that something is not quite right with Sir James." Captain D'Villiers tapped his own temple. "Something not quite right in the top hamper."

For a few seconds, Maximus tried to hold on to his temper. It was no good, and he burst out, "Do you mean to say ye've left Lord Q's most valuable operative behind enemy lines, with a man who's gone off his nut?"

Much spluttering in French ensued. Had not Mademoiselle been sent in expressly for the purpose of turning Broke's mind? Then Maximus realized he'd not been quite fair. Miriam's mandate of late was dealing with nut cases. Together they must put their minds to ending that.

From that point on, Maximus wasted not a moment in ordering his jolly boat to take him into Kuching. He paused only long enough to shave, and give orders to Mr. Dashwood concerning the disposition of the ship, naming three separate rendezvous where Maximus might rejoin. With Miss Miriam Albuyeh Kodio Blackwell Thorpe in tow, Maximus privately hoped and trusted.

"Let us not be too particular, for all love," Maximus said now to the coxswain of his jolly boat. He pointed toward a wide strand of beach fringed with sago palms where a group of men were gathered beside their boats, watching fish flop on the exposed sand. "That will do very well."

Alijah jumped out as soon as the jolly boat ground ashore, and ran over to the knot of fishermen. Maximus followed, watching the fishermen gesturing at the low water level of the Sarawak and the soot gray sky pressing down from above. They spoke in excited tones to Alijah.

"These men say Great Spirit, *Hantu Grassi*, so angry by Astana killings, gone suck out all Kuching waters and rain ash down us."

"What killings?" Maximus said.

A pain sprang up in his chest. He stood there feeling paralyzed, staring downriver at a stone bridge that ended the other side on rising ground topped by a great mansion. He set off at a sprint for the bridge.

"Tuai Torpe! Tuai Torpe!"

Alijah, supple as a forest deer, ran after and caught him up. "Tuai Torpe, stop mad rush. You no go there, no one go there now!"

Maximus fetched up at the foot of the bridge on the Kuching village side. Lined up blocking access across the river was a row of Iban tribesmen, faces drained of color beneath their ochre and yellow paint. One European stood among them, a youthful man with dark wavy hair and a pale frightened face, looking as though he'd just seen hell.

"What's happened here?" Maximus asked.

"They are all dead over there." The dark-haired man pressed white lips together, then said in Malay, "One of Muda Hasim's captives—Sir James was negotiating their release—ran amok and killed them all. They are all dead or run off."

"Sir James is dead?" Maximus said, his heart never ceasing its painful thud.

"No, at least...his is not among the bodies—"

"Show me these bodies," Maximus instantly demanded.

"Tuai Torpe," Alijah cried, "you some kind crazy? Place full evil spirits, no one go there now!"

Maximus pushed past the Iban tribesmen, who clutched their weapons to their chests and let him by. He heard someone at his heels, and knew the dark-haired young man was following him.

"I'll...I'll show you," the man said, catching up to Maximus on the path between the bridge and great house. "I'm amanuensis to Sir James, my name—"

The young man gagged and clapped a hand over his mouth. The tall double doors of the mansion stood wide open. From the shadowy interior of the house came a smell of blood and putrefaction, along with the high-pitched whine of busy insects.

"I'm sorry sir, I can't," the young man said through clenched teeth. "They are all downstairs in the great hall."

He turned and ran back toward the bridge, dark curls flying. Maximus untied his neckcloth and, securing it over his nose and mouth, walked up the steps into the great hall of the manse. He'd seen his share of pitched battles on the decks of ships, and one or two bloody land actions, and except for his desperate fear for Miriam, Maximus thought he was prepared for what he would encounter.

Yet the scene in the great hall was one far outside of Maximus's experience, and for several moments together he was rooted in place. There were men and women with their throats slashed, lying in copious pools of coagulating blood, on which insects were merrily skating. At Maximus's feet were a pair of sliced off fingers, and not far from them laid out on the blood covered tiles was a long gray colored fleshy member. It didn't seem an appendage that could belong to man or beast. Everything and everybody in the great hall was covered in blood, a fine white-gray ash, and splinters and shards of glass.

Maximus swayed in place, dizzy with nausea, and then inwardly chastened himself. He'd been around corpses, wounds, and blood, all his adult life and for much of his youth. How old had he been when he'd dissected his first corpse? He wanted to take a deep strengthening breath, knew that was a bad idea, and began to move methodically round the room. He saw blunt force trauma, caved skulls, and many, many stab wounds and dismemberments. Toward the back of the great hall the glass fronts of two long wall-sized cabinets were shattered, half the glass intact and the other half strewn round in a wide trajectory.

In spite of the reek and carnage Maximus's heart began to beat easier, for he'd examined nearly all the corpses. Three bodies caught his eye. They were laid out side by side with straightened limbs on the floor, in contrast to the disorderly death throes attitudes of the rest. Maximus moved over to the group and knelt down.

One of the victims was known to him, it was Charles Vintner. The red gaping slash across his throat matched the color of his skin in life. In death, the ugly character of the man was displayed on a dreadful drained white face. A small rotund native man lay by his side, part of his head smashed in with what appeared to be the corner of a glass box, still protruding from one eye. Maximus spent little time examining them, and moved to a woman on Vintner's other side. A tall elegant woman dressed in a flowing robe, her blue eyes open to the world, with a fierce expression on her face. She appeared to have no wounds, until Maximus noticed the place between her eyes where the bullet had entered.

What gave Maximus a severe jolt, just as relief at not finding Miriam in this nightmare hell-scape was creeping in, was spotting his own sword lying on the floor. Right beside the blue-eyed dead woman's open hand. He went gingerly round and stooped to collect the sword, registering in a remote part of his mind the two-day growth of beard on the woman's cheeks. Maximus straightened, momentarily unsteady, caught movement out of the corner of his eye and jerked his head toward the open door of the great house.

Staring back at him was a Hell-Cat. The creature

hissed at him and streaked away. Maximus leapt up and darted after it.

The elephant's lowing cries woke Miriam, they were followed by a rending, cracking noise that seemed to come from all directions at once. The floor beneath her undulated. She heard the flapping and beating of many wings passing over the house, and the shrill calls of birds that normally spent all day making their living at sea. Rolling over and up on to her hands and knees, she crouched there with her head hanging down like a dog's. Once Miriam was sure the pounding in her skull had stopped, and the floor beneath her was stable, she rose to her feet and wobbled over to the wash handstand.

She gulped down the greater part of the water in the jug, reserving a last portion to wet her face, neck, and hair. The coverlet she still wore was stuck to her back with sweat and humidity, its pattern no doubt imprinted semi-permanently in her skin. Miriam went and tried the still locked door of her room, remembering screams and cries that made her back away with a cold tight feeling in her chest.

She went over to the window, the shutters were open and a fine ash was drifting through the air inside and out. Miriam grasped hold of the iron bars and shook them. Just as with the set outside Poonah's chamber, these bars creaked at the hinges fastening them to the house.

"Maja!" Miriam called, leaning against the iron rails. "Maja, come, it's me. Come!"

The White Elephant was pressed against the gate on the far side of the pen, near where her depleted stash of food had been. Her eyes were closed and she moaned pitifully.

"Maja!" Miriam thrust one shoulder and arm through the bars, and motioned the elephant over. "Come, Maja, come speak to me."

The elephant opened her large amber brown eyes and swung her head in Miriam's direction. She lifted her trunk and tasted the air, and plodded toward her, Miriam calling encouragement. Maja raised her trunk, her head came to just below Miriam's window, and stuck it through the bars. The elephant first caressed Miriam's hand and then the top of her head. Miriam closed her eyes, at last the comfort she'd craved during these past few fever days had arrived.

She was reluctant it should end, but at last Miriam gently took Maja's powerful trunk and wrapped it round one of the iron bars.

"Pull!" Miriam commanded in the language of the uzis.

Maja gave a mighty jerk and the ironwork creaked and groaned, but held to the house. The elephant knew what she was about, and stepped back a moment to consider. Miriam had no doubt Maja understood the task was to bust her out of that room. Maja stepped up and locked her trunk more securely through several of the bars, braced her back legs, and pulled while twisting her head. The iron framework came loose, dangling open on one side while still fastened to the house on the other.

"Bless you, Maja, the best of all elephants!" Miriam cheered.

Miriam thought of stepping out of the bed chamber window onto Maja's back, but rejected the idea. It might not be the wisest thing to do, unbidden, to a half-starved elephant known for man-killing. Clad in a bedcover and barefoot, she scooted out onto the window ledge.

From there Miriam crawled on to the iron cage, praying it would hold a little longer, and scrambled from it to the top of the pen wall. Scrapped and bruised, Miriam rested on the rough-cut enormous logs, straddling the wall awkwardly, contemplating how she was to crawl or tightrope her way to the tree branch ladder she hoped still rested against the outside of the pen.

Maja was good for much more than acts of great strength. She grasped the situation, and lumbered over to Miriam, raising and offering her trunk. Miriam crouched with one foot in front of the other, braced her hands on the wall and then pushed upright to her feet. Maja's trunk was there to hold on to, and slowly Miriam stepped out. She teetered this way and that, calculating if she lost her balance, falling inside the pen might be better than outside it. There she'd be at the mercy of the powerful, wise elephant, outside of it god only knew what awaited.

High up on the stout log wall, Miriam chanced one or two glances around. What she saw frightened her almost as much as anything that'd happened so far. She reached the juncture of the fence with the pen gate, and to her infinite relief found the tree-trunk ladder still leaning against the outside.

"I shall have you out in a trice, Maja, my dear." Miriam patted that sustaining trunk, and lowered herself onto the top of the ladder.

When her head disappeared below the enclosure wall, Maja let out a trumpeting roar that blasted Miriam loose of her hold. She slid haphazardly down the tree limb, scrapping more flesh from her legs, and tearing off her bedcover wrap.

Landing with a naked plop at the bottom of the

ladder, Miriam sprang up and retrieved the coverlet from the mud with an indignant huff. She'd be damned if she'd come it the Lady Godiva in Borneo, or anywhere else in the world.

Miriam rushed to the pen gate, her ears ringing with Maja's trumpeting cries, and heaved up the solid wooden latch. She remembered to stand clear as several tons of elephant came charging through the open gate, making straight for the tall grasses beside the river.

Ash floated in the air like snowfall. Miriam leaned against the heavy wooden gate, trying to make sense of her surroundings. There must be an enormous fire, and somewhere close, by the drifting soot in the air and sun blotted out sky overhead. Miriam gazed at Maja, nearly hidden by the dense riverside reeds and grasses, shoveling trunk loads of food into her mouth. The same chill of fright ran through her that she'd experienced up on the pen wall, because of the Sarawak. There was hardly any water in it.

Miriam pushed away from the wood gate of Maja's prison. Wherever the fire was, it was not in the great house. The manse stood whole and quiet and still before her, despite the violent shaking earlier. Miriam hiked up her bedcover and marched over to the French doors where she'd last entered the house. She stopped short, seeing one-half of the double door ajar, and craned forward to peer into the room. Inside was a scene of hasty departure, the low wood center and side tables overturned, and the door leading into the grand hallway left wide open.

Through that open hall door Miriam glimpsed shattered glass, and blood splattered on the tall curiosity cabinets. A powerful reek reached her. Miriam gagged, yanked a corner of the bedcover over her nose, and was turning to flee outside when her eye fell on her tunic, long trousers, and boots. Her clothes were neatly laid atop a settee against the wall, in a pile exactly as she'd leave them before bed, with her boots on the floor below.

Miriam darted in and dressed in seconds. Her small clothes were folded inside her shirt and trousers, just as her mother had taught her, so no one should see them. She sat down to pull on her boots, a cry of joy escaping her when she found the *sgian dubh* inside the right one.

She was straightening, after strapping the weapon to her leg, already feeling stronger—the effects of the drug must be leaving her—when she heard a fleshy whomp sound. There was James Broke, ricocheting off the door frame, careening into the room stark naked except where the blood dappled his skin.

Miriam leaped up and ran. She pelted out the door in the direction of the river and ran, ran for all she was worth. Any thought of Lord Q, of taking a madman hostage, gone right out of her head.

"Maja, Maja!" Miriam called, sucking air. "*Hmit!*"

The elephant swung her head up, still munching, and for a moment regarded Miriam with an exasperated, annoyed eye. Then the great White Elephant saw and smelled what was coming after Miriam. And she sensed, in the distance, the greater danger racing toward them at top speed. The elephant folded at the knees, and Miriam, the bedcover still draped round her neck, grasped hold of the veiny ear and fairly swarmed aboard.

"Go! Let's go, Maja!" Miriam leaned forward over the elephant's back. "To the Queen of Heaven!"

Maja rose. From atop her bony ridged back, Miriam allowed herself one glimpse behind. James Broke was lurching after them down the riverbank, shouting something that sounded like "*Mine!*"

Her eye moving from one horror to another, Miriam looked at the gray and red streaked horizon away out at sea, and a single wave. A monster wall of water, many feet high, barreling inland.

A single line of foam ran the length of the wave's great crest, a white noose closing in.

But Maja was already across the near dry riverbed to the village side. And then the elephant really began to stretch out, all her senses urging her to flee. Miriam clung to her, bouncing like a sack of goods. She coiled the bedcover under the reed rope, wrapping it round her own waist and back again under the rope band passed round Maja's mid-section.

The village of Kuching went by in an uninhabited blur. No one came out from the deserted huts to stare and point at the spectacle. A charging elephant with a woman, a little flea, clinging on her back. Was the mad red and white rajah still chasing them too?

Away on the far side of Kuching, Maja slowed on a rising mountain path that wound through several more villages. Relief washed over Miriam. They'd made it to high ground. She glimpsed several Iban and one white face peering out the window of a hut. Miriam jerked on her high seat. Could it be him, or was it just her morbid imagination? A resounding roar interrupted these tortured thoughts. A great smashing crash like a full broadside of cannon, and the wave overtook them.

Great Maja was swimming, stroking out bravely, her trunk held above the surface. Miriam coughed and choked out sea water, crouched jockey style, with her arms hooked under the elephant's belly rope, water hitting her in the face. Miriam, the great White Elephant, and a kaleidoscope of vegetable, mineral, and animal life, was pushed and whirled round and carried along by the wave.

Clinging to the canopy of an enormous uprooted tree was a whole family of gibbons, shrieking and reaching out their tiny hands to Miriam as Maja swam past.

A clouded leopard with a head the size of a boulder, holding a cub in her mouth, swam in their direction. Until the elephant and leopard spotted one another, paused, and veered off in different directions.

A troupe of orang-utans riding an overturned canoe floated past. One stood on its hind legs and saluted Miriam with a gesture very much like that of the British officers.

Clusters of Iban tribesmen clung in the tops of coconut palms and to the boles of the towering honey-bee trees. One of the honey-bee tree groups launched themselves into the water, swam to the orang-utans' boat, and started a battle royal.

More people were in the water. Most were dead. Some floated upright, surprised eyes open to the grainy sky. Others were face down revealing where skulls had been bashed in, and even more dreadful wounds.

A small bobbing creature was directly ahead in Maja's path, it reached up a little fist and opened five fingers in a starfish signal of distress. As she came upon the creature, Maja curled her trunk round it, and sent it backward with a gentle shove toward Miriam.

A baby girl was in the water. Eyes open she reached her arms up to Miriam, water washing over her face as she floated next to the elephant's side. Miriam pulled one arm free of the rope and leaned down. A myriad of tiny bright fishes was swimming through the girl's hair, just before Miriam plucked the infant from the water.

She dragged the little girl onto the elephant's back, opened her mouth to say something encouraging, and nearly dropped her again.

"You there, Harlot!" a high English voice screamed. "That's *my* elephant!"

Floating toward them was the thatch roof of a native hut, with six or seven wild eyed people riding atop it. Maja changed direction, but not before the most deranged among them hurled a string of invective that made Miriam want to cover the little girl's ears.

"*My* elephant! *Mine!*" Sir James howled.

Then, to Miriam's horror, he took a running start off the thatch roof and launched a swan dive straight into the water.

"Alright," Miriam said, clutching the child against her midriff. Reaching down, she pulled the black blade from its sheath. "Let's end this."

She never took her eyes from the surface of the water, watching for Sir James's head to pop up, clinging to Maja's sides with her knees.

With surprising athleticism Sir James surfaced on the far side of Maja. Miriam instantly shifted the child away, and changed her weapon hand.

"Don't do it!" Miriam shouted, trying to warn him off. "Keep clear, none of us belongs to you!"

Sir James paused in his determined stroke long enough to rear up and hurl a word at Miriam so foul, this time she was sure both the child and Maja felt and understood it at a gut level. Maja put on a burst of speed. The baby began to wail. Sir James reached for Miriam's leg to drag her from the elephant's back. Miriam's last recollection before water surged over and engulfed them all, was of stabbing down with the *sgian dubh*. That, and the horrible high-pitched animal scream that followed, cut short even as she yanked out the blade.

CHAPTER SIXTEEN

Miriam came to her senses, her clothing soaking wet though Maja no longer breasted the waves. Her heart gave a great lurch of fear for the baby, until Miriam realized the child was pinned between her body and the elephant's back. The little girl was wide awake, perfectly sensible, and reached out and patted Miriam's cheek.

Pulling herself upright, Miriam wiped her face and tamped down her tangled hair with one hand. She sat the little girl astride in front of her, Maja plodding along uphill. Miriam felt the ever so slight trembling of Maja's legs. The dear elephant was about at her limit of endurance. She wanted to call a stop, give the command for Maja to kneel so that she might get down. She'd no right to ride any elephant, much less a White and sacred one that had just saved all their lives.

"Maja," Miriam croaked.

By way of acknowledgement, Maja swung her trunk back and briefly allowed Miriam to shake the tip of it with her hand.

The difficulty was they were not alone on the steep and muddy uphill climb to the temple of the Queen of Heaven.

Laboring up the mountainside both ahead and behind Maja were the wet, bedraggled, limping survivors from Kuching and the surrounding villages. Miriam turned around on her high swaying seat and gazed back at the people straggling away far down the slope. Up close to her, three brave little boys had joined hands, with the tallest and oldest one holding fast to Maja's tail. As soon as they reached level ground Miriam must ask Maja to halt, so that the children and any wounded might take her place.

The sight of the enormous swath of destruction cut by the great wave through Kuching and halfway up the mountainside made Miriam's stomach clench. She turned to face forward and shut it out, closing her eyes. She would allow her blurred vision to clear and the rising wave of nausea to pass.

When she opened her eyes again, the black, green, and red streaked stones of the temple complex were rising out of the jungle. The trumpeting calls of elephants penetrated the mists in Miriam's brain. Maja plodded a few last steps before halting beside the temple stairs. On the open ground surrounding the stone structures, refugees were already constructing small huts and *bashas*. Many more people wandered about dazed, examining the newcomers, and looking for lost family members.

The throng gave way when Miss Chief, in the lead, with Miss Temper and Miss Fat Bottom close behind, rushed up hot foot to greet Maja. A great rumbling, swaying, and touching of trunks broke out between the cows. Hoola was nowhere to be seen. But Miriam thought she would fall off Maja's back, so great was her relief, when she spotted Dena, Inghai, Le No, and Pin Ho in the crowd near the elephants.

A single high cry rose above the confusion of people and elephants. It drew the attention of other animals lurking nearby, clusters of the diminutive forest deer peering in from the fringes, gibbons milling on the tiled roofs of the temple complex, and the orang-utans down by the pools. A woman wailed and shoved, plowing her way through the crowd.

No power in heaven and on earth could resist a determined mother. The woman, reaching Maja's side, cried, "Kondima! Kondima!", holding out her arms.

Maja knelt without being commanded, for the child's sake. The little girl Miriam fished from the water, the floating creature with wrasse in her hair, screamed and twisted toward the woman. Miriam managed to hand the child down safely. Kondima would've hurled her small body from the elephant's back, straight into her mother's arms.

Kondima sank her crumpled face on her mother's neck and shoulder, and wrapped small arms round to cling to her. They were fellow survivors.

"*Khun*! Maryam!" A familiar voice was calling.

"Krunk!"

Miriam stepped from the elephant's bent knee directly into Krunk's arms. She was kissed on both moist cheeks, and then on the lips.

"Oh, dear goddess!" Krunk said, holding her tight. "We thought you dead."

"I stabbed James Broke," Miriam said.

Krunk stood back and gazed into Miriam's face. Miriam saw in the bruise like circles below Krunk's eyes, with their yellow-red whites, the signs of recent illness that were likely all over her own face too.

"Deserved it, no doubt." Krunk put her fingertips on Miriam's flushed cheeks. "Speak no more that man name. Here your friends."

Tuai Rumah Dena shook Miriam by the hand. Inghai patted her shoulder, and Miriam received kind congratulations from Pin Ho and Le No on her survival. The elephants, Maja standing at their center, began to turn together for the pools that cascaded at the bottom of the temple complex.

"Wait!" Miriam said, pulling away from Krunk. "Dena, please. I want a word with Maja."

She'd assumed the head uzi would take charge of Maja, once a working elephant. Perhaps, Miriam hoped, to lead her far into the jungle to liberty, and retirement.

Dena spoke to the group of cows, who heeded his voice and swung their heads in Miriam's direction.

She walked up to Maja and made a deep bow, hands pressed together before her heart.

"Peace be with you, great Maja," Miriam said. And then, the words of the other half of her religious upbringing surfaced. "May goodness and mercy follow you all the days of your life."

Maja draped her trunk over Miriam's head in caressing fashion. In every fiber of her being, Miriam felt the elephant's rumbling response, 'and also with you, peace.' Miriam and Maja stood together, caressing and patting one another, until Hoola, away out of sight at the pools, began trumpeting for the cows to join him.

Krunk led Miriam, weak and unresisting, and bathed in tears, through the inner temple complex. The courtyard surrounding the temple was crowded with people, all under the beneficent gaze of the Queen of Heaven, refugees swelling the numbers of the former inhabitants. Miriam, holding to Krunk's hand, wished for a glimpse of Hawwa's sensitive face and dark eyes.

"Indoors mostly wounded," Krunk told her, as they

ducked into the familiar, crumbling, tree-grown dormitory.

Am I wounded, am I sick, do I lie trapped on the floor of James Broke's Astana, with the odor of brimstone in the air? Miriam was lying on several layers of woven mats on a stone floor. But no bed coverlet was pressing patterns into her skin. Miriam considered the light in the dormitory, a faint strip of sunshine picked out the green and black moss where the tops of the walls met the ceiling. Twilight, Miriam judged, in Iban the time of day called *lagi lemai*.

There was one other sleeper in the dormitory. Sia, warrior and hairdresser, lay not far from Miriam, arms and legs flung wide, her face work-worn and exhausted. Miriam sat up and put her back to the wall. After a moment's hesitation, she was not wounded and felt only slightly sick, Miriam rose and walked outside.

She took a place in the queue for one of the cisterns and when it came her turn, dumped two buckets of water over her head by way of bathing. Squeezing water from her hair, Miriam made her way through the maze of *basha*s. Women squatted cooking outside improvised dwellings, while gangs of naked children ran playing and screaming in the spaces between the huts. Miriam smiled at them, though feeling world weary and far removed as she climbed the temple steps.

Miriam paused at the top, on the temple platform, keeping her gaze on the near view of graduated pools. At the end of the pools, she searched for uzis and elephants—their number increased by one sacred addition—and caught a glimpse of them exiting the water. The elephants would soon be turned loose to feed in the forest, their favorite time of day.

She watched the little group of five elephants amble into the jungle upcountry, away from the destroyed mud-yellow covered mountainside. Miriam took a few deep breaths of the moist, cook-smoke laden air, and headed down the temple steps toward the hospital wing. The gods or goddesses, the spirits of land and sea, had granted her survival when so many others had perished. It was her duty to find Nisa and help with the wounded, or ask Krunk and the other warriors to put her to work among the refugees.

In the doorway of the first hospital chamber Miriam paused, closing her eyes, the shocking sights and smells of her last visit flooding back. The scene now was different. Those overburdened women had moved to a more private chamber. Their places were taken by many more contused, abraded, half-drowned victims of the great wave. Miriam gazed round at the mud stained, shocked faces, wondering where and how she was to begin. And then her heart gave a great leap in her chest.

A heavy Scottish burr reached Miriam's ears. "I have the greatest respect for your abilities, dear colleague, a more delicate hand with a prolapsed uterus I have never seen. But that, madam, is a broken collarbone."

Heart pounding, Miriam dashed through the first hospital chamber and into the second. At the far end of the chamber, near the archway into the next, Nisa stood hands on hips gazing down at a white man squatting next to the patient he was examining. The doctor looked up, opening his mouth to speak. But as his mismatched eyes—one green and one pale blue —fell on Miriam across the chamber, he clapped it shut again and reeled to his feet.

They met halfway down the chamber, clasping their outstretched hands together. Neither spoke a word as they gazed at one another, a little disbelieving. At last Maximus let go one of Miriam's hands, to wipe a tear from her cheek. She raised a hand to his face, dried his tears in turn, and cupped his beard-stubbled jaw gently in her hand. Maximus kissed her hand, pressed it to his heart, and then enfolded Miriam in a close embrace.

He was murmuring endearments in Gaelic in Miriam's ear, when there came a cough and a loud 'ahem'.

"Persia, Edinburgh, there," Nisa said. "Give you joy of your reunion. You've had your moment, now back to work."

"Right, there's not a moment to lose," said Maximus, straightening to his full height, and looking, to Miriam, impossibly tall and noble in that low roofed dormitory. "It is after the battle, dearest Miriam, and we are triaging the wounded. Those in the outermost chamber you came through require the least attention. In this room are the more serious cases, and the far chamber is our surgery and operating theatre."

"I must beg your pardon for running away, and leaving you in that charnel house."

Under a starlit sky, with a brilliant moon magnified and reflected in the cascading pools, Miriam and Maximus sat side by side on the temple steps. Before them lay the graciousness and wrath of nature, illuminated by the same stars and planets as yesterday, yet somehow different—because they were together again. After hours of working in the hospital, Maximus and Miriam were at last having a private word. They began by recounting how they'd ended up in that place, under the stars at the temple of the Queen of Heaven.

"I ran after a Hell-Cat, like a great numpty. Dismissed

my gig and gig's crew—"

"May she have made it out before the flood."

"Amen, amen." Maximus looked at her with great affection. "I was convinced the Hell-Cat would lead me to you. It brought me here, where I discovered that Hell-Cat was no Thrax, and you yourself come and gone."

"Most likely Newt," Miriam said. "Nisa's...that is to say, the Hell-Cat of this place. A beautiful spotted creature the people here very much hoped might be got with kitten by Thrax."

Maximus chuckled. "Or vice-versa. What's in the scabbard is not known till it's drawn." Then he sobered. "What happened down there? I shall no soon forget the great hall of Broke's Astana. Like a scene out of Dante's Inferno. Some brute cut off an elephant's trunk and threw it right down on the floor, full upon the blood and gore."

"A fool's errand is what happened." Miriam shivered. "Where I played the fool—Lord Q's fool. None of it was ever any use. Neither I, nor anyone, could have convinced James Broke the rights and privileges over land and people he wanted, were not his to claim. Even had he been in his right mind." She paused, ordering her thoughts, at once relieved and dreading to speak. "There were a number of wome—people, captive in that house. Hostages of Muda Hasim. Sir James was negotiating their release, or at least that's what he told them. I suspect abuses. It was a false, tainted, poisonous atmosphere in that house. What you saw was the rebellion of nature, Poonah's at least. Nature's power to make all our animal strivings meaningless."

She waved toward the devastation on the mountainside. Roofs and walls of huts were strewn down the hillside. Great forest trees planted head down and roots up. Worst of all were human bodies, torsos, heads, and limbs, poking out of the yellow mud, and the hooves of dead water buffalo and the paws of countless other beasts waving up at an indifferent sky.

Miriam sniffled and wiped her face. "That was no elephant's trunk, by the way. Do you not know a rhinoceros penis when you see it?" And then, quite at random, she added, "I lost the *sgian dubh* you gave me."

She wouldn't tell him she'd stabbed James Broke with it, remembering Krunk's words of caution. With an inward pang of grief, Miriam realized the things she couldn't share with the people she loved were increasing upon her with each new mission of Lord Q's.

Maximus relieved her weary heart with his reply of, "Och, never mind it. I shall get ye another."

"And your big book of Birds of the Malay Archipelago too," she said. "Lost quite early on, when we were hit by a sky waterfall."

"Weelll, now, I make no doubt—in time—I shall be persuaded to forgive you. One day I should very much like to hear about this waterfall, and all your jungle adventures."

They were silent for a space, contemplating the beauty and ruin of their immediate surroundings, reaching for the language that would knit them back together again.

"*Capitaine de corvette* D'Villiers found you then, and the *Nonesuch*? I gave him your coordinates, after he threw out the private signal. Yet I could not be easy in my mind."

"Never trouble yourself, m'dear. As the case fell out, I found him. D'Villiers and I have known one another almost since we were in short pants. He is a classics scholar, a most prodigious intellect, and an eminent natural philosopher. But no one ever accused Jules Sébastien of excellence in navigation."

"How happy I am to hear it," Miriam said, distracted, thinking of Maximus's own prodigious store of books, his intellect, and the fact he was a physician. "When I walked into the hospital chamber you were speaking to Nisa of prolapsed uterus. Have you examined a child, a patient, named Hawwa?"

"Aye," his tone turned grave, "aye, so I did. She died of her terrible wounds the day after I arrived here. The poor wee lassie."

"Oh!" Miriam's voice wavered, "Oh!"

After a decent pause, he said, in a gentle tone, "Dearest Miriam, you no longer wear the veil?"

In a short while Miriam recovered her voice. "No. The black blade was not all I lost this mission." Without conscious thought, she reached out and took Maximus's hand.

CHAPTER SEVENTEEN

During the long odyssey in Borneo, through shipwreck, natural and man-made disaster, Miriam and Maximus had formed deep attachments to their Iban, Dusan, and other tribal friends. This was to say nothing of the elephants. Miriam visited the elephants every day, entwining her arms with their trunks, exchanging pats and caresses, communicating through sound and the gazes of their intelligent brown eyes. She and Maximus stayed in the aftermath of the great wave to help treat the wounded, and begin the work of digging out and rebuilding.

They remained until the day Captain D'Villiers popped out of the jungle. D'Villiers dressed not in the attire of the French naval service, but in canvas trousers parting at the seams, a linen shirt so worn it was see-through in places, and a battered straw hat from Chile. All over his person were hung small wicker cages, collecting baskets and pouches. D'Villiers, captain and natural philosopher, also carried with him orders from their mutual chief.

The time for leave-taking had come. Aside from her very real attachment to the place—the temple of the

Queen of Heaven and Borneo—and her people, Miriam was apprehensive because she couldn't be sure who would go with her. Krunk had found a fragment of her people here, the Amazons, after a protracted and painful separation. Aboard ship was no place for the dear elephants and her uzi friends, and so Miriam knew they must part forever. And then there was Thrax.

Into the general disorder and chaos of the refugee encampment, which radiated outward from the inner temple complex of the Queen of Heaven, seven Hell-Cat kittens made their appearance. Four were spotted jungle beasts, while three were striped with ticked fur perfect for blending into the Thracian steppes. Nisa and the people of the temple, if not quite the whole of the camp, doted upon the kittens. Attempts at kissing and cuddling often resulted in vicious swipes, and a number more injuries, scratches and bite wounds, for the physicians to treat. Meanwhile nothing was seen of pater and materfamilias—Newt or Thrax—though it was assumed they somehow cared for their thriving fat-bellied offspring.

"Thrax cannot abide most humans, much less a crowd of them." Maximus attempted to console her. "You are the only one it has ever had any use for."

"I doubt that will still be the case, now Thrax has greater concerns," Miriam said, a whiff of self-pity in her voice.

They were gathering at the bottom of the temple stairs in preparation for departure, and to make their way to the coast where Captain D'Villiers' boat awaited them. Tuai Rumah Dena, the uzis, and three of the elephants had appointed themselves their guides down the mountainside.

The two great elephants, Hoola and Maja, wouldn't

be joining the traveling party. Hoola was in *musth*, his season of sexual activity. Some days before, Maja led him away deep into the jungle. The tinkling of the bells round their thick gray necks no longer reached the uzis. Dena, wise in the ways of elephants—and in what could happen to humans who intervened—was letting nature take its course. One day, he hoped, the elephants might return of their own will, bringing with them a new sacred baby elephant.

"Pray do take care of those," D'Villiers cried out, darting forward as Inghai was loading the *bohongans* hung over Miss Fat Bottom's back with his specimens and collections. "That sack contains the skin of a tree-shrew I was at some pains to shoot."

"That what smell?" Inghai wrinkled his nose, tamping sacks of D'Villiers' plant cuttings atop the Insectivora.

"There is also a pangolin, a small inoffensive loris, a red-colored leaf monkey. And the wealth, the bounty of coleoptera and lepidoptera of this country!"

D'Villiers turned to Maximus, hands clasped before his breast. "How I long to dissect and catalogue the whole aboard my ship!"

"I'm sure you do, old cock," Maximus said. "But let us no interfere while Dena and Ingy-Pingy make all fast. They are the masters of this environment."

From over near Miss Fat Bottom, Inghai raised his brows at Maximus and turned away to conceal a smile.

The last preparation, the hoisting up and lashing in place of a *basha*-like platform atop Miss Fat Bottom's back, was almost completed when a great cry of voices and stir of people arose near the temple stairs. Out of it emerged Krunk, head shaved bald and in seaman's tunic and trousers, with a new woven red and yellow dyed fiber belt slung over her shoulder. Fastened to the weapon belt were the sacred *kris* and *parang*.

Krunk strode straight up to Miriam. They clasped forearms, looking into one another's faces. Tears filled Miriam's eyes. The illness, the jungle fever, had left Miriam weak, vulnerable, and emotional. The bamboo platform the uzis were securing to Miss Fat Bottom's back was for her—and now for Krunk too—when the fever overtook them every odd day, and they were prostrated, unable to walk.

"You will come with us?" Miriam blubbered out.

Krunk, still clasping her arms, leaned in and said, "You not know how I love you? Besides, I do about anything go fly again."

"Dear Krunk," Miriam said, wiping tears and sweat from her face. "Me too! How happy you've made me."

Though Miriam loved and valued her Borneo friends, she too wanted to be back aboard ship. To rise above the steaming land, into the cool airs and soaring clouds. Far beyond sickness, struggle, and the eternal dripping sweatiness of earth. Even though she'd no idea where they were bound. Maximus hadn't shared his orders with her, the orders D'Villiers carried, and she was too well-brought up to question him.

They said final farewells to the people of the temple. Nisa, Sia, and the other warrior guards, who were at once disapproving and positively distracted by their excess of affection for Krunk.

"Persia, Edinburgh," Nisa said gruffly. "May the Goddess bless you for what you did for Her people. May She go with you on your travels to foreign-devil lands."

"Handsomely now, handsomely!"

Miriam heard Maximus's voice as she was lowered

from Miss Fat Bottom's back, soaked to the bone with rain and her own fever sweat. She and Krunk were carried into a guest hut by Maximus, Captain D'Villiers, and the uzis, surrounded by a crowd of excited villagers that seemed to know Maximus intimately well. 'Tuai Torpe', they called him, asking after the 'maiden-faced one' with great concern and interest.

It was disconcerting, slipping in and out of consciousness. Miriam next woke on the floor of a hut, and became aware of Maximus moving quietly between her and Krunk. How many days she'd lain there or been on the trek to the coast, she didn't know. At least Miriam remembered they were journeying toward the ships. She was to go aboard *Nonesuch* again, and the knowledge brought a glowing happiness to her heart and a smile to her face.

From a screened off section of the hut came the sound of voices. Miriam recognized Captain D'Villiers' French accents, mingled with the uzis' and other native voices, engaged in a drinking game. Their revelry didn't quite drown out the woofing noise Krunk made as she vomited into a tight-woven basket. Maximus was holding Krunk up, her shaven head resting against his shoulder, until she leaned forward to heave.

"There she go again," Inghai said, "spewing away like volcano what threw up great wave."

"Hush that unlucky talk!" Dena said. "Krunk my very best friend. Tuai D-Vil cup empty, Ingy-Pingy, for shames."

"Maximus," Miriam whispered, reaching out her hand as Maximus reentered the hut after taking out the slops. "Will you shave my head too?"

"No, m'dear," Maximus said, coming to squat beside her, after helping Krunk to a half coconut full of water steeped in bark of the *langsat* tree. "No unless you wish it. Nisa suggested as much, she it was who shaved our Krunk." He motioned toward Krunk with a uniquely Scottish jerk of his head. "But I told her it was all great stuff and nonsense, and you should do just as well without a bald pate."

"Do you really think so?"

Maximus eased her upright against his chest, and put a fresh decoction of *langsat* bark to her lips.

"I might wish to have it all off," Miriam said. "It weighs on me so, not unlike the veil."

"Never you mind it. Tomorrow you'll feel more the thing."

Maximus gave her forehead a gentle caress, pressing her limp-necked head against his chest. He nodded to a string of women making their way on tiptoe through the main room of the hut, and disappearing behind the screen. Furious giggling and mutual attempts to shush one another broke out the other side of the wall.

"Should you like me to plait your hair, at all?"

"Could you?" Miriam said. "I mean, can you?"

"Och, woman. Am I no a seaman?"

He took her by the shoulders, and tried to steady her upright. Miriam slumped sideways as soon as he let go of her, so he braced her against his shoulder while his hands went quickly to work. Maximus braided her hair into a fine, thick, bedtime queue. He arranged the pigtail over her shoulder, and eased her to lie down again on the mats.

Sounds of hilarity, games of slap and tickle, were wafting from the other side of the hut. Miriam patted the split bamboo flooring next to her.

"You must lie down with me," she said.

Glancing round, Maximus said, "Must I?" and

prepared to stretch out beside her.

"What 'bout me?" A voice rose out of the dark.

Maximus leaned down, and picked Miriam up in his arms. He carried her to the other side of the room, and set her on the mats near Krunk. He then stretched out between them, so that either need only put out a hand to reach her physician. Her *baboolian*, and he was trying to be a better one to all his peoples.

In the morning a disagreement arose between Alijah and the people of Durian village on the one side, and the head uzi on the other, about who was to carry the foreigners the rest of the way to the coast and their ships. While Dena and Alijah argued in loud voices, Mookit and the other uzis calmly loaded Captain D'Villiers's collections and specimens into two canoes that would carry the party downstream to the rendezvous on the coast.

"Elephants no go mangrove swamp," Inghai whispered to Miriam, early on.

Today was a good day, and Miriam and Krunk, fit to travel, waited on the bank near the two canoes and the disputing chiefs. Captain D'Villiers was up and down the embankment, anxiously looking after his Borneo treasures. Maximus loaded their meager possessions. All was prepared, with the party assembled on the river bank.

"Take them then!" Tuai Rumah Dena shouted.

The two chiefs rejoined the group gathered on the embankment.

To ease the tension, Krunk asked, bending her elbow, "Who won game last night?"

All heads swiveled toward Captain D'Villiers. Laughter and hoots broke out, the men of Durian village and the uzis slapping D'Villiers on the back. The Europeans kept their title for holding their wine.

"Not best at, you know—" Inghai made a hip waggling motion, to further hoots and calls. "Womens get too friendlies, Tuai D-Vil run away."

This was translated for Captain D'Villiers at everyone's insistence.

D'Villiers blushed deeply. "I'm a married man," he said. "And a Catholic."

Miriam and Krunk said their final goodbyes to the uzis, feeling the particular pain of parting with friends they might never meet again this life. Earlier, and since they were well enough, they'd paid one last visit to the dear elephants, shedding buckets of tears.

Dena clasped both Miriam's hands. "Jams no longer my very best friend. You and Krunk are."

Tuai Rumah Dena, Inghai, Le No, Pin Ho, and many of the men and women of Durian village from last night's carouse, took a hand in pushing Alijah's boats into the middle of the stream. Their cheeks were wet, and their vision blurred, by unashamed, unchecked tears as Miriam and Krunk gazed at the group waving to them from the riverbank. The native craft glided inexorably downstream.

Very soon even the large gray and brown outlines of the elephants were swallowed by a bend in the river, and the layers deep silvan green of jungle foliage.

Long after Durian village had slipped astern, Miriam remained alert, outward looking, gazing with great attention at the shore. Floating downstream, guided by Alijah and Mookit—men who knew the river and countryside intimately well—a method of travel that demanded far less of her than trekking behind elephants, Miriam was able to better appreciate her last glimpses of the intense flourishing life of Borneo.

At times the way narrowed and a hundred species of tree, vines as thick as a man's thigh, ferns and parasitic orchids closed bower-like round them. Gibbons with white hands and masks, and fiery red-furred monkeys chattered and stared at them with round inquisitive eyes. Fish broke the surface of the water hunting insects, while jewel-colored kingfishers and sharp billed herons darted after the fish. When the boat broke the cover of overhanging trees, the flapping of strong wings was heard. Swarms of green parrots, and, to the great delight of the naturalist, the Rhinoceros Hornbill, appeared overhead. Its red and gold curved horn was clearly visible as it tilted its head, massive wingspan fairly blocking out the sun.

"There, there she is!" Captain D'Villiers cried, following the flight of the enormous bird. "*Buceros rhinoceros!* Give me joy, *mon ami,*" turning to Maximus, "now I have nothing more to wish for. My sojourn in this remarkable country is complete!"

Once the excitement of the hornbill sighting was over, Captain D'Villiers settled back into his place in the stern of the boat near Miriam and Maximus. The French captain took notice of how quickly Miriam's attention turned back to an intense scrutiny of the passing shore.

"What are you in hopes of seeing, Miss Blackwell, before you quit this remarkable land?"

"Thrax," Miriam said, straining hard for a glimpse of fast-moving fur against the raging green of the jungle.

The course of the tributary of the Samarahan narrowed and narrowed until at last it flushed out into a wide flooded plain of mangrove swamp. The smell of the sea reached them here, and the two naval officers nodded to one another with satisfaction. Alijah and

Mookit guided the canoe in unerring fashion through the channels between the tall mangrove roots rearing out of the swamp, as though following a well-worn track. Overhead, whole families of bulbous nosed monkeys crowded the wide spreading tree branches. Indifferent to their passage, the monkeys went about their business; suckling their young, feeding on leaves, and coupling with great energy.

Captain D'Villiers raised his rifle and took aim. "Look at those ugly creatures!"

Alijah held up his hand and made a sharp remark to Maximus.

"He says it's very bad lucks to shoot one's ancestors, Jules Sébastien. Pray stow the rifle, if you please."

D'Villiers looked defiant, as though he would argue, while a fierce blush rose to his fair face. The blush intensified when he turned his attention to a large monkey, penis dangling, mounting one female after another. Maximus said, "No doubt they are man and wives."

They emerged at last onto the coast where a gentle surf lapped the shore. Trading their long poles for stout paddles, they maneuvered the canoe out past the breaking surf and turned her prow up the coast. After a flurry of activity, a single matt sail was set and drawing well. Alijah's canoe shot through the sparkling waves.

Miriam's stare was fixed on the receding swamp, and on the forest it gave way to, here and there interspersed with limestone cliffs. In her heart was a distinct longing and ache that she wasn't sure she'd any right to feel. She had no boots or weapons, she'd lost Maximus's precious books, and the clothes she wore were rotting off her back. Even her religion—and the visible sign of it, the *hijab*—was left behind in the jungle. Yet, she wasn't leaving Borneo empty-handed. It wasn't for any of those reasons her heart ached. After all, Maximus and Krunk were here beside her, and somewhere over the horizon waited the ship *Nonesuch* and the life she'd always wanted.

Captain D'Villiers's boat was spotted, pulled up on a wide strand of beach, with the tricolor flag of France waving and snapping over it. Mookit and Krunk lowered the single sail, the nose of the little craft swung round, and they paddled and rode the surf right up onto the sand beside the large wooden ship's boat.

Everyone leaped out of the native craft, and a confusion of languages ensued, with the French seamen coming forward to bear a hand with their captain's collections. Miriam walked away up the strand from the milling group, leaving Maximus, Alijah, and Mookit to a private goodbye. The men were clapping one another on the shoulders in the way of clansmen everywhere. She paced the edge of the beach where the scree of jungle took over, straining and half convincing herself she caught a flash of dun-colored fur. But no, it must be her imagination, her willing imagination, and now they were hailing her. With the usual naval precision, all was in readiness in *Astrolabe's* boat. Her crew in their white duck trousers and blue jackets looked far smarter than poor tattered *Capitaine de corvette* D'Villiers, to say nothing of the rest of them.

Miriam took her seat in the stern, on a thwart between Captain D'Villiers and Maximus. Krunk, more part of the lower deck than the upper, was settled in the bows.

Cries began to ring out from the French sailors.
"Zut allors!"
"Allons!"

Miriam whipped round in time to see Alijah and Mookit rushing away and launching their canoe into the surf. Streaking down the beach, kicking up fine white sand with its speed, came Thrax.

The Hell-Cat executed a splashing two-part bounding leap and vaulted into the cutter, carrying some unidentified lumpish creature in its mouth. Miriam had a fleeting sensation of horror—of Thrax making her a present of some dead monkey ancestor—but this was deep down below her joy. Then Thrax landed in her lap, first flinging a spotted kitten straight into that of Captain D'Villiers.

In the bows of the cutter, one of the French seamen said, "Pah! It is only a pussy-cat. A pet belonging to the foreign gentlewoman."

"Wrong on both counts, mate," Krunk said, startling the men with an Africanized French dredged up from childhood. "That ain't no *animal domestique*, and just you cross *khun* Maryam and see where it gets you." Being the very soul of discretion, this last part Krunk uttered only within her own bosom.

As the cutter was pushed into the surf and the seamen began to pull away, Miriam's hands remained in constant contact with Thrax, caressing its fur. They looked into one another's eyes, Thrax squinting back at her in its well-remembered loving way. Miriam turned to Captain D'Villiers, who was crying, "Oh! Oh!", as he gazed on the kitten.

"If ever you think of skinning that creature and stuffing it for a specimen," Miriam said, with a look so savage Captain D'Villiers and Maximus recoiled. "Know that you do so at your peril, and shall answer to me!"

CHAPTER EIGHTEEN

Two ships swung placidly to their cables, anchored in the harbor of Singapore. The French *Corvette l'Astrolabe* and His Britannic Majesty's Hired Vessel *Nonesuch*. A third vessel was expected to complete Maximus's little squadron, for as the most senior captain he was given command of the expedition. The new ship would bring with her additional seamen to complete *Nonesuch's* accident, battle, and shipwreck depleted crew.

Anticipation of this third vessel, *Dolphin*, had Mr. Dashwood dancing on his toes with excitement for his hopes centered on being promoted into her as captain. Was he not a connection of Lord Exmouth, Admiral of the Pacific Fleet, who had influence with Lord Q, head of British intelligence and airships? Had he not survived a most desperate shipwreck when others had perished? While awaiting *Dophin's* arrival, the rest of them— officers and crew of *Nonesuch* and *Astrolabe*—did their best to sort themselves out.

Mr. Dashwood took up the long promised and differed astronomical lessons and training with the Mechanism he'd promised Miriam. Captain D'Villiers examined, sorted, dried, and described his collections, sending lovingly prepared packages off in homeward bound ships for the herbariums of botanical colleagues and the *Académie des sciences* in Paris. Maximus attended to the innumerable duties of a commodore; provisioning the ships for another six-month cruise, overseeing repairs, procuring and installing replacement balloons, sails, rigging, powder, shot, and small arms.

A captain at sea, let alone a commodore on a foreign station, had great powers of decision and promotion. In his elevated capacity, Maximus rated Miriam volunteer first class. She was become a sort of officer in training.

There was no one to naysay females aboard an airship's crew—indeed, *Nonesuch* now carried two such extraordinary persons—not within a thousand sea miles of the ships at their present location. After all the intimidation, the veiled threats in his previous letter to remove her from the airship, Lord Qs orders for the squadron, or what Miriam knew of them, were silent on the topic of her presence aboard. Not even a hemi-demi-semi-mention of her, her late mission, or a future one. Not that Miriam wanted or would accept another mission but she fumed, felt the slight most keenly, and in her breast lived a riot of emotions.

Though she seethed inwardly from the disrespect she perceived in Lord Q's silence, his discounting of all she'd confronted and endured in Borneo, outwardly she was calm. She studied astronomy and the workings of the ship with Mr. Dashwood. Navigation and mathematics were taught by the ship's captain—in the absence of a sailing master—to the young gentlemen, the officers in training. So, Miriam set to work with Maximus as her tutor, when he could spare the time. Captain D'Villiers even extended an invitation to her, to assist him in his dissections.

"Delicate female hands, those elegant tapered digits, are ideally suited to the fine work of surgery and dissection," the French captain said. "Do you not agree, *mon ami*?" he asked Maximus.

Maximus's face closed down, and he replied in an abrupt tone, "What tasks suit her best are for Miss Blackwell to decide."

Miriam couldn't quite get past the smell. She recognized she was foregoing an opportunity to advance her anatomical understanding, to contribute to important scientific knowledge, perhaps even the discovery of new species, but she's seen these creatures in life. The hornbills, the brightly colored kingfishers, herons, the singing, extravagantly plumed forest birds. The varieties of monkeys and gibbons pursuing their busy, involved, and highly social lives. One memorable Borneo morning she'd awakened to find herself staring into the bright black eyes of a tree shrew, waggling its long delicate snout at her with intense curiosity and disapproval. As though it knew she'd no business in that jungle. No, she couldn't dismember them with cold dispassionate precision, holding her nose before their decomposing little bodies in the name of science.

She'd declined that particular honor. Nevertheless, she looked forward to viewing the collections of beetles and butterflies D'Villiers promised them, as she and Maximus were rowed across to dine aboard *Astrolabe*.

The rain fell in unremitting sheets, in great curtains of water, soaking them down to their small clothes in a matter of minutes. Miriam followed Maximus up *Astrolabe's* side to the shrill call of the bosun's pipe, concentrating on not losing her hold on the manropes, or her footing on the slippery wood rungs carved in the ship's side.

She waited behind Maximus as he returned the salutes of *Astrolabe's* quarterdeck. Maximus stepped forward to shake Captain D'Villiers's extended hand, and then they both turned to Miriam. She stood there, a moist and peculiar sight, with her round hat held to her head by a scarf tied and knotted under her chin. She was otherwise decently clad in a modified version of midshipman's dress and, her greatest delight, she wore a new pair of half-boots bought of the cleverest cobbler in Singapore. Oh, the joy of shoes that didn't smell of meat! Tucked into one supple new boot was a three-inch black blade. How Maximus managed to find a Scottish dagger on an island in the South China Sea, she couldn't tell.

"Come below at once," Captain D'Villiers said, "you are wet to the bones, and shall catch the bad humors from the falling damps."

Inside D'Villiers's cabin, Maximus winked at Miriam over all the fuss. They stood together, dripping discretely, puddles forming at their feet. D'Villiers and his steward ran in and out bringing towels with which to mop them and the pristine canvas covered deck.

"There is nothing so wretched and uncomfortable as wet feet!" Captain D'Villiers said. "*Madame aspirant* Blackwell, should you like to remove your boots?"

"You are very kind, but no sir, I thank you," Miriam said. "I have on a new pair, and they are ever so snug and water tight."

D'Villiers smiled, reassured, and at last considered they were dried sufficiently to be allowed to move about the cabin. It held many interesting—and to the natural philosopher—precious things. Miriam went to greet the most precious of all, curled on the stern lockers with one eye open and fixed on the newcomers. The Hell-Cat rose at her approach, arched its spotted back in a luxurious stretch, and lolled out a rough pink tongue. It reared up and bumped its head into the hand Miriam outstretched to caress it. The cat then leapt off the stern locker, hissed vehemently at Maximus, and hardly deigning to glance in D'Villiers's direction padded out of the cabin, twitching its tail in annoyance at being disturbed from its slumbers.

"Allow me to show you the coleoptera and the lepidoptera. Oh! The butterflies, *mon ami*, the butterflies! Such exquisite colors, such enormous size!"

In his enthusiasm, D'Villiers seemed to have forgot that both Maximus and Miriam just spent the better part of the last months crawling round the Borneo jungle. But, Miriam considered, she didn't know the scientific names of all the teeming life she'd encountered. D'Villiers did, and Miriam listened attentively while he pointed out the species he believed were unknown to natural science. She and Maximus walked round, guided by D'Villiers, and viewed the many colored, shining, iridescent, bugs and butterflies pinned neatly in wooden drawers.

Over the last drawer of beetles, graduating in size from tiny to monstrous, all of the same genus, the two captains fell into a discussion of cryptogams and phanerogams. Miriam wandered a few steps away to examine *Astrolabe's* Mechanism, nestled against the curving side of the ship. It was a more modern astronomical instrument than the table sized behemoth that never left *Nonesuch's* cockpit. *Astrolabe's* Mechanism was smaller, more refined, portable, a French version in every way superior to the British.

Miriam smiled, just touching her fingertips to the discs and the tilting axis around which they orbited. Lord Q had apparently considered the changing world landscape, like the revolving parts of the Mechanism, and come away with a plan for a cross-national mission of exploration.

"*Astrolabe* is an exceptional ship," Maximus had confided to her, "the sweetest of sailors, the longest serving airship. Weatherly, dry—she must be to preserve her captain's treasured collections—fitted out with every conceivable instrument, and they of the finest French design. Is it any wonder Lord Q should wish to associate himself with such a prodigy? So, I am to become an English explorer. And I say this to you as one gentleman to another, m'dear, was there ever such a useless, unwanted creature in the world?"

She reminded him he must take comfort in the fact they could be set upon by hostile tribesmen, meet with piracy, or be fired upon by ships of the Russian navy, vying for supremacy in the Pacific with the European nations. In short, a thousand accidents of fortune might befall that would call for the skills of a fighting airship captain, and save Maximus from the ignominy he imagined. Secretly, in her inmost heart, Miriam thought the only fate they both dreaded was the command to return to so called civilized society.

"Shall you ever marry her, my friend?" D'Villiers asked Maximus in Latin.

Miriam bowed her head lower over the Mechanism, to hid the grin that leapt onto her face. Poor D'Villiers didn't realize—he had a penchant for trying to speak in code: English when aboard his ship, and French when aboard the *Nonesuch*—he was unaware there was hardly any language he could select that Miriam wouldn't understand. Maximus, however, knew all.

With a little ahem, Maximus said, "You are very impertinent, Jules Sébastien, as usual. I asked her once, in point of fact, and she declined the honour. I rather think it now up to her, to do the asking, if she be so inclined."

"And you, Maximus, are the most possible unconventional. What was it your god-father used to say? Weak heart will never win wise wife?"

"He used to call me woman-hearted, the creature," Maximus said. "I thought it was to wound and bring me low. Now I can't help but wonder if he meant instead to do me great credit."

Miriam turned from examining the Mechanism, and her gaze met Maximus's across the cabin. Such a warm look of regard and understanding passed between them, it was as though they'd reached out and shook hands in metaphorical agreement. Now they were captain and junior officer, however, she and Maximus could neither touch nor cohabitate openly. Which was not the same as giving up all the pleasurable things of the past.

"Ah, Maximus!" cried D'Villiers. "Here is my steward with the cloth, the pickles, and our wine. Pray help me with the lepidoptera. Miss Miriam, I beg! Do be careful with that drawer of butterflies you so forcefully seize upon. Most delicate!"

Once the dead insect life was tucked away into its purpose-built cabinetry, D'Villiers invited them to take seats round the white cloth covered table in his cabin, barely stopping himself from offering Miriam his arm and holding her chair.

"He is an old-fashioned soul," Maximus had said, by way of explaining D'Villiers's difficulty with a woman in the service. "A dear woman and bairns in their proper places six thousand mile away, while he cruises the world topping it the philosophical cove."

Miriam took a seat across from Maximus. D'Villiers was in his rightful place at the head of the table, beaming and rubbing his hands together in anticipation of the feast.

"We are to have none of your grand English dinners, I must warn you," D'Villiers said. "Nothing too heavy, my liver could not stand it in this heat. No. Merely these sweet little pickled fishes with root vegetables, they go very well with a glass of Chateau Lafite. My cook is most excellent with the seafoods, and the Singapore langoustes are the size of..."

D'Villiers broke off as though searching for inspiration. In walked the spotted Hell-Cat kitten, attracted by the scent of seafoods. D'Villiers rushed upon it in a way that made both Miriam and Maximus flinch, and grasped the kitten in a crushing embrace.

"Why! The size of my dear little Frou-Frou."

"Good God!" Maximus almost spat out his mouthful of wine. "Is that the name you've given it?"

"And what goes wrong, exactly?" D'Villiers retorted, mashing the cat's delicate little round head to his face. The Hell-Cat watched with intense concentration as D'Villiers plucked out the flesh of the fish and raised it in his fingers.

"Nothing at all, at all. But unless you fancy smiling out the other side of your face, I should recommend removing that beast a safe distance away from it."

D'Villiers set the kitten on the deck with a small dish of pickled fish in front of it, and the munching and crunching began. "Really, Maximus. Look at it! Frou-Frou is a mere nut, an insignificant little bean. How can you imagine such a precious thing could do harm?"

"How indeed?" Miriam said, having witnessed some things first hand. "The mighty bean."

The French captain stared at her. Miriam wondered if she'd spoken out of turn, offended naval etiquette—or D'Villiers's sense of it. Fortunately, D'Villiers was distracted by the entrance of the steward and his mates, balancing a great gleaming silver soup tureen between them.

"The broth is made of shells and heads of those Frou-Frou sized langoustes," D'Villiers said. "Then we shall have langoustes alamode, a brace of local, tufted duck, soused, then lacquered. Along with *quelque chose*. How do *l'Anglais* put it, Maximus—various of kickstraws?"

"Kickshaws."

Maximus nodded politely at his dinner companions, different colored eyes dancing, while Miriam might just have snorted a small amount of bisque into her napkin.

D'Villiers pursed his lips and glared at the seaman standing behind Miriam's chair.

"Pray serve *Aspirant* Blackwell a fiction more *bisque de homard*, Jeannot," D'Villiers ordered the seaman, in English. "You will take a very little more soup, Miss Blackwell?"

By the time the truly prodigious crustaceans had come and gone from the table, and the gentlemen, at least, reduced several ducks to well-picked bones, superior vintages of wine flowing all the while, D'Villiers was magnanimous, mellowed and relaxed.

Observing with approval Miriam's determination, in the tradition of the service, not to speak until spoken to, D'Villiers asked in a benevolent tone, "Tell us, Miss Blackwell, about the cuisine of the people of Borneo. I myself was not in country long enough to truly experience it. What was the best thing you ate? Oh, and do not leave out the worst!"

"I very much liked their sweet rice cakes, made with coconut flesh and the milk of the coconut. It was a special occasion dish, needing many hands to make. They wrap them in green leaf parcels like little purses. Another was *pooloot*, a steamed fowl, cooked with rice in lengths of green bamboo."

"And the worst?" Maximus asked.

"The worst was the tail of a monitor lizard. Tuai Rumah Dena caught it near the Sebauh, a lizard half the size of a canoe. Like eating pure suet." Miriam shuddered, remembering the quivering viscous yellowish flesh of the tail, and the way Inghai stuffed himself with it. She made the mistake of glancing down at the duck fat on her plate, and had to swallow a mouthful of the excellent Chateau Lafite to calm her stomach.

"You obviously never eats the Haggis, my dear Mada...er, Mak Blackwell."

Maximus let out a strangled sound and reached for his own glass of wine. The seamen standing behind their chairs exchanged wary, knowing glances, each drawing himself up, on guard.

"Indeed, I have not, sir," Miriam said. Avoiding Maximus's eye, and spurred on by that impromptu Miriam Albuyeh Kodio—Mak Blackwell remark, she said, "Is it so very terrible?"

D'Villiers emitted a few inarticulate puffing breaths, perhaps awakening to the possibility of having offended his commodore and his guest on several fronts. His men relaxed, perceiving the source of their captain's discomfort was social and not martial.

"Oh aye, Haggis is vera terrible." Maximus, as ever acting the commander, took pity on D'Villiers, who'd given them an excellent dinner. "Though whether it be worse, now, nor quivering lizard's tail, I could no say. Miss Blackwell shall enlighten us, should she ever encounter Haggis. Then she will have et of both."

Maximus lifted his glass to salute his companions. The seamen serving them left the cabin, clearly believing their captain in no danger from the wild Scots and his odd sidekick.

"A glass of wine with you both," Maximus said. "To Scotland and Borneo, homes of the worst cuisine in the known world!"

"Scotland and Borneo!" Miriam echoed with all her heart, though she'd never seen the former and barely survived the latter.

The cabin door opened and in came the seamen bearing a floating island on a long elegant silver salver, borne atop a great door-like wooden slab. The French seamen banged it down on the table before them, making the islands skip around in their ocean of cream. Miriam wondered about the construction of such a dish here in humid Singapore. What animal gave of that cream, and in this swelter, how much had D'Villiers's cook sweated into that ocean, frothing up such a confection?

"Ah!" cried D'Villiers, clasping his hands together. "He has fashioned it into the islands of the South China Sea. *Aspirant* Blackwell, may I help you to a slice of Borneo?"

"Thank you, sir," Miriam said, accepting of her plate and her fate with it. "Though I rather think that is the Spanish Philippines, sir."

"She has you dead to rights," Maximus said, with a wave of his dessert spoon. "The large misshapen one would be the East Indies and the kingdom of Brunei."

When they all had their dishes of swimming island before them, D'Villiers said pointedly to Miriam, "What do you make of our mission? Nothing more than a complete tour of the *Terres Australes*, carrying out investigations of great importance wherever we call. Indeed, operations of the first importance to science and the advancement of human knowledge."

D'Villiers smirked down at his meringue, his spoon poised, while Miriam tried to work out if she was required to respond. Then a booming concussion hit the ship. All three of them grabbed for the table edge to keep themselves upright as the ship canted to one side. Miriam's dish of floating island slewed sideways off the tabletop and smacked a wet dessert mess into her chest, dribbling thickly onto her lap. It felt exactly as though *Astrolabe* had been fired upon.

The ship righted, rocking back and forth. The two captains were on their feet, rushing for the after hatchway companion ladder. Miriam followed close behind, catching up her round hat and Maximus's second best scrapper on her way. The officer of the watch all but collided with D'Villiers, actually stepping on his captain's pinky finger, in his haste down the ladder to make his report.

"We thought it was the roast-beeves, sir, firing on us." The officer cut a glance in Maximus's direction. "But it appears to be an airship, sir." He lowered his voice as they emerged on deck. "Firing in distress and coming down fast."

"Mother of God!" D'Villiers declared, calling down to his steward to bring his best perspective glass.

Maximus strode over to the ship's rail and in a strong voice called out, "Mr. Dashwood, send my boat across at once, and prepare to make sail."

"Aye, aye, sir!" Mr. Dashwood raised his hat across the water.

D'Villiers and Miriam, Maximus and Mr. Dashwood, and everyone on the decks of both ships, was scanning the sky in the direction of the gun report, searching for another glimpse of the airship's great balloons. Between them and the airship was a lowering gray sky and a choppy cross-grained sea, peppered by ceaseless heavy rain.

"Captain D'Villiers," Maximus said, extending his hand. "Thank you for a most splendid dinner, and for my wine. Please to keep your station here in Singapore harbour, while I take *Nonesuch* out to offer aid to that ship. We shall attract as little attention as possible, in parting and rejoining you." He bowed. "And so, Miss Blackwell and I will take leave of you."

D'Villiers wished them god's speed, bowing Maximus over the ship's side. *Astrolabe's* bosun and his mate were forbidden from springing their calls, and Maximus and Miriam slid silent into *Nonesuch's* gig. Krunk was one of the oarsmen. She put hand to forehead to salute the ship's captain as he took his seat. The smear of cream down Miriam's shirt and trousers was beginning to wash out under the downpour of rain. She squelched onto the thwart beside Maximus in the boat.

A collective *Ahhh* rose up from the French and British ships, in spite of all their officers could do to impose silence fore and aft. A break in the distant squalls revealed the distressed airship. She wobbled and plunged, her balloons going slack one moment and filling the next, jigging her up and down in her descent. Maximus stiffened and tensed beside her. Their own precipitous plunge and crash on the coast of Borneo perhaps in his mind.

Nonesuch's gig was halfway between the two ships, the oarsmen pulling hard, when Maximus said in Gaelic, "Dost see yon pennant a-flying on the mainmast betwixt her sad balloons?"

Miriam could not suppose the remark was meant for anyone but her, and she, only understanding the bare edge of his speech, said, "Aye, aye, sir."

"It signalizes an admiral aboard." Maximus went quiet a moment, as the boat approached *Nonesuch's* side. "Which in the case of *our* service may mean himself, that right bastard."

There was only one right bastard in Maximus's lexicon, and that was Lord Q. Miriam murmured another quavering, "Aye, aye, sir."

Maximus called out, "Larboard," loud enough for the boats' crew and the men on *Nonesuch's* deck to hear him. Krunk and the other oarsmen rowed the boat round to the leeward side of the ship, where her captain could go aboard—again without ceremony.

The gig latched onto *Nonesuch's* main chains, and Maximus, with a fierce glare in his eyes, leaped up the side of his ship. Miriam, Krunk, and the rest of the gig's crew scrambled to the deck in his wake.

An anxious yet ebullient Mr. Dashwood met them. He was wringing his hands while dancing on his toes. He'd put everything in motion for sailing that could be done, without her captain aboard.

"Mr. Dashwood, take us out, if please." Out of compassion, quietly, for Mr. Dashwood's ear alone, Maximus said, "I wonder too, what great numpty is bringing her down in this squall. Yet, we will both be knowing how changeable is the weather in these seas."

He raised his voice. "Let us proceed to sea, Mr. Dashwood. No shouts, no calls."

Miriam ran forward to her position in the bows, until she could report to the first lieutenant the ship's anchor was, "Up and down, sir."

The anticipated series of orders for weighing were given, and Maximus's surviving crew limped and scurried about in creditable fashion. One or more of them, and not always Krunk, spared an eye, a word of caution, even a stabilizing hand, for their new midshipman. Miriam climbed the shrouds with the foretopmen, once the headsails were on the ship, and the order came to set topsails.

All the monkey climbing up the hills and mountains of Borneo had conditioned Miriam for the ratlines, different on a swaying ship of course, but she wished she'd more of the ape in her when it came to easing out along the yard. There was only a rope beneath her feet and the tight rolled canvas sail to hold onto. It was the foretopsail they would untie and loosen, and let fly at the word of command from the deck.

Miriam gritted her teeth, trying to concentrate on Krunk and the seaman on her other hand. Not on the plunging sensation in her stomach, nor the vertigo from the height, as the ship breasted the seas. She was a midshipman now, a reefer, and this work in the dizzying foretop was the reefing part. If she couldn't do the work of a junior airship officer, whatever that entailed, then whomsoever the distressed ship carried and whatever news she bore mattered little.

She called on the physical strength the Borneo jungle run had given her, and the toughness of mind she was still in process of building. Concentrating on Krunk at the exposed end of the yard and the experienced old hand on her left, Miriam did what they did exactly as, and when they did it.

For a few brief moments, before the foretopmen were called down, Miriam gazed out over the top of the billowing sail. Clouds and rain obscured the view of the airship they were chasing. Rain was slanting down out of control, visibility poor, sea and sky equally gray and leaden. Way up here on the swaying, dipping foretop yard all the senses came into play. Miriam forced down the nausea, the rising up of the rich French cuisine. The last thing she wanted in life was to see that lobster alamode again. She threw her whole being into the sensation of flying, now by sea, and in the not too distant future, she hoped and trusted, in the heavens.

"*Khun!*" Krunk hissed. "Budge along! Look sharp and jump at the word, or it look bad on us."

Krunk jerked her head in the direction of the deck. Miriam made her way carefully sideways like a crab back along the yard, and down the ratlines, holding fast to the rough hemp hand and footholds. Maybe she'd best do more of the monkey thing and go barefoot as the seamen did. She hit the deck, relieved, and was immediately summoned by the captain.

Maximus was hanging on with one arm wrapped round the starboard mainmast shrouds, leaning out as the ship surged along, his red hair flying loose behind him.

"Miss Blackwell!" he cried. "My perspective glass, if you please."

Lord Q's face was bright red as the airship plummeted, his skull shining with sweat beneath his white hair. He was not flushed with fear. Far from it, he'd survived worse than this—though he should see to it the fool captaining this airship never commanded another one—no, it was frustration and anger that was the cause.

The wounded man strapped next to Lord Q all the way aft in the captain's cabin groaned, and Lord Q's lip lifted in disgust. They'd plucked the man off the coast of Borneo, out of a capital city so wreaked Lord Q calculated he could safely leave the country's exploitation for a later date. The native bushmen would never recover sufficiently to mount a concerted defense, before Lord Q meant to send the British back in. The wounded man next to him with the livid dagger slash from hairline to jaw, angered Lord Q. The only reason he was alive was as leverage against young Miss Blackwell. Otherwise, the man served as a reminder of failure.

The ship jerked up suddenly then plunged again, bringing their stomachs into their mouths. The wounded man squealed.

"Stop that whinging, man." Lord Q turned his face away. "No one will be a-dying this day."

He'd miscalculated was all, believing the wounded man any match for Miss Miriam of Persia. She'd survived the mission, and no doubt continued paramour to Maximus. Not the outcome Lord Q intended, or most desired, when he'd planned the mission. Still, his was a supple mind, used to formulating and reformulating the attack, just as circumstances demanded.

Another precipitous upward wrench and downward fall, and Lord Q clenched his teeth. The trick was to turn it to account, Miss Miriam's survival, and his foster-son's misguided, besotted attachment. Perhaps it wasn't, came a voice from a corner of Lord Q's consciousness, and what was instead mistaken was his own notion that they needed separating. But he wasn't ready to accept Miriam and Maximus might be stronger together, not before testing them further.

Determining who would lead the airship service into the future was no light matter. Lord Q had always envisioned his successor as a man; a known entity, a relative was ideal. Turning the mantel over to a partnership, especially when one half of it was foreign-born—and the young Miss was as foreign as one could get, the black shame of it—was what Lord Q struggled to wrap his head around. As Lord Q's schemes solidified in his mind, his color gradually returned to its normal pinky-white. A luster lingered in his reptilian green eyes.

When the first impact of landing came, with the man beside him screaming, Lord Q locked onto one solid fact: whatever else might be true of her, Miss Miriam Albuyeh Kodio Blackwell was a survivor.

Miriam scurried below, a brief respite from the rain while the sound of it continued drumming the deck over her head. She scrambled back up the aftermost hatchway companion ladder, glass tucked under one arm. Maximus met her, where there was some protection from the elements, below the break of the quarterdeck.

She held the telescope out to him.

Instead of taking it Maximus stared at her, keen and direct. "Whatever comes down in yon ship, m'dearest and most cherished friend, we shall be well enough together. I can build a ship with me own hands, come to it, is what I learned in Borneo." He waved his free arm, the one not holding to the ship, sending a stream of water from his sleeve that hit Miriam right about heart level. "This is how we live!"

Maximus grasped the other end of the telescope, and through the instrument they were joined. Miriam felt a jolt, from his words, from touching him—even through the medium of the perspective glass. Her enthusiasm for the mission of exploration, the first she'd ever truly wanted, lay somewhere between D'Villiers's full on eagerness and Maximus's reserved pragmatism.

In that moment danger and uncertainty were at a distance and Miriam was filled with curiosity, and a willing spirit for what came next.

"A life worth living," she said, feeling her heart glow.

Romance, Intrigue, and Airships - Code Black Book 1

Miriam Kodio Blackwell is caught between East and West. When a Code Black arises she is recruited by Lord Q, head of British intelligence and airships, who helps Miriam escape Iran only to press her into service of the Crown. Will Miriam survive when she's put aboard the airship *Nonesuch*—with her captain, crew, and a Hell-Cat of fearsome reputation—and the assignment to rescue the niece of a Dutch ally taken captive in the South China Sea?

Golden Dragon is a witty new steampunk adventure, set in the Romantic age of Byron and Shelley.

www.ingramcontent.com/pod-product-compliance
Lightning Source LLC
Chambersburg PA
CBHW022357110726
47902CB00002BA/322